PROGENITOR

STAR TREK®
STARGAZER
BOOK TWO
PROGENITOR

Michael Jan Friedman

Based upon STAR TREK: THE NEXT GENERATION®
created by Gene Roddenberry

POCKET BOOKS
New York   London   Toronto   Sydney   Singapore

This book is a work of fiction. Names, characters, places and incidents are products of the author's imagination or are used fictitiously. Any resemblance to actual events or locales or persons, living or dead, is entirely coincidental.

An *Original* Publication of POCKET BOOKS

POCKET BOOKS, a division of Simon & Schuster, Inc.
1230 Avenue of the Americas, New York, NY 10020

STAR TREK is a Registered Trademark of
Paramount Pictures.

This book is published by Pocket Books, a division of
Simon & Schuster, Inc., under exclusive license from
Paramount Pictures.

ISBN: 0-7434-2794-7

First Pocket Books printing May 2002

10 9 8 7 6 5 4 3 2 1

POCKET and colophon are registered trademarks of
Simon & Schuster, Inc.

For information regarding special discounts for bulk purchases, please
contact Simon & Schuster Special Sales at 1-800-456-6798
or business@simonandschuster.com

Printed in the U.S.A.

**Poul Anderson,
knight of ghosts and shadows**

Acknowledgments

I find myself once more indebted to a handful of good people, without whose loyalty, help and hard work I'd never have had the opportunity to put this book in your hands. I gratefully acknowledge the efforts of John Ordover, editor; Scott Shannon, publisher; Paula Block, executive director of publishing at Viacom Consumer Products; Dave Van Domelen, science maven; Gene Roddenberry and the illustrious writers and producers of *Star Trek: The Next Generation,* who invented Jean-Luc Picard and the good ship *Stargazer.*

I'd also like to thank my wife and sons, who are kind enough to open my office door and throw in mail from time to time; my parents, who have been known to bring me citrus fruit so I don't get scurvy in the manner of some fifteenth-century sailor; and my friends, who understandably have trouble believing I'm smart enough to write this stuff.

Chapter One

JEAN-LUC PICARD HAD LOST his fencing partner.

His name was Daithan Ruhalter. Ruhalter had also been Picard's captain, his predecessor as commanding officer of the *Stargazer*.

Picard had been happy to discover that there was another fencer on the ship, a security officer by the name of Pierzynski, who had a good few inches on Picard and outweighed him by perhaps thirty pounds. Unfortunately, as Pierzynski had subsequently discovered, size and skill didn't always go hand in hand.

At the moment, Picard enjoyed a four-touches-to-none advantage in a five-touch match. To this point, Pierzynski had failed to take advantage of his longer reach, just as he had failed to do so in the four matches that preceded this one.

Picard could have postponed the inevitable and toyed with the fellow for a while. However, he didn't want to give Pierzynski the illusion that they were competitive enough for the captain to consider doing this on a regular basis.

It was unfortunate. Picard had hoped a good fencing session would distract him from what he was obliged to do when the *Stargazer* reached Starbase 42.

But Pierzynski hadn't provided much of a distraction for him. The disposition of Caber and Valderrama still weighed heavily on the captain's mind, making him wonder how he could ever have allowed himself to embrace those individuals in the first place.

Picard sighed. "En garde."

Pierzynski raised his blade in response. Then, aggressive by nature, he took a step toward the captain.

Picard frowned. He didn't even have to parry to create an opening. Taking a couple of steps back, he waited for Pierzynski to follow him. Then he planted his back foot, extended his point and launched himself forward—all in one quick, fluid motion.

He hit Pierzynski in the ribs, just below his elbow. Point and match. "Alas," he said.

Pierzynski reached for the top of his mask and pulled it down, exposing his flushed, fatigued-looking face. Then he tucked the mask under his sword arm and extended his hand to the captain.

"Good one, sir. One more?"

Picard removed his own mask and clasped the security officer's hand. "Perhaps some other time, Mr. Pierzynski. I'm due on the bridge in half an hour."

Pierzynski nodded. "Of course, sir." He smiled sheepishly. "I hope I didn't disappoint you *too* much, sir."

The captain smiled back and lied through his teeth. "You didn't disappoint me at all, Lieutenant. I simply had a good day."

That seemed to make Pierzynski feel a little better. At least, it seemed that way to Picard as he showered, dressed, and made his way to the bridge.

He arrived just in time to receive word from his communications officer that a message was arriving for him. Naturally, the captain reckoned it was from Starfleet Command, since his only orders at the moment were to exchange personnel at Starbase 42.

He was wrong. It wasn't from Command, after all. Apparently, it was from the *Crazy Horse*.

"Really," Picard said, wondering what it might be about.

"Really, sir," Lt. Paxton confirmed for him.

"I'll take it in my ready room," Picard told his comm officer, and went there to receive the message.

Phigus Simenon, chief engineer of the Federation starship *Stargazer*, eyed the knot of scarlet-clad specialists standing at attention in front of him. There were twelve of them in all, males and females representing six different species.

They didn't seem happy. But then, he didn't *want* them to be happy. Not after what he had just seen.

"Disgraceful," he spat, feeling his anger constrict the flow of blood in his throat vessels. "Absolutely disgraceful."

"Sir," said Dubinski, one of Simenon's senior officers, "in all fairness—"

Simenon cut the man short with a snap of his tail. "Fairness?" he repeated, giving the word a bitter twist as it echoed throughout the engineering section. "You want fairness after you let this ship go up in a ball of matter–antimatter fury?"

In reality, the *Stargazer* hadn't suffered so much as a

scratch. But that was because the events of the last several minutes had only been a simulation of a warp core containment failure, not a real one.

Simenon ticked off his section's failings on the digits of one scaly clawlike hand. Each accusation snapped and cut like the business end of a very sharp whip.

"First," he hissed, "you relaxed and assumed the internal sensors would detect the beginnings of the failure. Second, you allowed the computer to respond to the situation, when you should have taken the initiative yourselves."

Both were grievous errors, considering Simenon had shut down the sensors and the computers for a five-minute period. But then, what good was a test if it was too easy?

"And third," he finished, "you hung onto the core too long when you should have ejected it immediately."

The assembled engineers seemed to strain under the weight of their superior's charges. They weren't used to this kind of talk—even from the likes of *him*.

But it wasn't Simenon's job to mollycoddle them. His job was to make sure the ship got what it needed in the way of power and propulsion and a number of other critical areas, and he would be damned if he was going to fall short of accomplishing that.

That was why he was ripping into his engineers, right? To ensure that they didn't falter in their vigilance? To make sure the *Stargazer* didn't fall victim to some ridiculous and avoidable oversight?

"Sir," said Dubinski, now that Simenon had vented the worst of his figurative spleen, "I'd like permission to speak."

Simenon fixed the fellow with his lizardlike gaze.

"Permission granted, Mr. Dubinski. I can't wait to hear the excuse you're going to give me."

The engineer frowned. "It's not an excuse, sir. I'd just like to try to put this...exercise...in perspective."

Simenon shrugged. "By all means."

"First off, sir, we *did* conduct periodic checks of the core—even more frequently than Starfleet directives recommend. And while it's true we gave the computer a chance to respond to the situation, we had every reason to believe it would do so—since our boards told us it was running fine."

The engineering chief harrumphed. "And your slowness in dumping the warp core once you realized the computer wouldn't do it?"

"It just didn't feel right," Dubinski explained. "After all, complete, irreparable and rapid failure is virtually unheard of without apparent cause—enemy fire, a collision with another ship, *something*—and we couldn't identify anything that might have triggered a breach of the containment vessel."

It was a good answer. Simenon had to admit that, if only to himself. In fact, it bothered him that he hadn't considered it.

Just as he hadn't considered that every control console in engineering would show the computer was on-line—something the chief should have taken into account if he were to make the test a fair assessment of his people's preparedness.

It wasn't like him to gloss over important details. But then, it wasn't like him to conduct unannounced drills in the first place. He had always judged the efficiency of his section by virtue of daily observations, not contrived exercises.

So what had come over him? A sudden lack of confidence in his security measures? Or something else—something unrelated to the continued welfare of the *Stargazer?*

Something that had been bothering him more and more over the last several days, keeping him awake at nights and insinuating itself into his thoughts during his waking hours.

Inwardly, Simenon cursed and crossed the room to a sleek, black control console, where he made a show of inspecting what was on its various screens. It gave him time to think—to gain that sense of perspective of which Dubinski had spoken.

Maybe he hadn't been fair to his engineers, he thought. Maybe—gods help him—an apology was in order, as hideously distasteful as the concept seemed to him.

Then Urajel, the Andorian on his staff, breathed something to the woman next to her. Obviously, she hadn't intended for Simenon to hear it. But he heard it, all right.

He heard it all too well.

Turning from the console and glowering at the Andorian with slitted yellow eyes, he said, *"What* was that, Ms. Urajel?"

The engineer's face suffused with blood, giving it a dark blue tinge beneath her fringe of silver-white hair. No doubt, she was tempted to deny she had said anything. But she couldn't do that.

Urajel steeled herself. "I said I wonder what crawled up your hindquarters, sir."

Another time, Simenon might have let the remark slide, insubordinate as it was. But not *this* time.

This time, his anger surged. "You'll run safety drills for the balance of this shift," he rasped, not just to Urajel but to all of her colleagues as well. "And for the next shift, and the one after that and the one after that, until I'm confident that what I saw today won't happen again."

Simenon knew he wasn't being fair to them. He knew he was abusing his power as engineering chief. But even knowing these things, he couldn't help it.

Before he said something he would *really* regret, he whirled and made his way to his office.

Picard considered Starbase 42 as it loomed ever larger on his bridge's main viewscreen.

Like many of the interstellar bases Starfleet had built in the last twenty years, 42 was comprised of a long cylinder, a protruding ring in the vicinity of its midsection and an even more prominent ring near what was generally recognized as its top.

Both rings were liberally dotted with brightly lit observation ports. At this distance, the captain imagined he could see uniformed figures framed in the ports, peering out at him in curiosity even as he was peering in at them.

Where had all those figures come from? Where were they going? There were so many uniformed personnel in the fleet, it was barely possible to keep track of even a fraction of them....

Much less to know who would become an asset to his crew and who would become a burden. Or who would choose to leave just when she seemed to have found her niche.

"You look positively grim," said Gilaad Ben Zoma, Picard's friend and first officer.

"Do I?" the captain asked.

"If I didn't know better, I'd think your shields were down and you'd just fired off your last photon torpedo."

Under most circumstances, Picard would have smiled at the metaphor. But not under *these* circumstances.

"I'll do my best to cheer up," he said.

Ben Zoma leaned a little closer. "That would be nice. And while you're at it, you may want to give the order to establish orbit."

The captain glanced at Idun Asmund, his primary helm officer, and realized that she was waiting patiently for instructions. Feeling his face flush, he said, "Establish orbit, helm."

"Aye, sir," came the response.

Picard frowned at his lapse as he watched Idun manipulate her controls and activate the ship's braking thrusters. *Keep your mind on what you're doing,* he told himself.

"You know," Ben Zoma said in a voice only the captain could hear, "none of this is your fault. It wasn't even your decision to bring these people aboard."

"I know that," the captain replied. "But that doesn't mean they're not my responsibility."

"And as for that *other* personnel situation—"

Picard stopped Ben Zoma with a gesture. "Let's contemplate that later, shall we? I can only take so much change in one day."

"Orbit established," reported Idun's twin sister Gerda, who was seated at the bridge's navigation console.

The captain nodded. "Hail the base."

"Aye, sir," said Ulelo, who had minutes earlier taken over for Paxton at the comm panel.

In a matter of moments, the officer in command of Starbase 42 appeared on the viewscreen. He was a broad, squared-off fellow with pronounced crow's feet at the corners of his eyes and a thatch of thick, gray hair. And though he gave Picard his name readily enough, the captain couldn't have repeated it if his life depended on it.

Despite what he had told himself, he was still distracted by what was happening to his crew. More to the point, he was still wondering if he could have done anything to prevent it.

There's one *thing you could have done,* he reflected. *You could have denied the captain of the* Crazy Horse *his request to speak with one of your officers.* But that would have been neither fair nor in keeping with Starfleet protocol.

The commander of the starbase asked if Picard would be beaming down himself. When he indicated that he would not be, the man said something polite and signed off.

As the image of the base was restored to the screen, the captain turned to Ben Zoma. "Shall we?"

The first officer stood aside for him. "After you."

Reluctantly, Picard got up from his seat and made his way across the bridge to the turbolift.

Chapter Two

AS PICARD AND BEN ZOMA ENTERED Transporter Room Three, one of half a dozen such facilities on the *Stargazer,* the captain saw that there were two uniformed figures waiting for them beside the hexagon-shaped transporter platform.

One of them was Juanita Valderrama, a middle-aged woman with a kind, round face and dark hair. The other, a man in an ensign's uniform, was the tall, sturdy-looking Joe Caber.

Picard turned to the morning-shift transporter officer, who was standing off to the side at his black, streamlined console. "Mr. Refsland," he said, "is the base prepared to receive Lieutenant Valderrama and Ensign Caber?"

"They are, sir," confirmed Refsland, a husky, blond fellow in his middle twenties.

The captain nodded. "Good." He indicated the platform with a gesture. "If you please."

Caber ascended without any further encouragement. Valderrama, on the other hand, hesitated.

"Is something wrong?" Picard asked her.

The lieutenant lifted her chin. "May I speak candidly, sir?"

The muscles worked in Picard's jaw. *Here it comes,* he thought. *The disclaimer. The "I was wrongly accused" speech.*

"By all means," he responded.

Valderrama's nostrils flared. "I want to apologize," she said softly. "Not only to you and First Officer Ben Zoma, but to Ensign Jiterica as well. What I did was reprehensible. I wish the idea had never even occurred to me."

It was the last thing that Picard had expected to hear after Valderrama tried to take credit for someone else's idea—in this case, Ensign Jiterica's. Glancing at Ben Zoma, he saw a look of surprise on his friend's face—although it must have been only a faint shadow of the surprise visible on his own.

Still, he couldn't accept Valderrama's apology. What she had done truly *was* reprehensible, and there was nothing she could do now that would change that.

Meeting her gaze, the captain said, "I'll be sure to relay your apology to Ensign Jiterica."

If Valderrama had hoped for absolution from him, she didn't show it. In fact, she looked considerably more at ease simply for having made her peace with her commanding officer.

"Thank you," the lieutenant said. Then she joined Caber on the transporter platform.

A part of Picard naturally disapproved of what she had done. However, another part of him wished her well and hoped she might regain what she had lost of herself.

Unlike Valderrama, Ensign Caber had yet to make a

sound. He looked bored as he stood on the platform, as if his being there were something of an inconvenience to him.

The captain could have let him go on that way. But he didn't. He approached the ensign and said, "What about you, Mr. Caber? Do you have any regrets concerning your actions?"

The young man smiled thinly, exposing perfectly spaced white teeth. "None at all, sir," he replied with undisguised arrogance. "And when my father hears what happened here, I don't think *I'll* be the one with cause for regret."

The threat wasn't lost on Picard. Caber's father was an admiral in Starfleet. Never having met the fellow, the captain had no idea how he would react.

Not that he could allow it to affect his decision. Caber had assaulted another member of the crew, exhibiting a certain amount of what appeared to be bigotry in the process. His presence would no longer be tolerated on the *Stargazer.*

Picard turned to Refsland and said, "Energize."

"Energizing," Refsland responded.

Almost instantly, Valderrama and Caber were reduced by the transporter to shimmering columns of light. Then they vanished altogether, their molecules dispatched through space to their destination.

Picard sighed. Ben Zoma was right, of course. Valderrama and Caber had brought this fate on themselves. Their departure wasn't anyone's fault but their own.

Nonetheless, the captain regretted the loss of his most promising ensign and his science officer. Any commanding officer in the fleet would have felt the same way.

Fortunately, Caber and Valderrama were not his only

reason for being there that morning. "Mr. Refsland," he said, "are our new crewmen ready to beam up?"

The transporter operator nodded. "Aye, sir."

"Then," said the captain, "advise the base that we are ready to receive them."

As Refsland relayed the information to his counterpart at Starbase 42, Picard turned to Ben Zoma. "Feeling lucky?"

His friend smiled. "I was just going to ask *you* that."

The two who would replace Caber and Valderrama, unlike their predecessors, had been handpicked by the captain and his first officer. In fact, they were the first additions to the crew Picard had made since the day he assumed command.

He regarded the empty transporter platform. "To tell you the truth, Number One—"

"Too late," said Ben Zoma. "Here they come."

In a reversal of the dazzling effects that had accompanied the departures of Valderrama and Caber, two brilliant columns of light appeared on the platform. Moments later, a pair of figures materialized in the midst of them.

One of them was human, a fair-haired young man with boyish features that contrasted with the seriousness of his expression. The other was a Kandilkari, his long, striated face distinguished by the heavy, purple jowls characteristic of his species.

"Welcome aboard," the captain said.

"Thank you, sir," the human replied crisply. "It's a genuine pleasure to be here."

This was the crewman Picard and Ben Zoma had had their eyes on weeks earlier, before Admiral McAteer foisted his own choices on them. Like Caber, the fellow came from a Starfleet family with a long and prestigious track record. And like Caber, he was an ensign with a high career ceiling.

But that, the captain hoped, was where the resemblance between the two men ended. Caber had been an anomaly, an aberration. Picard expected much more from the likes of Cole Paris.

"I, too, take pleasure in joining this crew," said the Kandilkari in a slow, surprisingly musical voice.

Stepping down from the transporter platform, he extended a long, four-fingered hand in Picard's direction. His eyes, which were as purple as his jowls, seemed to dance with enthusiasm as he spoke.

"Lieutenant Nol Kastiigan," he added by way of an introduction. "At your service, sir."

The captain shook Kastiigan's hand, feeling the unusual metacarpal structure. "You come highly recommended, Lieutenant."

"Captain Sannek and I had the utmost respect for one another," Kastiigan told him. "I only regret that he chose to retire when the *Antares* was decommissioned."

Picard smiled. "Captain Sannek spent more than forty years in the center seat of one Starfleet vessel or another. His retirement is no doubt well-deserved."

He turned to Ensign Paris again, who was waiting to be invited before he descended from the transporter disc. It was a formality few observed in this day and age.

"Please," the captain told him, indicating the deck beside him.

Only then did Paris come down from the platform. "If it's all right with you, sir," he said, "I'd like to take the first available shift. No time like the present and all that."

Picard glanced at Ben Zoma, who looked equally impressed. It was difficult to decide who was more eager, their new lieutenant or their new ensign.

"I think we can arrange that," said the captain.

Ben Zoma nodded. "Absolutely. But you'll want to settle in first," he told the ensign.

The fellow smiled a little. "Of course, sir."

"Come on," said Ben Zoma, heading for the exit. "I'll see to it you're shown to your quarters. Both of you."

The newcomers fell in behind the first officer, leaving Picard alone with Refsland. He turned to the transporter operator, who was already in the process of locking down his console.

Refsland looked up at him. "I guess that's it, sir."

Picard nodded and replied, "So it would seem, Mr. Refsland." But inwardly he added, *For now.*

Nikolas was lying in his bed with his uniform on, enjoying the feeling of just doing nothing, when the doors to his quarters slid apart. Reluctantly, he opened his eyes.

The guy that came in was his new roommate. He had to be. Otherwise, he wouldn't have walked in as if he owned the place.

As Nikolas watched, the guy made his way to the naked mattress that had been Joe Caber's and took stock of the linens piled on top of it. Then he began unfolding them.

"You don't waste any time," said Nikolas, "do you?"

His roommate looked at him as if noticing him for the first time. "Excuse me?"

Nikolas smiled and sat up. "Sorry," he said, offering the guy his hand. "Andreas Nikolas, widely known as the only indispensable member of the crew."

The newcomer just looked at him.

"That was a joke," Nikolas told him.

Finally, the guy cracked a smile, albeit a weak one,

and shook Nikolas's hand. "Cole Paris. Pleased to meet you."

"Just so you know," Nikolas said, "I haven't had much luck with roommies lately. The last one got himself kicked off the ship. But then," he quipped, "what do you expect from an admiral's son?"

Paris's smile faded.

"What?" said Nikolas.

"I'm an admiral's *grand*son."

Nikolas felt a rush of heat in his cheeks. *Nice going,* he thought. *Offend the guy right off the bat.*

"Tell you what," he said, "just give me a moment and I'll get my foot out of my mouth."

The new guy dismissed the notion with a wave of his hand. "Don't give it another thought," he said with the utmost seriousness. "I'm sure I'll make my share of stupid remarks."

Nikolas didn't know Paris very well, but he had a premonition that the guy was right. Paris seemed a little off somehow, a little too stiff for his own good—like a toy soldier Nikolas had seen once in the window of an antiques store.

Different from Caber, he thought. That was for *damned* sure. As different as high noon and midnight.

"So what do you do," Nikolas wondered, "when you're not busy saving the universe?"

Paris stared at him for a second, a knot of flesh gathering over the bridge of his nose. Then he said, "Another joke?"

Nikolas nodded. "Sort of. But a question, too."

His roommate shrugged. "I do like to read."

Now we're getting somewhere, Nikolas told himself. "Anything in particular?"

"Uh huh. Piloting manuals. That sort of thing."

Inwardly, Nikolas cringed. "Really."

"Can't get enough of them."

Nikolas managed a smile. "How about that."

Paris looked thoughtful. "You know," he said, "I could go for something to eat."

The guy was talking Nikolas's language. "Why don't we head for the mess," he said, "and I'll—"

"But I've got an orientation meeting with Commander Wu," his roommate finished, "and I don't want to be late. First impressions and all that. See you later, all right?"

"Yeah," said Nikolas. "See ya."

As he watched Paris leave their quarters, he couldn't help thinking how much Paris and Wu were going to love serving together. Between them, they didn't have a relaxed bone in their bodies.

To a casual observer, Dikembe Ulelo would appear to be sitting at his console on the bridge of the *Stargazer,* exchanging routine data with the comm officer on Starbase 42.

But in reality, he was focused on another matter entirely. He was reflecting on the progress of his mission.

The junior communications officer had accomplished quite a bit since his arrival on the *Stargazer* a few weeks earlier. He had examined the engineering section, the shuttlebay, and a critical component of the deflector array. However, there was still a good deal more that he could learn.

For instance, Ulelo had yet to get a look at the ship's weapons control center. Vigo, the chief weapons officer, had agreed to give him a tour of the place when an occasion presented itself, but to date that hadn't happened.

Ulelo might have expressed a stronger desire to take Vigo's tour, but he didn't want to arouse the weapons chief's suspicion. So he had decided to wait until the next time Vigo invited him to play sharash'di, and then remind his colleague about his invitation.

Eventually, he reflected, he would get Vigo to show him what he wanted to see. It was just a matter of time.

A green light began to flash in the corner of one of Ulelo's communications monitors. It alerted him that the ship was in the process of receiving a subspace packet from the nearest Starfleet relay station.

It was part of his job to go through the packet and distribute its component messages to the appropriate parties. After all, only some of it represented official business. Much of it was personal mail intended for individual members of the crew.

The comm officer would also make a copy of each message for his own use. Then he would download the lot of them to the computer terminal provided in his quarters.

Of course, this would constitute a clear-cut violation of Starfleet regulations. But he would accept the risk if it meant knowing just a bit more about his colleagues—because knowing them better might gain him easier access to key operating areas of the ship.

And the more Ulelo learned about the *Stargazer,* the better equipped he would be when the time came.

Chapter Three

As Jean-Luc Picard contemplated the computer screen in his ready room, he heard a chime. "Come," he said.

The doors parted and Ben Zoma walked in. "There's a rumor going around that that last packet contained new orders. Any truth to it?"

The captain smiled. "Quite a bit, actually."

Ben Zoma sat down opposite Picard. "So where are we going?"

"The Egreggedor system. There are a couple of planets there that Admiral McAteer would like us to survey."

The first officer looked skeptical. "Wasn't that system surveyed less than a decade ago?"

Picard shrugged. "Slow day at the office, I suppose."

"Must have been." Ben Zoma frowned thoughtfully. "You think McAteer's trying to take another shot at us somehow?"

"I wouldn't put it past him," the captain said. "Not

after he unleashed us on the trail of the White Wolf, hoping to make us look bad when we failed to find him."

"Unfortunately for our friend the admiral, we managed to disappoint him in that regard."

Picard nodded. "Which no doubt made him feel that much more bitter toward us."

Ben Zoma seemed to take pleasure in the notion. "No doubt," he said with a mischievous gleam in his eyes.

The captain clucked in mock disapproval. "I don't think you're showing the proper respect, Number One."

"You're probably right," the first officer told him. "And believe me, I feel terrible about it."

"You don't *look* like you feel terrible about it."

"I hide it well," said Ben Zoma. He got to his feet. "Well, I would love to stay and gloat some more, but I think it's time we started out for Eggregedor."

"I would appreciate it," Picard responded.

He watched his friend leave the room to apprise Idun and Gerda of their destination. Then he turned back to his screen and sent a message to Admiral McAteer, confirming that the *Stargazer* had received her orders and would endeavor to carry them out.

No matter *what* the admiral had in mind for them.

Second Officer Elizabeth Wu of the Federation ship *Stargazer* sat down at the desk in her quiet, tastefully decorated quarters and opened the message that had come for her just that morning.

Wu had learned of it when she arrived on the bridge to go over supply reports with Captain Picard. As she passed Ulelo at his comm station, he had told her, "You've got mail, Commander. From Captain Rudolfini on the *Crazy Horse*."

Picard was the only one close enough to hear Ulelo. At the mention of Rudolfini, it seemed to Wu, a shadow crossed the captain's face. Of course, it might just have been her imagination.

In any case, her curiosity was piqued. In fact, it was increasingly difficult for her to keep her mind on her work until her shift was finally over.

Then she went straight to her quarters. And now here she was, opening the message—wondering what her former captain had to say as his image filled her monitor screen.

Enzo Rudolfini was tall, painfully thin and almost completely bald, with a prominent nose and a chin that seemed to want desperately to crawl into the flesh of his neck.

But if his looks were less than felicitous, his ability to command a starship more than made up for them. Rudolfini had a way of drawing people to him that Wu had never seen in any other human being. A week after she came aboard the *Crazy Horse* as a raw ensign, she would have given her life for the man.

And she wasn't alone in that regard. People loved Rudolfini. They adored him—enough to stay on his ship for the duration of their Starfleet careers in some cases. And Wu had envisioned doing exactly that herself—at least, in the beginning.

But after her third year as head of security on the *Crazy Horse,* she had craved a change—a challenge. And with the second-officer and first-officer slots filled with individuals as enamored of the captain as she was, it wouldn't be possible for her to find that challenge under Rudolfini's command.

So she applied for a transfer to a ship willing to give her a chance to serve as second officer. And she had found that opportunity here on the *Stargazer.*

Rudolfini hadn't been happy about it. He had loved Wu like a daughter. But what could he do? He couldn't offer her what she wanted. So like the good man he was, he had wished her well as she embarked on a new phase of her career.

He smiled at her from the screen. "Hello, Elizabeth. I hope this message finds you well."

It was good to hear Rudolfini's voice. Wu had only been gone a few weeks, but it felt like forever.

"Before I go on," he said, "I should tell you I've already discussed this with Captain Picard and received his permission to speak to you. So don't feel like you have to sneak around."

Wu's heart began to pound—and her heart *never* pounded, not even in the midst of a space battle.

"When you left the *Crazy Horse,* you said it was because you had nowhere to go. T'lar and Omalayak had locked down the first and second officers' slots and it seemed they would stay there for the long haul. Well, guess what?"

They're leaving, Wu thought wildly.

"They're leaving," Rudolfini said. "T'lar accepted a captaincy on the *Resilient* and she's taking Omalayak along as her first officer. Looks to me like I've got not one but *two* slots open. That is, if I can find someone capable of filling them."

Wu couldn't believe it.

"I had Mecir in mind for the second officer's post. If anyone deserves it, she does. But I don't have anyone qualified to be an exec, and I'd sure hate to have to look outside the family...."

Wu knew exactly where he was going with this. He was going to ask what she had dreamed about for years.

"So what do you say, Elizabeth? I know you just got

used to being a second officer, but they say it's easier to be a Number One than a Number Two. And I can't think of anyone I'd rather have standing beside me on the bridge of the *Crazy Horse*."

Wu drew a deep breath and let it out slowly.

"Get back to me as soon as you can, all right? Rudolfini out."

A moment later, his image blinked off and was replaced by the Starfleet logo. Wu sank back in her chair, stunned.

She had given up on the possibility of ever receiving another promotion on the *Crazy Horse*. And suddenly, a promotion had fallen right into her lap.

The question was...did she dare pass it up?

Phigus Simenon stood in his quarters and contemplated the small white stone in his scaly hand.

The stone, which had come from his homeworld, had a series of black characters carved into its otherwise smooth surface. As Simenon wasn't an expert in the area of ancient writings, he had no idea what the characters meant.

Nor did his father, to whom the stone had been given three long decades ago. But then, one didn't have to understand the characters to appreciate their significance in the scheme of things.

Simenon glanced at the computer terminal on the opposite side of the room. He had known this day would come. Hell, how could he *not* know? But he had put the prospect from his mind, concentrating instead on his duties as a Starfleet engineer.

Now he had no choice. He had received the summons. He was compelled to answer it.

With a sigh, Simenon crossed the room, pulled out

the chair in front of his terminal, and sat down. Then he placed the stone on the desk beside his keyboard and called up the message he had received from Gnala earlier in the day.

Typing out a return message, he had the terminal translate it into a language his people would understand—one that bore a vague resemblance to the characters on the stone.

Then he dispatched it to the communications queue for inclusion in the next subspace packet to that part of space, sat back in his chair, and absorbed the import of what he had done.

Carter Greyhorse, the *Stargazer*'s chief medical officer, blew on a spoonful of steaming hot corn chowder. "Yes, Pug," he replied, "I remember your misgivings."

"Well," said Pug Joseph, the ship's acting chief of security, "I think I'm getting past them. The way my people respond to me lately, I feel sometimes like I'm the *permanent* chief of security."

Joseph was sitting across the table from Greyhorse, twirling his fork in a plateful of pasta. To that point, the doctor noticed, Joseph had been too talkative to actually place any of it into his mouth.

"That's good," said Greyhorse.

"I'm gaining confidence," Joseph told him.

"I hear it in your voice."

Joseph grinned. "Really?"

"Would I lie to you?"

The physician took a mouthful of soup, savored its taste, and glanced across the mess hall. Right on schedule, Gerda Asmund was sitting down to eat with her sister Idun and a couple of other officers.

Greyhorse could have been one of them if he wished. But it would have been torture for him to share Gerda with others, to engage in conversations he didn't care about when what he really wanted was to take her in his arms.

And she knew how he felt about her. He had told her himself, right there in one of the ship's corridors less than a month earlier—just after she had lashed out at him in anger.

"You're all I can think of," the doctor had confessed, the bulkheads echoing with his pain. *"All I want to think of. I can't go on like this. If I haven't got a chance, I need to hear you say it."*

That's when Gerda had told him to meet her in the gym, where she would teach him "to fight like a warrior." It wasn't exactly an answer to his question. But then, in a way it *was*.

So Greyhorse met her in the gym as she suggested, and continued to meet her afterward at regular intervals. And little by little, despite his pronounced lack of athleticism, he was beginning to learn what she taught him.

But it wasn't his thirst for learning that kept him coming back. It was the chance to touch her, however fleetingly—to smell her scent, to hear her voice, to feel her intoxicating presence.

In the gym, where they were alone. Where it was just the two of them, locked in a dance of violence and grace—at least on her part.

But Greyhorse didn't sit with her in the mess hall. He sat with men like Joseph and listened to them go on about their personal trials while he kept his own very much to himself.

"So what's going on with you?" Joseph asked.

The doctor turned back to him and shrugged. "The usual."

Picard smiled politely at Wu as he regarded her across the sleek, black expanse of his ready room desk. "I believe I know why you asked to see me," he said.

Wu smiled back. "Captain Rudolfini asked me to respond on a timely basis. I did that."

"And what was your decision?" Picard asked, though he believed he already knew.

"I told him," said Wu, "that I would accept the position of first officer aboard the *Crazy Horse*."

The captain felt a sting of disappointment—no less sharp for his anticipation of it. "I see. As of when?"

"Your earliest convenience," said his second officer.

Picard nodded. "I will ask Mr. Paxton to contact the *Crazy Horse* and arrange a meeting in accordance with our schedules. I don't imagine it will take more than a week or two before we can get together."

"Thank you, sir," said Wu. She looked contrite for a moment. "I hope I haven't given you cause to disapprove of me."

"Disapprove?" he echoed.

"Yes, sir. For leaving so soon after I arrived."

Picard shook his head from side to side. "Not at all, Commander. Opportunity knocked. You answered."

Wu looked relieved. "Thank you for putting it that way, sir."

"If there's nothing else?" he said.

"Nothing," she confirmed.

"Then you are dismissed, Commander."

With a slight inclination of her head, Wu got up and left the captain's ready room. As soon as the door closed behind her, Picard sat back in his chair and shook his head.

In fact, he thought, he *did* resent Wu's coming and going in so short a time. He *did* disapprove of her behavior.

However, it wouldn't have accomplished anything if he had stood in the way of her transfer. The *Crazy Horse* would have missed out on Rudolfini's first choice of exec and the *Stargazer* would have been stuck with a disgruntled second officer.

It was too bad, Picard thought. He liked Wu. He had come to appreciate her dedication and efficiency, and she had even begun to overcome her tendency to be overzealous at times.

He tapped his communicator. "Picard to Commander Ben Zoma."

"Ben Zoma here," came the response.

"We've got a personnel matter to discuss, Gilaad."

There was a pause on the other end. *"The one you mentioned to me earlier?"*

The captain frowned. "Yes. *That* one."

"I'll be right there," his first officer promised. *"Ben Zoma out."*

The disappointment in his voice was unmistakable. But then, Ben Zoma had come to value Wu's contributions as well.

Picard swiveled in his chair to face his computer terminal. Tapping out a command, he called up Starfleet's periodically updated list of qualified second-officer candidates.

Unfortunately, there was no one on the *Stargazer* whom the captain could name as Wu's replacement. With so many of his officers having received battlefield promotions, command experience was in drastically short supply.

Funny, Picard thought. When Wu had been foisted on

him by Admiral McAteer prior to their hunt for the White Wolf, he hadn't looked forward to working with a stranger. Now he wasn't looking forward to seeking out a candidate on his own.

Nonetheless, the captain reflected with a sense of resignation, *that is* precisely *what I will have to do.*

Chapter Four

GERDA ASMUND WAS RUNNING a long-range sensor diagnostic at navigation when she saw a fair-haired young man approach the helm console manned by her twin sister.

Idun looked up at the fellow—an ensign she had never seen before—as he stopped beside her. "Yes?" she said, posing a challenge as much as a question.

"I'm your replacement," the ensign told her.

Gerda glanced at the chronometer readout in the upper right-hand corner of her control panel. In fact, Idun's shift was over, though Gerda's still had two hours to go.

It was the captain who had decided to stagger the schedules of the helm and navigation officers. What's more, it made perfect sense. The remaining officer could apprise the new one of any concerns that had arisen in the last couple of hours.

Nonetheless, Gerda hated to see anyone but her sister at the helm. Idun was a skilled pilot and a cool head in an emergency—and one never knew when a crisis might arise.

"So you are," Idun told the ensign.

She got up and gave him her seat. Then, with a glance at her sister, she left the bridge. Knowing Idun, Gerda imagined she would be in the gym in a matter of minutes.

Turning her attention to the new helmsman, Gerda watched him go over his monitors to make sure everything was in order. The navigator felt a rush of indignation. Did he think that someone like Idun would leave a mess for him?

Ben Zoma, who had the center seat, glanced at the ensign. "Steady as she goes, Mr. Paris."

The ensign nodded. "Aye, sir."

Paris, Gerda repeated to herself.

So *this* was the new crewman she had heard about. The one whose Starfleet lineage went back to the Stone Age, or so it seemed. He didn't look like much to Gerda.

But then, *no* human did.

Gerda had grown up among Klingons after the death of her natural parents. Her *human* parents. In the process, she had adopted a Klingon's way of looking at things—a Klingon's appreciation for the drama and spectacle of life.

Her Klingon father had been an impressive individual. He had carried himself with confidence, with dignity. One had but to look at him to know one was in the presence of a warrior.

Very few humans possessed that kind of bearing. Captain Ruhalter was one of them, though his spirit had gone to *Sto-Vo-Kor.* Captain Picard was another, at least at times.

And Greyhorse...

The navigator didn't know what to make of him. He was often passive, willing to let others make his decisions for him. But he showed a certain *promise,* she was forced to concede.

Ensign Paris, on the other hand, looked to the navigator like any other human—fragile, timid, too focused on expediency to give any thought to matters like dignity and honor. If he had a warrior's spirit, he concealed it well.

Abruptly, Paris's fingers began crawling over his control console. Clearly, he was busy with something. But to Gerda's knowledge, he hadn't been given an order to make changes.

"What are you doing?" she asked.

He looked at her. "I beg your pardon?"

Gerda pointed to the ensign's console. "You did something to the thrusters. What was it?"

He shrugged. "I changed the timing."

"Who told you to do that?"

Paris hesitated. "No one."

"Then why did you do it?" the navigator asked.

"To make the ship more responsive," he explained.

"Thruster timing is a delicate matter—one that requires special expertise. By tampering with it, you have likely made it necessary for someone to spend hours readjusting it."

"That's certainly a possibility," Paris conceded. "And if the thruster timing was all I'd worked on, it *would* be out of sync."

Gerda scowled. "You worked on *other* flight functions as well?"

"Sure," he said.

He tapped out a command and Gerda saw a graphic come up on her monitor. It showed her a bright yellow cross section of the *Stargazer*'s shield configuration.

Paris leaned over and pointed to the graphic. "By making complementary changes in thruster timing and shield geometry, I've picked up a tenth of a second of response time."

The navigator made some quick calculations, which—to her great surprise—precisely supported the ensign's contention. She looked at him with new respect.

"Of course," the ensign said, "it'll only make a difference if we find ourselves in a battle. And who knows when *that* will happen."

In her short time on the *Stargazer,* Gerda had already taken part in her share. "Soon enough," she assured him. She eyed his controls. "Where did you learn to do that?"

"Back at the Academy," said Paris.

"A professor taught it to you," Gerda concluded.

"Professor Rehling," he told her. "But he didn't teach it to me. We came up with it *together.* In fact, the professor insisted that my name appear above his when the monograph comes out."

"The monograph...?" Gerda echoed.

The ensign nodded. "They say it'll be required reading for all Starfleet helm officers."

"Impressive," the navigator muttered.

And Gerda Asmund wasn't easily impressed.

Vigo, the *Stargazer*'s Pandrilite weapons officer, had a bit of a problem on his hands.

His friend Charlie Kochman had introduced him to a clever diversion called sharash'di, having purchased it for Vigo from an Yridian merchant at a bazaar on Beta Nopterix. However, Kochman no longer seemed to wish to play the game.

In fact, he told Vigo he wished he had never bought it for him in the first place.

Of course, the weapons officer had challenged his friend to a sharash'di match a couple of times a day for the last several weeks. In retrospect, it was to this that he attributed Kochman's growing disaffection with the game.

Vigo, on the other hand, never seemed to grow tired of it. Every time he played sharash'di it was as if he were playing for the first time, discovering new complexities and new delights.

So when Kochman's interest in the game began to flag, Vigo found other opponents—among them the ill-fated Lt. Valderrama and Ulelo, the new man in communications. But the weapons officer was finding that none of these others wished to play him again, either. Valderrama, the only one who had seemed at all eager for a rematch, had changed her mind when Captain Picard stripped her of her responsibilities.

Hence, Vigo's problem.

But a few hours earlier, while he was still at his post, the *Stargazer* had picked up a couple of new crewmen—a new science officer and a new ensign. To Vigo's colleagues, the newcomers might have represented a great many things—expertise, reliability, new viewpoints to spice up mess hall banter.

To the Pandrilite, they represented only *one* thing: prospective sharash'di partners.

Which was why he had made it his business to get to this place as soon as his shift was over. The other newcomer was on the bridge according to the ship's computer. But *this* one was in his quarters.

Pressing the metallic pad set into the bulkhead, Vigo stepped back and waited. *Nol Kastiigan*, he repeated to himself. *Science officer first class. Formerly of the* Antares.

A moment later, the duranium doors to Kastiigan's quarters whispered open, revealing the science officer's anteroom. But the science officer himself was not in evidence.

"I will be right there," someone called in an oddly musical voice from the next room.

Kastiigan, Vigo thought.

"Don't hurry on my account," he advised the newcomer. Then he came in and looked around—and to his surprise, found himself wondering about what he was looking at.

The Pandrilite wasn't sure what he had expected to see here, but he was pretty certain this wasn't it.

"Thank your for your patience," said Kastiigan as he entered the room, wearing a black-and-white tunic and loose-fitting pants that featured the same color scheme. "As it happens, you are my first visitor."

Vigo nodded, still wondering. "I guess you haven't had a chance to unpack," he allowed.

His host looked at him. "I beg your pardon?"

Vigo indicated Kastiigan's quarters with a sweep of his hand. "There's nothing here."

The newcomer followed his gesture, but seemed at a loss. "On the contrary," he maintained, "there is quite a bit here. Chairs, computer, carpet…and that is in this room alone. In the next room, there is a bed, a set of drawers and a closet. And in the bathroom—"

"That's not what I mean," said the weapons officer. "Those things were here before you got here. They're permanent furnishings. I'm talking about *your* things."

Kastiigan seemed even more perplexed.

"You know," Vigo elaborated, "the items you brought with you from your previous assignment. Standing sculptures, hanging artwork, images of your loved ones…"

The science officer smiled. "I did not bring any such items."

Vigo looked at him askance. "You didn't bring any mementos from your homeworld? Or from the planets you've visited? No parting gifts from friends or family?"

Kastiigan shook his head from side to side, indicating that he had done nothing of the sort.

It was a big galaxy, the weapons officer reminded himself. Different cultures had different customs. Still, he was curious as to the reasoning behind the Kandilkari's behavior.

"Why *not?*" he asked.

"Because," Kastiigan explained, "such possessions would only be a burden to my crewmates after I perish."

For a moment, Vigo thought he was kidding. "Are you planning on perishing sometime soon?"

"Oh, yes," the newcomer responded cheerfully.

Vigo blanched. "You *are?*"

"Most definitely. As soon as possible. And when I do, I will consider it my great honor to give my life for my captain and my comrades—you included, Lieutenant."

"Er...thanks," said Vigo.

"You are quite welcome. Perhaps we will even have the opportunity to perish *together.*"

The Pandrilite managed a smile, albeit a weak one. "That would be...something to look forward to, wouldn't it?"

"It would indeed," said Kastiigan. "Now, what was it you wished to speak to me about?"

It wasn't often that Vigo could say he didn't have a yen to play sharash'di. This was one of those rare times.

"Nothing," he assured the Kandilkari. "Really. I just wanted to...welcome you aboard."

Kastiigan inclined his head. "You are kind to do so. Would you care to stay and join me in meditation?"

Vigo had never been one for meditation. He said so.

"I understand," the science officer told him. "For some, the manner of one's death is a personal matter."

"Right," said Vigo, jumping on the excuse with both feet. "It's personal. *Very* personal. So if you don't mind, I'll go back to my quarters and meditate on my own."

"May you find fulfillment in your meditation."

"You, too," the weapons officer told him. Then he backed out of Kastiigan's quarters and made his way down the corridor as quickly as he was able.

Phigus Simenon took a deep breath, waited for the turbolift doors to open, and headed directly for Picard's ready room.

He knew the captain was there because the ship's computer had told him so. Still, he glanced at the bridge's center seat to make sure the situation hadn't changed.

Picard wasn't there, but Commander Wu was. And in Simenon's experience, Wu was the sort of individual who wanted to know everything that was going on.

Everything. Without exception.

Seeing Wu's head turn in his direction, Simenon looked away again. The last thing he wanted to do was engage the second officer in conversation. He just wanted to take care of what he had come to the bridge for and beat a hasty retreat.

But Wu didn't seem inclined to let him do that. Rising from her seat, she intercepted the engineer and asked, "Can I help you?"

She couldn't. Only Picard or Commander Ben Zoma could do that. "No," Simenon told her emphatically.

He must have surprised Wu with the forcefulness of his response, because she recoiled a bit. What's more, the other bridge officers turned to look at him.

It was exactly what he had hoped to avoid.

"All right," Wu said, regaining her composure. "Then perhaps—"

The engineer didn't wait for her to finish her suggestion. Instead, he turned and made his way back to the turbolift, having embarrassed himself quite enough.

As he reached the double doors, they slid apart for him. He was about to enter the lift compartment when he heard a familiar hiss.

Picard's ready room door was opening. Simenon turned his head in time to see the captain and Ben Zoma emerge.

Before they could go anywhere, the Gnalish hurried over and planted himself in front of them. Picard looked surprised. But then, he had probably never seen his chief engineer move so quickly before.

"Mr. Simenon," he said.

Ben Zoma smiled. "Everything all right?"

The Gnalish wasn't in the mood for niceties. "Can I see you in private?" he rasped. "Both of you?"

Picard's eyes narrowed. No doubt, he was trying to divine the reason for Simenon's discomfort.

"Of course," he said at last.

"Good," the engineer snapped, and led his superiors back into the captain's ready room.

Ensign Nikolas was whistling to himself as he made his way to the bridge for his training session with Commander Wu.

Wu wasn't exactly known as an easy taskmaster. People didn't often whistle on their way to meetings with her. But this once, Nikolas felt justified in doing so.

To that point in his career on the *Stargazer,* he had earned a reputation for arriving at his training sessions just in the nick of time, raising the eyebrows of the officers in charge of them. In fact, some of the ensign's friends had picked up on his habit and given him the obvious moniker: "Nik of Time."

But this time he wasn't going to show up exactly when he was due. For once, he was going to be early for something.

That was his intention, at least.

But as Nikolas passed the doors to the ship's gymnasium, which were situated between his quarters and the nearest turbolift, he saw them slide open. And out of the corner of his eye, he saw a feminine figure come out of the gym.

Of course, he wouldn't have allowed himself to be detained if it was just *any* feminine figure. But it wasn't. It was Idun Asmund, her cheeks flushed with evidence of her exertions, her skin glistening with a thin sheen of sweat.

Nikolas didn't know he was slowing down to acknowledge her until he had already done it. "Lieutenant," he said a little awkwardly.

She glanced at him, her eyes the blue of polar ice, and said, "Ensign." Then she made her way down the corridor.

As he watched her retreat, he couldn't help smiling. Idun Asmund was a living work of art. No, he corrected himself—*better* than that. She was a genuine masterpiece.

"Nikolas?" said a familiar, high-pitched voice.

The ensign looked away from the object of his admiration just long enough to see who had greeted him. He found himself peering down at a small, pink humanoid who—as the ever-sensitive Joe Caber had gleefully pointed out—looked a lot like a plucked chicken.

In this case, a plucked chicken in midnight-blue gym togs.

"Obal," said Nikolas.

The Binderian, who worked in security under Pug Joseph, looked up at him with a distinct glint of curiosity in his eyes. "What are you doing?" he asked.

Nikolas resumed his admiration of Idun Asmund. "Appreciating one of the finer things in life."

A moment later, the helm officer vanished around a bend in the corridor. The ensign sighed. *All good things come to an end,* he mused, and he couldn't think of anything better than the sight of such an attractive woman.

Nikolas turned to his friend—and realized something. "Hey...you were working out in the gym just now, weren't you?"

"Why, yes," said Obal.

The ensign smiled. "You know what? You're one lucky guy."

"And why is that?"

"Well," said Nikolas, "it's not everybody who gets a chance to share a gym with one of the Asmund twins."

The Binderian's brow wrinkled over his big, round eyes. "What does luck have to do with it? Are the Asmunds less likely to make use of the gym than other crewmen?"

Nikolas chuckled. "You don't get it, do you?"

Obal shrugged his bony shoulders. "I suppose not."

The ensign wasn't all that surprised. As humanoid development went, Obal's people were pretty far off the beaten track. Nonetheless, he did his best to explain.

"You see, buddy, by human standards, the Asmund twins are hot. I mean *really* hot."

Obal looked just as perplexed as before. "Hot?"

Nikolas sighed. "They're...how can I put it? Extremely desirable mating partners. Get it?"

A light went on in the Binderian's eyes. "Ah," he said knowingly. "*Hot.* Of course."

Nikolas pointed to his friend's chest. "And *you* got to get sweaty with her. You know what that makes you? The envy of every human male on board—me included."

Obal shrugged again. "If you say so. But, you understand, we didn't engage in any mating practices. We merely fought."

It was the human's turn to be perplexed. "You mean you...sparred with her? With Idun Asmund?"

The security officer nodded. "It was her idea, actually. She said she had heard of my prowess as a hand-to-hand combatant and wished to see if the stories were true. As it turned out, it was an exhilarating experience for both of us."

Nikolas smiled. After all, he had seen Obal in action. His friend was as fast as lightning and twice as devastating.

"Then you must have pulled your punches, my friend. Otherwise, the lieutenant wouldn't have walked out under her own power."

Obal let a smile of his own leak out. "I suppose I did pull my punches a *little.*"

It had to be more than just a little, Nikolas mused. But what he said was, "That's what I thought." Then an idea came to him—a brillant, absolutely inspired idea. "Say, do you think you could set up a sparring session for *me?*"

The Binderian looked at him. "With Lieutenant Asmund?"

"Yup. With Lieutenant Asmund."

Obal thought about it. "You're sure you'd like that?"

"I know I would. It would give me a chance to get to know her a little better—and there are few things I would rather do in life than get to know Idun Asmund."

Obal seemed to understand. "All right. I'll try."

"That's the spirit," Nikolas told him. "And if she agrees, I'll treat you to dinner."

His friend eyed him suspiciously. "But dinner is available to all crewmen free of charge."

"Picky, picky," said Nikolas, already dreaming about his sparring session with the statuesque helm officer.

Unexpectedly, Obal made a face. "Wait a second…"

"What is it?" the ensign asked.

"Shouldn't you be on the bridge? I distinctly recall your saying that you had a training session scheduled with Commander Wu."

Nikolas felt the blood drain from his face. "Gotta go," he blurted and sprinted down the corridor, hoping he could catch a turbolift before it was too late.

Picard sat down behind his desk and watched Ben Zoma fill the chair on the other side of it. But their chief engineer remained on his feet, pacing back and forth across the captain's ready room with his hands clasped behind his back.

Picard had seen Simenon agitated before, but seldom like this. It worried him.

"Won't you sit down?" he asked Simenon.

The Gnalish shook his head. "That won't be necessary." Suddenly, he stopped and looked directly at Picard. "I need a leave of absence. For personal reasons."

"Personal reasons?" Ben Zoma echoed.

Simenon hesitated, his ruby eyes blinking. "Yes," he said finally.

It was clear that he didn't wish to go into any detail regarding his request. However, the captain felt compelled to make sure his officer was all right.

"Is there a problem?" he asked.

Again, Simenon hesitated, as if that were a difficult question to answer. Then he said, "Everything is fine."

Picard frowned. "You're not ill, are you?"

The engineer looked at him askance. "Why do you ask?"

The captain smiled. "Isn't it obvious? You seem to have something on your mind."

"That's for sure," Ben Zoma chimed in. "Come on, Simenon. You're among friends. What's going on?"

Leave it to Ben Zoma to cut to the chase, Picard reflected. He regarded the engineer. "Phigus?"

For a moment, he thought Simenon might let them in on his problem. Then the Gnalish's lizardlike features hardened with resolve. "I have to go back to Gnala," he said. "That's all. And if you're my friends, you won't ask me any more questions."

Picard and his first officer exchanged glances. The captain didn't like the idea of letting the matter drop. However, Simenon wasn't leaving him any other option.

"Very well," Picard said reluctantly. "I'll respect your privacy. And I'll grant your request for a leave of absence."

Ben Zoma looked at him and shrugged. "There's nothing urgent about Egreggedor, is there?"

"Nothing," the captain agreed. He glanced at the intercom grid. "Picard to Gerda Asmund."

"Asmund here," came the response.

"Chart a course for Gnala, Lieutenant. Best speed."

"Aye, sir," said Gerda.

The Gnalish looked from one of them to the other. "Thank you," he told them. Then, before they could engage him in further conversation, he left Picard's ready room.

As the door whispered closed in Simenon's wake, Ben Zoma whistled. "I've never seen him like that."

"Nor have I," the captain noted.

"I wonder what's bugging him," said Ben Zoma.

So did Picard. But he had given his word not to pry into Simenon's business and he meant to keep that promise unconditionally.

Chapter Five

Captain's Personal Log, supplemental. We are more than halfway to Gnala, the world of Simenon's birth, and he has yet to volunteer any additional information regarding his business there. In fact, he has become rather close-mouthed in general, leading me to believe that what awaits him on Gnala may be something less than pleasant for him. Still, I continue to respect Simenon's wishes and allow him to deal with the matter on his own.

FOR THE UMPTEENTH TIME THAT DAY, Elizabeth Wu's thoughts wandered in the direction of her return to the *Crazy Horse.* And for the umpteenth time, she reeled them back in.

For the time being, she was still serving on the *Stargazer.* Captain Picard and everyone else on the ship were depending on her to carry out her duties faithfully and efficiently, and she would be damned if she would fail them in any way.

Hence, her decision to visit the science section. It wasn't that she didn't trust Lt. Kastiigan, who appeared to be a capable individual. It was just that new section chiefs often had questions, and it was the second officer's job to answer them.

Just as soon as the double doors slid open in front of her, Wu began to look around for Kastiigan. As it turned out, he was nowhere in sight. All she could see was the section's horseshoe-shaped bank of sleek, black sensor stations, through which all incoming data was available.

Half the stations were occupied—in every case but one by a science technician who had received prior authorization to access sensor data. The crewman who represented the exception was easy to identify, even when seen from the back.

After all, most of the 240 people serving on the *Stargazer* only donned a Starfleet-issue containment suit when they went *outside* the ship. Only one of them—a Nizhrak ensign named Jiterica, whose molecular structure was radically different from any of her colleagues'—was in the habit of wearing a suit on board.

Wu crossed the room to join Jiterica. But it wasn't until she was standing beside the ensign that her presence was noted.

Turning in her chair, Jiterica looked up at the second officer. There was an expression of surprise imposed on the ghostly visage visible through her transparent faceplate.

"Commander," she said, her voice sounding tinny as it emerged from her specially designed vocalization unit.

"Ensign," Wu responded with the same note of formality.

Jiterica glanced at the monitor, then at Wu again. "I apologize. I accessed sensor data without the proper authorization."

She was right. And the fact that she had violated regulations with full knowledge of what she was doing made her violation an even more grievous one.

The second officer's first impulse was to come down on Jiterica for blatantly breaking the rules. However, she managed to hold that impulse in check.

Not so long ago, Ben Zoma had made Wu the object of a strict interpretation of the rules, giving her a taste of how it felt. Since then, she had become less of a stickler about regulations, and her relationships with the crew had improved as a result.

Nor, to her surprise, had anyone's efficiency suffered. It was a lesson Wu now wished she had learned years earlier.

"It's all right," she told Jiterica. "It's a minor infraction. There's no need to apologize."

The ensign gazed at her for a moment, her ghostly visage unreadable. "Thank you," she said at last.

"Don't mention it," Wu assured her.

Peering over Jiterica's shoulder at the monitor, she saw that the ensign was studying the file on Gamma Barchedden V, a gas giant in a distant star system. She wondered why—until she remembered that Jiterica had grown up in the atmosphere of a gas giant.

When Wu regarded Jiterica again, she thought she saw a sadness in her strange, translucent eyes. A melancholy, as if she had lost something dear to her.

"Are you...homesick?" Wu asked.

Jiterica didn't give her an answer right away. And when she did, it was an elusive one. "I was just trying to gain a better understanding of Gamma Barchedden."

Understanding that the subject might be an emotional one, the second officer didn't probe any deeper. "I see," was all she said.

The ensign got to her feet—a less than graceful maneuver, thanks to the cumbersome suit she wore. "I'm due on the bridge in a few minutes," she told Wu. Then she brushed past her and made for the exit.

Wu's heart went out to Jiterica. After all, the Nizhrak hadn't had an easy time of it on her last vessel, nor had she made any friends to this point on the *Stargazer.*

And yet, if not for her contribution to their search for the White Wolf, they might never have had an opportunity to find the pirate. Obviously, the ensign had a lot to offer.

But she might never get the chance unless someone took her under her wing. *Someone like me,* Wu thought.

She might not have planned to serve on the *Stargazer* much longer, but while she was there she was going to see what she could do on behalf of Ensign Jiterica.

Vigo wasn't exactly a stranger to the *Stargazer*'s engineering section. As chief weapons officer, he often had occasion to check on the various systems that generated and delivered the energy used in phaser and photon torpedo barrages.

But he hadn't come to engineering to check on any systems this time. He had come to see his friend Pug Joseph.

Vigo found him in his office, a small cubicle that lay just past the weapons diagnostic room and opposite the locked phaser armory. As the Pandrilite filled the doorway with his bulk, he saw Joseph look up from whatever work he was doing on his computer terminal.

"Vigo," said the security chief. He swiveled around in his chair. "What's up?"

"I…wanted to speak with you," the Pandrilite told him.

Joseph's brow pinched over the bridge of his nose. "You don't look so good. Is everything all right?"

Vigo averted his eyes. "Perhaps not everything."

The human leaned forward. "What's the matter?"

"I've had a…bad experience," Vigo said.

"Bad in what way?"

Vigo frowned. It was an awkward expression for him. A smile would have felt much more natural.

"I just spoke with Lieutenant Kastiigan in his quarters. Apparently, he intends to die."

Joseph stared at his friend. "I hate to tell you, buddy, but I don't think any of us has a choice in the matter."

"No," said Vigo, struggling to explain. "He doesn't *expect* to die. He *intends* to die."

The security officer looked strained as he tried to figure out the difference. "I'm not sure I follow you."

The Pandrilite heaved a sigh. "I don't suppose I'm explaining this very well."

"Why don't we try it again? You spoke with Kastiigan, right? And he told you…?" Joseph held his hands out, palms up, indicating that it was Vigo's turn to speak.

"He told me that he wanted to die. He wanted to give his life for his captain and comrades."

Joseph shrugged. "People say those kinds of things."

"And he wanted to do it *as soon as possible*."

Finally, the security officer began to show signs of concern. "As soon as possible? You mean he's in a hurry?"

"So it would seem."

Joseph grunted. "Are you saying Kastiigan is… suicidal?"

Vigo shook his hairless, blue head. "I don't think so. I just think he's got a warped sense of duty."

Joseph looked at him with a hint of suspicion in his expression. "Then why are you so shaken up?"

The weapons officer frowned again. "On Pandril, we don't speak of...the sort of event Kastiigan is contemplating. It's considered bad luck. Tempting fate, a human would say."

The security chief seemed to see the entire picture now. "He's giving you the heebie-jeebies."

"That would be another way of putting it."

"So what are you going to do? Try to avoid Kastiigan?"

"As much as I can," Vigo told him.

"It's a big ship," Joseph said, "but it's not *that* big. You're going to run into him sooner or later."

"I thought you might suggest a way for me to avoid doing so."

The security officer considered the question for a while. Then he said, "You could find out what shift he's working and work a different one. But that's not going to work all the time."

"I know," said Vigo, who had already discarded that option on his own. "As the senior weapons officer, I have to be available when the captain *wants* me to be available."

Joseph gave it some more thought. "Well," he said finally, "you could try talking to him. You could let him know that all his talk of dying is disturbing you."

That had occurred to Vigo as well. He had rejected it because he was a Pandrilite—because his people weren't the kind to impose their values on others. But maybe it was time to break with tradition.

"Perhaps I will do that," he told Joseph. "Thank you."

"Hey," said the security officer, "I'm glad to help. Let me know how it goes, will you?"

Vigo agreed that he would do that.

As Dikembe Ulelo waited for a turbolift on Deck 10, his hands locked behind his back, he considered the contents of the subspace mail he had read to that point.

Commander Wu had been offered a position on another vessel. Lt. Iulus's sister had given birth to a girl. And Ensign Montenegro's father had survived a serious illness.

None of this news succeeded in moving the comm officer to any great degree. However, he filed it all away in his mind, knowing he might need to draw on it sometime.

"Dikembe?" someone said, intruding on his thoughts.

Ulelo turned and saw a woman approaching him. A crewman in the science section, judging by her uniform.

But she didn't look at all familiar to him. And judging by the pucker in the woman's brow, she wasn't entirely certain that *he* looked familiar to *her*.

Ulelo's first impulse was to leave the vicinity. To *escape*. But how could he do that? The *Stargazer* wasn't so big a place that he could lose himself once he had been identified.

Eventually, the woman would find him. Better to face her now, the comm officer told himself, than have to explain his abrupt departure at some later date.

The woman's expression of uncertainty became a smile as she came closer. "It *is* you," she said.

"Yes," Ulelo responded, not knowing what else to say.

"What are you doing here on the *Stargazer?*" she asked. "I thought you were still working for Lovejoy on the *Copernicus.*"

The comm officer frowned. Lovejoy was his former captain, the *Copernicus* his previous assignment.

The woman tilted her head playfully as she regarded him. "What's the matter?" she said. "Cat got your tongue?"

His frown deepened. Apparently, she had met him prior to his coming to the *Stargazer.* It was evident from her tone and choice of references. But he still didn't have a clue as to who she was.

Before he could consider the wisdom of saying so, it came out. "I'm sorry," he said, "but I don't know who you are."

The woman's smile faded a bit. "Since when did you become such a joker, Dikembe?"

Ulelo had no choice but to remain steadfast in his position. "I'm not joking. If we've met before, I don't recall it."

The woman's smile faded the rest of the way. "Stop it. We spent *hours* together at the Academy. You, me, Angela, Ragnar…"

He didn't remember Angela or Ragnar either. "I'm sorry."

She held her hands out in an appeal for reason. "It's *Emily,* Dikembe. Emily *Bender.*"

Ulelo just shrugged.

Her gaze went cold. "Right. Whatever you say." And with that, she turned and began to walk away.

But the woman didn't get far before she stopped and looked at him again. This time, her expression was one of unconcealed resentment. Clearly, he had caused her some discomfort.

"I don't know why you're pretending not to know me," she said, "but it's rude. Damned rude."

Then she walked away.

Chapter Six

"MIND YOU," SAID PICARD, "I didn't bring you aboard for this reason alone. But I would be lying if I told you I haven't been looking forward to this moment."

Ensign Paris inclined his head slightly. "That's high praise, sir. I'll do my best to prove worthy of it."

With that, he slipped on his fencing mask, raised his sword vertically in a gesture of respect, and dropped into an en garde position.

Picard smiled approvingly. If Paris was even half as good a fencer as his personnel file had indicated, this was going to be a most enjoyable bout indeed.

And it would have the added benefit of taking Picard's mind off other matters—the sort that hadn't even occurred to him before Admiral Mehdi made him a captain.

Personnel matters, for instance. Caber and Valderrama might be history, gone if not quite forgotten. But

Picard was plagued more and more by the looming prospect of Commander Wu's departure.

The woman had just begun to feel at home here, it seemed to him. She had just begun to accept the way her superiors conducted themselves on the *Stargazer.*

And what does Rudolfini do? He reels her back to the Crazy Horse *like a prize fish.*

Then there was Simenon. Though Picard had promised not to pry into the engineer's personal affairs, he wished he knew more about Simenon's reasons for visiting his homeworld.

But there was nothing he could do in either case, Wu's or Simenon's. They weren't children, after all. They had the right to make their own decisions, just as he did.

And right now, he chose to test his new ensign's mettle.

The captain slipped on his own mask and returned Paris's salute. Then he lowered himself into a crouch and extended his blade, savoring what was to come.

He wasn't disappointed. The ensign's initial attack was a flurry of high and low angles that drove Picard back almost to the limit of the strip. But before he could be driven off it, the captain launched a counterattack. Inspired by his opponent's speed and aggressiveness, he matched it lunge for lunge.

And Paris warded off each thrust. In fact, he almost turned the last one into a point with a deadly-quick riposte.

Again, Picard smiled. This was nothing like fencing with Lt. Pierzynski. Nothing at *all.*

Paris launched another assault, probing what he must have perceived as the captain's weaknesses. His point darted at Picard's lead shoulder, then his lead hip, then his shoulder again.

But the captain parried each move and answered it

with a thrust of his own. It gave the ensign pause, forced him to think about what he would try next.

And in that moment, Picard struck.

His attack wasn't just quick, it was devilishly precise—a long, low lunge of which his fencing instructors back in France would have been proud. As Paris retreated in desperation, the captain's point came at his chest like an angry viper.

But just when Picard thought he had won the touch, the ensign flung his bell-shaped guard in the way. It deflected the captain's weapon just enough to keep it from grazing his opponent.

Picard swore softly to himself and tried it again. This time, his attack was more explosive than precise. But as before, Paris managed to deflect it enough to save himself.

The captain was tempted to make the attempt a third time since Paris seemed to be off-balance. But the ensign recovered more quickly than Picard would have thought possible and nearly caught him off guard with a lunge of his own.

They were back in the center of the strip, the captain noticed, right where they had started. As if in mutual recognition of that fact, the combatants paused for a moment.

"Well played," Picard said, his breath coming hard.

Paris inclined his head. "Thank you, Captain."

"Especially that last counter. Brilliant, I thought."

"You're too kind," said the ensign. "Shall we have another go at it?"

"I'd like that," Picard replied sincerely.

And they went at each other again.

As Admiral Arlen McAteer gazed out the observation port of the modest and all-but-empty officer's lounge at

Starbase 37, he was reminded of how little he had enjoyed living on starbases.

Unfortunately, he had been forced to do so at various times in his career—including an eighteen-month stint shortly after graduation at Starbase 68. He had worked there as the attaché of Admiral Bailey, a man with an unsightly paunch, thick white hair, and an equally white mustache.

Bailey, as McAteer recalled, hadn't tried any new approaches to the management of his sector. He hadn't made adjustments in personnel and their responsibilities. All he had done, it seemed, was let matters follow their natural course.

Early on, McAteer decided that Bailey wasn't very impressive, either as a man or as an admiral. He figured he could do better—a lot better. It was while he was working at Starbase 68 that McAteer decided he would become an admiral himself one day.

He had reached that objective precisely according to plan. Of course, the admiral still felt compelled now and then to leave Starfleet Headquarters on Earth and visit a starbase, but that was an inescapable part of his job.

And sometimes it wasn't McAteer's job at all but he did it anyway, for reasons that might be considered more personal than professional. This was one of those times.

His thoughts were interrupted by the hiss of the lounge doors and the sight of a woman in officer's garb. *It's her,* the admiral thought, recognizing the woman from her file picture.

Her name was Rachel Garrett. She was the second officer on the Federation starship *Excelsior.*

McAteer decided that Garrett's file image hadn't done her justice. *She's a damned impressive-looking woman,* he reflected. Part of him wondered if she had dinner plans.

But then, he could have more easily obtained a dinner date back on Earth, if that was all he was after. He had traveled all the way to this base for a much more important reason, and one that precluded any kind of romantic liaison.

"Admiral," said Garrett as she approached him.

"Pleased to meet you," he said, offering the woman his hand.

She took it. "Likewise, sir."

"Something to drink?" McAteer asked.

Garrett shook her head. "No. Nothing, thanks."

"Please," he said, "sit down."

He indicated a chair across a low table from his. The commander took it and gave him her attention.

McAteer smiled at her, doing his best impression of a doting uncle. "I've been looking forward to meeting you, Commander. I've heard good things about you."

She looked pleased to hear it. "Thank you, sir."

He wrinkled his nose. "Nasty business with the Orazwari last month."

Garrett nodded soberly. "It was. I suppose my captain told you all about it."

"I read his report. He said he had no choice but to leave his landing party behind until he could regroup and determine what he was up against. He also said the party wouldn't have survived without the courage of its ranking officer."

Garrett shrugged. "I was in charge, sir. I did what anyone would have done in my place."

"As I recall," said McAteer, "you did a bit more than that. When you saw that the Orazwari were getting close to your hiding place, you led them in another direction single-handedly—risking your own life so that the crewmen in your care could survive."

"Most of them were wounded," she explained. "They weren't in any shape to lead the Orazwari away."

"Nonetheless," said the admiral, "a remarkable effort. And all the more remarkable when one considers the fact that you survived."

"I was lucky, sir."

"I don't believe that for a minute," he told Garrett, "and unless I'm mistaken, neither do you." He leaned back in his chair and regarded his monitor screen, which the commander couldn't see. "After all, this isn't the first time you've demonstrated remarkable courage or inventiveness. In fact, you've pretty much made a habit of it."

Garrett didn't seem to know how to respond to that.

"You know," said McAteer, approaching the real reason he had arranged to see her, "a woman with your extraordinary abilities should be moving up the chain of command. But I see that you've been a second officer for some time now."

His guest shrugged. "I like it on the *Excelsior.* It's a wonderful ship with a wonderful captain."

"So I understand," the admiral told her. "And I don't doubt that he values your services. But your fleet would benefit more if you were to make a change."

Garrett looked at him askance. "Such as?"

"Second officer on another ship."

Her brow creased ever so slightly. "I don't understand, sir. I'm *already* a second officer."

"Of course you are," said McAteer. "But on the *Excelsior,* there aren't any opportunities for advancement. Whereas, if you were to make a lateral move to another ship...you might find such opportunities materializing before you know it."

Garrett looked at him. "Is this a hypothetical question? Or did you have a ship in mind?"

"I have a ship in mind, all right. But for the moment, I prefer to conduct our conversation as if we *were* speaking hypothetically."

"I see," the commander said.

"So what would you do," the admiral asked, "if I were to say that I could arrange a berth for you on another vessel...where you would be the recipient of a captaincy in a short amount of time?"

Garrett looked tempted—just as he had predicted. "A captaincy," she said. "That would be quite a move."

"Are you saying you don't deserve it? Or that you're not eminently capable of commanding a starship?"

"I'm saying it would be most unusual, sir. In fact, this entire conversation strikes me as most unusual. I find myself asking why a Starfleet admiral would go to the trouble of meeting me out here in the hinterlands, much less making the kind of assurances you're making." She paused. "Hypothetical or otherwise."

McAteer smiled again. "You're a shrewd woman, Commander. But then, that doesn't surprise me in the least. If you were any less shrewd, I might be speaking with someone else."

"Obviously," said Garrett, "you want something. What is it?"

He continued smiling. "All I want is to help you help yourself—by supplying me with information on the officers with whom you'll share your new ship. When we've accumulated enough of it, I'll have them disciplined and stripped of their ranks. And you will move in to fill the breach created by their absence."

"And if I don't find anything objectionable?"

"You will," he told her. "Believe me."

Garrett seemed to consider the admiral's offer for

a moment. Then she frowned. "Permission to speak freely, sir?"

McAteer held his arms out in an expression of magnanimity. "By all means, Commander."

His guest leaned forward. "I'll be blunt, Admiral. I want to move up in the world as much as anyone in the fleet—but not at the expense of other qualified officers."

"They're *not* qualified," he interjected.

Garrett chuckled. "Why don't I believe that?"

"You need to trust me," McAteer said.

"Sorry," she replied. "I don't. And just for the record, Admiral, I don't ever plan on allowing myself to be used as a political pawn—yours or anyone else's."

McAteer had the distinct impression that his offer had been spurned. *Imagine that*, he thought.

"I don't suppose it would make any difference if I sweetened the pot?" he said.

Garrett smiled stubbornly. "There's nothing sweet enough in this galaxy to make me your puppet, Admiral."

McAteer scowled. Obviously, this conversation wasn't going anywhere. There was just one thing left to do.

"I'm sorry we couldn't help each other, Commander. I think you'll come to regret that in time. But in any case, what we've discussed here today is not for public consumption. If I learn that you've even mentioned this conversation to anyone—and I mean *anyone*—you'll be drummed out of the fleet. Understood?"

"What I understand," Garrett said, "is that you'll probably drum me out of the fleet anyway. Otherwise I'll be a danger to you—someone who can expose you for what you are."

"Come now," the admiral told her. "Do you really think I'd leave myself open like that? We haven't mentioned a name, remember? We haven't even mentioned a ship. So what is there to expose?"

That seemed to give Garrett pause.

"Besides," he added, "this sort of maneuvering happens a lot more often than you might imagine. You might say it's the *business* of admirals to maneuver."

"Not being an admiral," she said, "I wouldn't know."

He couldn't resist a gibe after the way she'd refused him. "And you probably never will. Dismissed, Commander."

Garrett stared at McAteer for a moment. Then she got up and left the room.

A pity, the admiral thought. The second officer of the *Excelsior* had seemed like the perfect candidate for what he was trying to accomplish. The perfect inside informant—though she might have suggested a slightly different term for it.

McAteer sighed. He would just have to find someone else to torpedo Jean-Luc Picard.

Chapter Seven

ELIZABETH WU WAS A WOMAN OF HER WORD, even if no one had heard her give it.

Stopping in front of Ensign Jiterica's quarters, she touched the security pad in the bulkhead. A moment later, the doors parted and gave her access to what lay within.

As it turned out, the ensign was seated at her workstation, the blue glare of its screen superimposed over the gray, vaguely human face she effected. Though her chair was bigger than the standard, she looked uncomfortable in her containment suit. Cramped, Wu thought.

"Hello," she said.

"Hello," Jiterica echoed.

"Doing some reading?"

The ensign paused for a moment before answering. "I am not accessing the sensors."

Wu waved away the notion. "I wasn't accusing you of anything."

"Then why are you here?" Jiterica asked.

The second officer shrugged. "If you have no plans tonight, I thought you might like to join me for dinner."

Jiterica looked at her. "I don't eat."

It hadn't occurred to Wu to consider that possibility. "You must eat *something,*" she said.

The ensign pointed to a valve on her containment suit—one that the second officer hadn't noticed before. "This mechanism allows me to create an aperture in my containment field. Through it, I can ingest air molecules, which my body is able to break down into their component atoms and use as sustenance."

Wu nodded. "I see. But humans—and a great many other species—don't just go to the mess hall to eat. We go to socialize, to—" She searched for the right word.

"Commune?" Jiterica suggested.

Wu breathed a sigh of relief. "Yes. May I assume that your people have an equivalent activity?"

"We gather in groups at certain times of day," the ensign explained. "We share experiences."

"That's exactly what I'm talking about," Wu said. "Even though your planet and your people are far away, you need to commune with someone. You need to share your experiences."

Jiterica seemed to absorb the advice. However, there was no indication in the cast of her ghostly features as to whether the second officer had swayed her.

"What do you think?" Wu asked, trying not to be too pushy. "Would you like to give it a try?"

The ensign considered it for a moment longer. Then she said, "When would you like to do this?"

Wu smiled. "I'll meet you back here as soon as our shifts are over. How does that sound?"

"As soon as our shifts are over," Jiterica echoed.

As the second officer left the Nizhrak's quarters, she felt a distinct sense of accomplishment. And for good reason.

She was about to make a difference in someone's life. She had convinced a lonely outsider to take the first step on a journey of immense personal enrichment.

Even after she was gone, she thought, Jiterica would remember the woman who had helped her find her place on the *Stargazer.*

Nikolas was sitting at the computer station he shared with his roommate, going over his new schedule of assignments, when he heard the sound of chimes.

Someone was calling on him. He hoped it was Obal.

After all, the Binderian had promised to try to get him a sparring session with Idun Asmund. And when Nikolas had looked his friend up at the end of his shift, the computer had informed him that Obal wasn't in his quarters.

He was in Idun's.

"Come in," said Nikolas, rising to his feet.

The doors opened and Obal entered. "Nikolas," he said, greeting the ensign exactly as he usually did.

"There you are," said Nikolas. "How did it go?"

He could tell from the change in the Binderian's expression that he wouldn't like the answer to his question. "Not well, my friend."

"What happened?" the ensign asked.

Obal shrugged his narrow shoulders. "Lieutenant Asmund declined your invitation to spar."

Nikolas was disappointed. Obviously, the woman was intimidated by the prospect of fighting with him.

"Maybe it would help," he said, "if you promised her I would go easy on her."

The Binderian didn't look very optimistic. "I doubt it."

Nikolas considered the lack of enthusiasm in his friend's response. "It's worth a try, isn't it?"

Obal's expression told the ensign he didn't think so.

"Okay," said Nikolas. "I'll tell her myself."

"She will not agree," Obal told him.

"We'll see about that," the ensign replied. And with that, he left his friend to pay a visit to Idun Asmund.

Gilaad Ben Zoma had met Tanya Tresh on his first day at Starfleet Academy.

Though their relationship had begun as a heated love affair, it had cooled off more quickly than either of them would have imagined, and settled into the kind of warm, intimate friendship only former lovers could enjoy.

Unfortunately, Ben Zoma hadn't actually seen his friend Tanya in more than a year. But then, he was the first officer of the *Stargazer,* and she was doing what she had always wanted to do—serving as an exobiologist on a Starfleet research vessel.

Still, they corresponded often by subspace packet. Usually it was just to say hello or send news of a mutual acquaintance. But this time, Ben Zoma had contacted his friend for a different reason.

"Gilaad," she said, as beautiful as ever beneath a fashionable pile of long, blond hair. "It was good to hear from you as always—even if all you wanted was to pick my brain."

The first officer smiled. Once, he had had other things in mind, but those days were long past. And Tanya did possess the particular expertise he needed.

"I don't know why you've suddenly developed such an interest in this subject, but here's your answer," she said. And she went on to tell him exactly what he wanted to know.

Ben Zoma frowned. He hadn't expected good news, but this was even worse than he had imagined.

"I hope that helps," Tanya told him. "Take care. And say hello to your pal Jean-Luc for me. I always did have a soft spot for Frenchmen."

Ben Zoma was so occupied with the information she had given him, he barely took notice of her teasing. He sat there for a moment as his friend's face gave way to the Starfleet insignia.

Then he got up and made his way to the captain's ready room.

Commander Wu looked around the surprisingly crowded mess hall for some open seats. Finding a couple at the far end of the room, she turned to her companion and pointed.

"We can sit there," she suggested.

Ensign Jiterica turned the transparent faceplate of her containment suit in the indicated direction. "If you say so," she responded, her voice as flat and tinny as ever.

"Good," said the second officer, making a conscious effort to sound cheerful for Jiterica's sake. "Let's go." And she led the way, threading a path between two rows of tables.

Glancing over her shoulder, she made sure that the ensign was following her. After all, Jiterica hadn't looked eager to accompany her here in the first place. And whenever Wu happened to glance at the Nizhrak's ghostly features, she had seen indications of uncertainty and trepidation.

On the other hand, that might not have meant anything. Wu wasn't one of the exobiologists who had worked with Jiterica at the Academy. She didn't know whether there was any real correlation between the Nizhrak's expression and her emotional state.

For that matter, Wu couldn't be sure Jiterica's people were even capable of emotion. Could they feel loyalty? Gratitude? Disappointment? Only Jiterica could answer those questions with any confidence.

Wu had believed that the ensign's actions back in the science section had their roots in a feeling of loneliness. But even that assumption might have been in error—a case of a human interpreting an alien's behavior on the basis of her own.

All the more reason for me to get to know Jiterica, the second officer told herself. *If I can reach her, understand her, I can help others to do the same.*

As she and her charge approached their seats, Wu became aware that they were being watched—and not just by a few crewmen here and there. Nearly everyone in the mess hall was staring at them, perhaps wondering what Jiterica was doing here.

Wu wondered if the ensign was aware of the scrutiny. For her sake, the commander hoped not.

"Here we are," she said, pulling out a chair for the Nizhrak. "Go ahead and sit down."

Jiterica studied the chair as if it were a rare celestial phenomenon, something she had never seen before. Then she tried to turn her suit around and settle into it.

It was a difficult maneuver—much more difficult than Wu would have thought. After all, Jiterica hadn't seemed to have any trouble sitting down in the science section or in her quarters.

But now that the commander thought about it, those places had swivel chairs without armrests. None of the chairs in the mess hall were of the swivel variety and they *all* had armrests. She bit her lip, wishing she had anticipated the problem before she invited the ensign to have dinner with her.

But she hadn't. She had acted blithely, confident that her good intentions would be sufficient. And now the ensign was paying the price for her shortsightedness, striving with the chair as if she were wrestling a *mugato*.

Wu looked around and saw people wincing in sympathy with Jiterica's efforts. She had to wince a little herself.

Finally, the ensign inserted her suit securely between the armrests. But her trials weren't over, because she then had to turn the chair around and slip it under the table.

Wu did her best to help, but it was still an arduous task. It took a full minute for the two of them to pivot Jiterica's chair ninety degrees and push it up to the table. And even then, she didn't look comfortable. The containment suit was too bulky to permit much movement, so the Nizhrak just sat there as if she were paralyzed.

Fortunately, she didn't *need* to move. As Jiterica had pointed out to the second officer in her quarters, she didn't take in nutrients the way that humanoids did.

Walking around the table, Wu sat down opposite her companion. It was then that she received an answer to at least one of her questions about the ensign.

Jiterica's face, pale and insubstantial-looking as it was, showed definite signs of embarrassment. Her brow was pinched and her eyes moved from one onlooker to another, making it clear that she was all too aware of them.

"So," said Wu, "how do you like it on the ship so far?"

The ensign looked at her. "I have no complaints."

It wasn't the kind of response Wu had hoped for. Obviously, this was going to take some work.

"You've been in every section of the ship by now," the commander noted. "You must have made some pretty interesting observations."

Jiterica seemed to weigh the remark for a long time. "I have made observations," she agreed at last. "However, it is difficult for me to say which of them you may find interesting."

Wu shrugged. "Try me."

The Nizhrak's ghost-visage frowned. "All right. Two days ago, I was assigned to the security section."

The second officer recalled the assignment. But then, one of her duties was to put together the weekly training schedules for all junior officers serving on the *Stargazer.*

"When I arrived, Lieutenant Joseph was engaged in phaser practice. Rather than interrupt him, which I thought would be rude, I stood and watched him."

Wu nodded. "And?"

"And," Jiterica continued, "I saw that his aim left something to be desired. Though his objective was to hit the center of his target, he occasionally missed."

The commander waited for the ensign to go on. But she didn't. She just sat there.

It was only after they had stared at each other in silence for several long seconds that the commander realized something: Jiterica had come to the end of her story.

"Really," said Wu, trying her best to seem enthusiastic.

"Yes," Jiterica replied.

"Any...other observations?" Wu asked hopefully.

With an effort, the Nizhrak extracted a handful from memory. However, none of them was any more entertaining than the first one. In fact, a couple were actually less so.

"How about that," said Wu.

Jiterica's eyes seemed to narrow. For a moment, the second officer had the feeling that her companion was onto her—that Jiterica had realized how uninteresting her stories were and how hard Wu was working to make it seem otherwise.

Then the ensign said, "You should eat, Commander. Otherwise, you'll be hungry when you start your next shift."

Wu *was* getting hungry—and she had a not-so-inexplicable desire to stretch her legs. "I'll tell you what," she told her companion. "You wait here and I'll be back in a moment or two."

"Agreed," said Jiterica.

As the commander got up and headed for the replicator slot, she considered the size of the gap she was trying to bridge in inviting the Nizhrak to dinner. Too large, perhaps.

But she wasn't about to give up. If there was a way to relate to Jiterica, a way to make her feel more at home here on the *Stargazer,* Wu was going to find it.

And she was going to do it *before* she claimed her post on the *Crazy Horse.*

Chapter Eight

As Jiterica made her way down the corridor, most of her attention was focused on coaxing her containment suit forward in a rhythm that accommodated ambulation.

She gave the rest of it to Commander Wu, who was walking alongside her. "Yes," she said, answering the question the second officer had just asked her, in a way calculated to spare Wu's feelings. "I *did* find our dinner a worthwhile experience."

"Good," Wu returned. "We'll have to do it again sometime."

But Jiterica didn't think that the human was quite as eager as her comment indicated. In fact, she was reasonably certain of it.

"Yes," Jiterica agreed, trying to be polite.

Truthfully, she hadn't been optimistic about the idea of a dinner exercise in the first place. However, she had gone along with it, partly to please the commander and partly to see if it might actually have a beneficial effect.

But from the moment Jiterica saw the chair in which she would be sitting, she suspected that she had made a mistake. And when she caught the look on Wu's face and realized how uninteresting the commander found her stories, she was sure of it.

She had been foolish to imagine that she could ever relate to humanoids the way they related to each other. Even species as divergent as Pandrilites and Gnalish might find a common ground here on the *Stargazer,* but not a being compelled to wear a containment suit merely to get around.

"See you later," said Wu.

"Yes," Jiterica responded. "Later."

The second officer's intentions had been good ones. The Nizhrak had no doubt of that. But they could never become friends.

Jiterica was gratified by the knowledge that she was making a contribution as a member of the crew. To expect anything more than that was simply unrealistic.

She watched Wu vanish around a bend in the corridor and recalled what real companionship had been like— how easy it had been, how effortless. Perhaps someday she would know such companionship again.

But not here, Jiterica thought. *Not on the* Stargazer.

Nikolas found the person he was looking for in the ship's gymnasium. *As if she would have been anywhere else,* he mused as he walked into the high-ceilinged chamber.

Idun was working out on the parallel bars, swinging her long legs back and forth with apparently effortless grace and precision. And as if that didn't make her tantalizing enough, she was wearing a form-fitting black warm-up suit that accentuated every luscious weapon in her arsenal.

The ensign didn't say anything right away. He just walked up to the bars and watched with undisguised admiration.

After a while, Idun noticed him. Finishing her routine with a simple side dismount, she went to the towel she had left on the floor and dried herself off. Then she glanced at him.

"Is there something I can do for you?" she asked.

"Well," said Nikolas, "our mutual friend Obal tells me you've decided not to spar with me."

Asmund nodded. "That's correct."

"I understand," he told her. "You're concerned that you'll get hurt. But I'm here to tell you that you needn't worry. I'm used to sparring with weaker opponents."

Her eyes narrowed. "Really."

"That's right," Nikolas assured her. "And if I can pull my punches for them, I can pull them for you, too."

The helm officer nodded. "I see."

"So," he went on, "there's really no reason not to—"

"Name the time and place," she said, interrupting him in the middle of his pitch.

Nikolas smiled. "Really? I mean…great. How about tomorrow, after second shift?"

Asmund's eyes seemed to glitter. "Fine."

"And afterward," he suggested, pushing his luck, "a cup of coffee in the rec? And a little friendly conversation?"

Her mouth pulled up at the corners, making her look even more desirable. "One thing at a time," she advised him.

The ensign was perfectly willing to go along with that. "One thing at a time," he agreed.

"I'll see you tomorrow, then."

"Absolutely," he told her. "Tomorrow."

Nikolas watched the doors to the lieutenant's quarters slide shut. Then, rather pleased with himself, he started to retrace his steps along the corridor.

This is good, he mused. This is very good. And it wasn't anywhere near as difficult as he had thought it would be.

Wouldn't Obal be surprised.

As soon as his shift was over, Ulelo returned to his quarters, stretched out across his bed and tried his best to concentrate on his mission. However, it was difficult to do so. Thoughts of Emily Bender kept intruding.

He had no reason to doubt that she had known him at the Academy as she had claimed. His memories of that time were incomplete, hazy at best. All he remembered was what he had learned in his classes.

It hadn't bothered Ulelo that it should be so. But it had bothered Emily Bender. It had bothered her a lot.

The question was…what would she do with her resentment? Would she discuss the matter with her fellow science officers? Would they think it strange that the junior comm officer couldn't—or wouldn't—acknowledge the experiences he had shared with Emily Bender?

And would the story spread eventually to Captain Picard and his command staff, raising doubts in their mind as to Ulelo's character…if not his sanity?

He couldn't afford that.

But what could he do about it? How could he keep Emily Bender from shining a light on his odd behavior?

He had barely posed the question when he heard the chimes that told him someone was standing in the corridor outside his quarters. Ulelo sat up on his bed and wondered who it might be. After all, no one had called on him before.

"Come in," he said. Then he left his bedroom and entered the smaller enclosure that served as an anteroom—just in time to see the doors part and reveal Emily Bender.

"May I come in?" she asked.

Ulelo frowned. "I don't—"

Before he could get the rest out, she slipped past him. "Thanks a bunch, Dikembe."

As the doors to his quarters hissed closed behind him, Ulelo watched his unwanted visitor take a look around. After a moment or two, she seemed disappointed.

"You know," she said, "I was hoping to find something from the Academy so I could pin you down. But you don't seem to have anything of that sort on display here." She turned to look at him. "Still, it's you. I know—I found your name in the personnel files."

Ulelo sighed. "Maybe we did know each other at the Academy. It's certainly possible—I met lots of people there. It's just that I don't remember you."

Emily Bender's eyes narrowed. "I don't believe you. We were a tight-knit group. Maybe we haven't kept up with each other very well, but there's no way you could have forgotten me."

He shrugged. "I'm sorry, but I—"

She put her forefinger to his mouth, silencing him. "Don't, Dikembe. I don't know why you're trying to give me the brush-off, but it's not going to work."

Ulelo moved her finger away from his lips. "It's not a brush-off. I just don't remember."

Emily Bender smiled. "Do you believe in Fate, Dikembe?"

He frowned. "What does that have to do with—"

Her finger slid back across his lips. "You probably

don't know this, but I had a crush on you back at the Academy. A *big* crush, and I always regretted not doing anything about it. Then I saw you in the corridor and I realized that I'd been given some kind of second chance."

Before he knew it, before he could say or do a thing to stop her, Emily Bender slipped her arms around his neck and kissed him. He couldn't say he didn't enjoy it. She was a woman, after all, and a rather attractive woman at that.

But Ulelo wasn't in a position to follow his instincts. Removing her arms from his neck, he shook his head.

"You're making a mistake," he said.

She looked at him disbelievingly. "What—?"

"A mistake," he repeated. "I'm going to have to ask you to leave."

Emily Bender stared at him for a moment longer. Then, her cheeks flushed with embarrassment, she said in an injured voice, "All right. If that's the way you want it."

And she left Ulelo standing there in his quarters, feeling that he hadn't merely failed to solve his problem. Somehow, he had increased the complexity of it.

Picard looked at his first officer as they stood in his ready room. "You did *what?*"

Ben Zoma shrugged. "I contacted my friend Tanya, who studied the Gnalish a number of years ago."

The captain winced. *"Please* tell me you didn't speak to her about Simenon."

"Actually," Ben Zoma said a little sheepishly, "I did. I wanted to find out what he was holding back from us."

Picard held his hands out in an appeal for reason. "Gilaad, that is *precisely* what he asked us *not* to do."

Ben Zoma nodded. "I know. I butted into his business. I betrayed the trust of a friend and a fellow officer."

"To say the least," Picard told him.

"But I may also have saved his miserable life."

That brought the captain up short. "What do you mean?"

Ben Zoma explained. In detail.

Picard frowned as he realized what his engineer was up against. The odds against him were considerable. But that didn't excuse what his first officer had done.

"We agreed not to pry into Simenon's affairs," Picard said. "You and I both. For pity's sake, we gave him our *word.*"

"So," Ben Zoma responded matter-of-factly, "does that mean you're not going to talk with him?"

The captain wrestled with the question. Finally, he came to the only conclusion possible. "Simenon is going to hate us for lying to him," he told his first officer.

"I know," Ben Zoma conceded. "But if you can't depend on your *friends* to lie to you, who *can* you depend on?"

Picard grunted. *Who indeed?*

Admiral McAteer sat back in his chair and tapped the rim of the bar glass on the table beside him. The previously clear liquid inside the glass began blushing with a host of different colors.

The admiral smiled appreciatively. "Best damned Samarian Sunset I ever saw. If it tastes as good as it looks, we're all set."

Of course, there was no answer. The replicator that had produced the cocktail had no more to say in response to his remark than any other inanimate object in the room.

McAteer didn't mind in the least. The truth was he *liked* being by himself once in a while.

Not everyone understood that, he thought, as he picked up the Sunset and conveyed it to his lips. Just because he was good with people, because he could *influence* them, didn't mean he wanted to be surrounded by them all the time.

The cocktail was sour and dusky sweet and a little bitter all at the same time, a riot of unexpectedly complementary tastes. And it went to his head like an exploding photon torpedo, exactly the way it was supposed to.

"Perfect," the admiral said out loud. "My compliments to the bartender." His words of praise echoed in the room for a moment, then faded to nothing.

He didn't normally drink by himself, especially when he was on a starship far from home. On the other hand, he seldom found himself in such a good mood.

Finding someone to undermine Picard hadn't been as simple as he had expected it would be. He had begun to realize that after he failed to enlist the services of Rachel Garrett.

After that, McAteer had felt the need to be careful. *Very* careful.

Any other strategy would invite the possibility of yet another second officer turning down his offer, and in that case he would be asking for trouble. The admiral was confident that Garrett, at least, wouldn't say anything about their discussion. But someone with less control or common sense might flap his jaws at the wrong time and expose McAteer's vendetta.

If it became common knowledge that he was after someone for personal reasons, it would be a difficult matter to explain away. He could ill afford that kind of embarrassment at this critical juncture in his Starfleet career.

So the admiral had resolved that his next attempt would be a successful one. That meant meant putting a lot more work into the winnowing-out process. A lot more research.

More than once, he had come close to his goal—or thought he had. But time after time, there had been something about the candidate that forced McAteer to rule him or her out.

Some weren't ambitious enough. Some were *too* ambitious. Some were too righteous while others couldn't be trusted, and still others simply lacked what it took to command a starship.

At one point, the admiral thought he had found his man in the person of Donald Varley, second officer on the *Invincible*. Varley had started out as a fast-tracker just like Picard, a fellow who would inevitably be placed in command of a starship.

Then he had slipped off the fast track by offending a superior officer. Judging from what McAteer had read of the incident, it wasn't really Varley's fault. Nonetheless, it had gone against him.

The experience appeared to make Varley a little more cynical—and a great deal more practical. McAteer got the impression that the fellow would compromise a few ethics if it meant obtaining the captaincy he had always wanted.

In the admiral's mind, Varley had been perfect—perhaps even more perfect than Rachel Garrett.

He had been all set to approach Varley with his offer. Then he had discovered one more tidbit of information—that Varley and Picard had become the best of friends in their last year at the Academy.

So much for perfect.

But McAteer hadn't given up. He had continued to rifle through personnel file after personnel file—and finally, his work had paid off. He found a candidate he believed would not only embrace his plan but act discreetly in carrying it out.

Then and only then had he made arrangements to meet the fellow at a mutually convenient starbase—the one he was headed for now, Samarian Sunset well in hand.

"It's only a matter of time now," the admiral told himself gleefully. "Only a matter of time."

And if his assessment wasn't greeted with encouragement, neither was it met with skepticism. But then, that was the way it went when one conversed in an empty room.

Chapter Nine

IN HIS SMALL BUT NEATLY KEPT OFFICE in sickbay, Carter Greyhorse considered what he was about to do. Then he tapped his combadge and said, "Greyhorse to Gerda Asmund."

The navigator's response came a moment later—from her quarters, according to the ship's computer. "Asmund here. What is it, Doctor?"

She still called him that—*Doctor* instead of Carter or even Greyhorse. Even in the aftermath of their most exhausting lessons, when they were both standing there on the gym floor with their chests heaving and their faces flushed and the musky scent of Gerda's sweat like perfume in his nostrils...even then, it was *Doctor.*

"It appears I won't be able to make our lesson this week," Greyhorse informed her.

He listened carefully for the tone of her reaction.

Please, he thought, *give me a crumb. Even a* hint *of disappointment.*

"Oh?" Gerda said.

"I'm going on an away mission," he elaborated.

"In the next few days?"

"Yes," Greyhorse told her.

In fact, all chief medical officers went on away missions at one time or another, so there was nothing inherently impressive about his announcement. But this was the doctor's first such mission since joining the *Stargazer.*

"I haven't been apprised of any away mission," she said, a hint of annoyance in her voice. "Is it classified?"

"It's not," Greyhorse assured her. And he described the endeavor in broad strokes, trying his best to wring some mystery and importance out of them.

Gerda chuckled, making his heart sink. "Oh, *that.* I wouldn't call it much of an away mission."

"There's danger involved," the doctor maintained. "I've been warned to expect casualties."

"Casualties?" she echoed.

He licked his lips. "Yes. The captain informed me that they were a distinct possibility."

Gerda paused, causing Greyhorse's heart to soar. Was it possible that she was actually *worried* about him? Was she perhaps wondering how she might feel if he didn't come back?

"Tell me more," Gerda said curtly.

The doctor savored the words as he might an exotic elixir. Then he did as the navigator asked.

Picard regarded the peaceful-looking sphere pictured on his viewscreen, half of its surface brilliant with sunlight and the other half blanketed in shadow.

He had never seen this particular world before, but he

had seen others very much like it. In fact, it was a good deal like his native Earth except for the predominance of red-leafed vegetation that gave its landmasses their striking crimson color.

"We've established orbit, sir," Gerda announced.

Picard nodded. "Thank you, Lieutenant." He glanced at Ulelo. "Contact the authorities, Lieutenant. Let them know we're here."

"Aye, sir," said the comm officer.

Next, the captain addressed his second officer, who was waiting patiently beside his center seat. "Commander Wu," he said, "you've got the bridge."

Wu inclined her head slightly. "Acknowledged, sir."

Picard had already briefed her thoroughly on his intentions. If she had had any questions, she would have asked them then.

He got up from his seat and headed for the turbolift. But before he could get there, he heard Wu say, "Captain?"

Surprised, he turned back to her. "Yes, Commander?"

She smiled. At least, it *looked* like a smile. "Good luck."

"Thank you," said Picard.

If his luck were *really* good, Wu would have been remaining with him on the *Stargazer* instead of returning to the *Crazy Horse*. But the captain didn't tell her that.

Instead, he entered the turbolift, watched the doors close, and punched in his destination. Then he waited for the compartment to take him to Transporter Room Two.

Phigus Simenon stood in the corridor outside his quarters, watched the duranium doors hiss closed behind him, and frowned at the thought that he might never see this place again.

Not that he was leaving behind the most *comfortable* living arrangement in the galaxy. At best, his suite was plain and uninspired, just like that of every other officer on the ship. At worst, it was poorly designed for someone of his size and physiology, not to mention his unique esthetic preferences.

But Simenon had called his quarters home, however briefly. He had looked forward to remaining in them for a while as a key component of the *Stargazer*'s command staff. And for that reason, he was reluctant to put the place behind him.

On the other hand, there was nothing he could do about the situation. He had received the summons. It was time to go.

Turning, he made his way down the corridor. But as much as he would have liked to reach the nearest turbolift without running into anyone en route, he hadn't even reached the first bend before two of his engineers appeared in front of him.

Urajel and Dubinski. The pair who had borne the brunt of his tirade a few days earlier.

Simenon put his head down and tried to walk past them. He desperately didn't want to engage them in conversation right now. He didn't want to engage *anyone* in conversation.

But of course, Urajel and Dubinski didn't know that.

"Sir?" said Dubinski.

I'm going to walk right past him, Simenon told himself. *I'm going to put my head down and pretend he doesn't exist.*

But of course, he couldn't do that. No matter how much he wanted to avoid contact with anyone, Dubinski was one of his engineers. If the man had something to say, it was Simenon's job to listen.

At least until he reached the transporter room.

"Yes?" he responded.

Dubinski shrugged. "I just wanted to apologize. I thought about what you said in engineering the other day." He glanced at Urajel. "We all did. And we came to the conclusion that you were right."

Simenon looked at him. "I was? I mean...of course I was."

Urajel nodded, her antennae dipping in the process. "No matter how many times we checked the warp core, we shouldn't have assumed there was nothing to worry about. Just as we shouldn't have assumed the computer was on top of the situation."

"And," Dubinski added, "while irreparable core failure is rare without an apparent cause, I'm sure there are causes out there we've never even heard of."

"In short," said Urajel, "we acknowledge our errors and we're going to try to do better." Her face turned a deeper shade of blue. "And I personally regret the—"

"Question you asked?" Simenon suggested, getting her off the hook. "About my hindquarters and what might have invaded them?"

Urajel nodded stiffly. "Yes, sir."

Normally, the chief engineer would have simply accepted their apology and moved on. But as he didn't believe he would be the chief engineer much longer, he said, "Don't give it a second thought. *Any* of it."

Dubinski looked perplexed. "I beg your pardon, sir?"

Simenon dismissed it all with a snap of his wrist. "You did fine, all of you. I was holding you to an unreasonable standard." He eyed Urajel in particular. "And for your information, something *had* crawled up my hindquarters—a personal matter. It was astute of you to notice."

Neither engineer seemed to know what to say to that. Taking unexpected pleasure in the looks on their faces, the Gnalish walked around them and resumed his trek to the transporter room.

If he wasn't coming back to the *Stargazer,* he thought, he would at least leave here with his conscience in good shape.

Ensign Nikolas put his tray full of food down on the table in front of him and pulled up a chair.

"Man," he said, "those replicator lines seem to get longer every day. Is the captain taking on new crewmen in secret or something?"

His friend Obal, who was sitting across the black plastic table from him, chuckled good-naturedly. "If he is, he is keeping it secret from me as well."

Nikolas savored the smell of his salmon in béarnaise sauce. And who did he have to thank for it? His old roommate, Joe Caber. It was Caber who had advised him to trust the mess hall's replicator and try some of the more challenging dishes.

Caber wasn't all *bad,* the ensign told himself archly. *Just* mostly.

He wondered what Caber would have said if he knew Nikolas had convinced Idun Asmund to spar with him. More than likely, the guy's jaw would have dropped— just as Obal's was going to.

Nikolas was still thinking about his old roommate when his new one walked into the mess hall. Paris wasn't alone, either. He was accompanied by Lt. Paxton and Lt. Pierzynski, the latter being the number two officer in Pug Joseph's security section.

And Paris had only beamed aboard a couple of days ago. "Like I said," he muttered, "the guy doesn't waste any time."

"Of whom are you speaking?" asked Obal, who

wasn't facing the entrance to the mess hall as Nikolas was.

"Paris. My roommate."

"Ah," said the Binderian. He swiveled in his chair and spotted the newcomer as he joined the end of the replicator line. "Ensign Paris is quite impressive."

Nikolas wasn't certain he had heard right. He looked at his friend questioningly. "Excuse me?"

"He's quite impressive," Obal repeated. He twirled some spaghetti around his fork. "Quite innovative."

Nikolas looked at the Binderian as he deposited the cluster of spaghetti into his mouth. It wasn't like his friend to use words like "impressive" and "innovative."

"Why do you say that?" the ensign asked.

Obal shrugged. "I heard Gerda Asmund say so. And the captain as well. I have no reason to doubt their judgment."

Nikolas frowned. "The *captain* said Paris was impressive?"

The Binderian nodded. "He did."

"In what way?"

"In the way he participates in a sport called fencing," Obal explained. "Apparently, he presented Captain Picard with a considerable challenge in that regard."

"Did Paris beat him?" Nikolas asked.

"It was never made clear to me who won. Only that the competitors were more or less evenly matched."

The ensign's frown deepened. "The captain was probably being generous, that's all. Gerda, too."

Obal seemed to find the comment interesting. He cocked his head to one side. "Is this an example of what humans refer to as jealousy?"

Nikolas made a sound of disdain. "What are you talking about?"

"You're normally generous with your praise for people, my friend. However, in Ensign Paris's case, you are denigrating his accomplishments. This suggests that you are jealous of him."

"Does it really?" asked Nikolas. He chuckled to show Obal how off base he was. "I'd only be jealous of Ensign Paris if *he* was sparring with Idun Asmund instead of *me*."

The Binderian looked surprised. In fact, he looked *exactly* the way Nikolas had expected him to look. "Are you saying you convinced Lieutenant Asmund to meet you, after all?"

The ensign nodded. "It wasn't even all that difficult."

Obal made a face. "I'm not sure this is wise, my friend."

"You're concerned that someone might get hurt," Nikolas speculated.

"Well," said the security officer, "yes."

The ensign dismissed the possibility with a wave of his hand. "I already discussed that with Idun and it's not going to happen, so don't give it a second thought."

Obal frowned. "You're sure?"

Nikolas nodded. "Absolutely."

He shot a glance in Paris's direction. His roommate was describing what looked like a space battle to Paxton and Pierzynski, who watched him with rapt expressions.

Jealous indeed, Nikolas thought, and let his mind drift in the direction of his appointment with the beautiful Idun Asmund.

As Simenon approached the double doors of the transporter room, he was pretty certain that the captain would be waiting for him inside. Probably Ben Zoma as well.

After all, he was leaving them. And though they didn't have any inkling of how permanent that departure might be, they had to know he wasn't looking forward to what he was facing on Gnala and would therefore want to wish him luck.

The doors whispered apart for him as he came in range of an unseen sensor. They seemed a little sluggish, though. *I should have someone check the trigger mechanism,* Simenon reflected.

And then he remembered—more than likely, that would be someone else's problem, not his.

The hard, unyielding nature of that reality stuck in his throat like a bone. Still, the engineer managed to swallow it back and enter the transporter room, his eyes trained on the floor so he wouldn't have to face anyone until the last possible second.

Finally, when he believed he had almost reached the transporter pad, he looked up. After all, he had to say his good-byes.

But to his surprise, the hexagonal platform was already occupied. The captain and four of Simenon's colleagues were standing on it in rugged civilian clothing.

It took the engineer a second to figure out what was going on. Once he had done that, he shook his head emphatically from side to side. "No, you don't," he rasped at them. "I'm going down to Gnala alone. This is none of your business."

"Wrong on both counts," Greyhorse told him flatly. "And that's the advice of your physician."

"We're your friends," Vigo said.

"Yes," Picard chipped in. "And this is a time when you need your friends around you."

"Come on," Ben Zoma advised him. "Lighten up." His expression turned arch. "That's an order."

Joseph didn't say anything. He just smiled.

Simenon took a deep breath and let it out again. He had never been so touched in his entire life—not that he would ever say so. But what his friends were doing wasn't right. They didn't have any idea of what they were getting into.

"You're all proud of yourselves," he observed, "aren't you? You think you're going to save me from a grisly end. But all you're going to do is get yourselves killed along with me."

"Nice speech," Greyhorse told him.

"*Very* nice," said Picard. "Now get on the platform and let's get this over with."

"Fools," Simenon spat.

"Careful," said Ben Zoma. "We don't like you *that* much." But the Gnalish knew the human didn't mean it.

Obviously, there was no dissuading them. Swearing under his breath, Simenon climbed onto the platform and took an empty spot. Then he turned to Refsland, the transporter operator on duty, and uttered a single word.

"Energize."

Chapter Ten

ONCE, SHORTLY AFTER PICARD had been accepted at Starfleet Academy, someone had told him that a man in a transporter could actually feel his molecules being dismantled and zapped through space.

Nothing could have been further from the truth.

There was no awareness of the process, no sensation associated with it. One moment, you were in one place. A moment later, you were somewhere else. It was that simple.

It's *so* simple, in fact, that it often surprised those unaccustomed to transporter travel. After all, they expected some intermediary state, some time to prepare oneself for the change in environment, and they didn't get even a fraction of a second in that regard.

Picard, on the other hand, had traveled by transporter more times than he could easily remember. But even a veteran of such travel could occasionally wish he had had a moment to prepare for what he was about to see.

He found himself wishing that now.

Ben Zoma whistled softly. "I've never seen anything like *this*."

"Nor have I," Picard confessed.

"It's beautiful," Vigo observed.

Joseph nodded. "You can say that again."

They were in an immense stone chamber, one that seemed to soar skyward with irresistible grace and power and majesty. And every inch of it, every twisting column and fluted wall, was the deep, scarlet color of human blood.

There were no energy-powered lights that the captain could discern, neither globes nor open flames. The only apparent source of illumination was a series of towering, splinter-thin windows that filtered the planet's sunlight and cast it in long, elegant shafts on the smooth stone floor.

It took him a moment to realize that he and his away team weren't alone in the place. At the far end of the chamber, a ceremonial gathering of some kind stood in a slash of light.

Shading his eyes from the glare of the windows, Picard was able to make out six elderly, white-robed Gnalish surrounded by at least a dozen towering individuals in loose-fitting black garments. The larger figures wore their hoods drawn low over their faces, so the captain couldn't tell what they looked like underneath them. However, the image they brought to mind was that of a team of medieval executioners.

Impossible, Picard told himself. Gnala was a civilized world. Its government didn't execute anyone, even for capital crimes. Then he noticed the long, deadly-looking blades that seemed to grow out of the larger figures' black sleeves.

For a moment, neither the white-robed Gnalish nor their companions said a thing. They just stood there, eyeing the away team much as the away team was eyeing them.

Finally, one of the Gnalish whispered something to one of his colleagues, his voice too low for Picard to discern individual words. The whisper was returned, its echoes fading on the air. Finally, one of the white-robed figures made his way toward Simenon and his companions and extended a scaly finger in their direction.

His mouth twisting, he rasped a single word of accusation: "Offworlders!"

It sent the hooded ones rushing at the newcomers like a powerful black tide. Before the away team knew what was happening, it had been surrounded. The captain saw that their captors were every bit as big as Vigo.

And of course, they had those *blades* in their hands.

"Tell me Refsland got the coordinates wrong," Ben Zoma whispered.

Joseph shook his head. "No such luck, Commander."

"Don't move," Simenon told his comrades.

"Believe me," said Greyhorse, "I hadn't even considered it."

Picard found himself wishing that they had brought phaser pistols. But Ben Zoma's friend Tanya Tresh had been explicit about the need to leave such weapons behind.

"What now?" Joseph asked Simenon.

The engineer didn't answer him. He just watched and waited.

Slowly and with great dignity, the Gnalish in the white robes advanced across the scarlet stones of the floor. And as they moved, they made hushed comments one to the other.

By the time they stopped in front of the away team, Picard could see that one of the Gnalish—the one who had pointed to them and initiated the stampede of black hoods—had a sickle-like blue mark on the front of his robe. The captain guessed that this one enjoyed a higher rank than the others.

The Gnalish with the blue mark regarded Simenon, ignoring the four humans and the Pandrilite. "Who are they?" he hissed imperiously, indicating Picard and the others with a sweep of his spindly hand. "And why in the name of Magdalassar have they come?"

Picard glanced at his first officer. He had an uneasy feeling that Ben Zoma's friend Tanya hadn't told them *everything*.

Elizabeth Wu felt awkward in Captain Picard's chair.

She hadn't expected to feel that way. After all, she had been in command of the *Stargazer*'s bridge at least once a day since the moment she beamed aboard.

So why the change?

In her heart, Wu knew the answer. To that point, she had felt like a legitimate part of the *Stargazer*'s crew. She had felt like she belonged there. Now she had one foot out the door, her return to the *Crazy Horse* imminent. It made her feel like an intruder, an interloper who had no right commanding these people.

Of course, she was the only qualified second officer present. In the absence of her superiors she *had* to command the *Stargazer,* and her subordinates had to obey her. But Wu didn't feel right about it and she wouldn't blame her officers if *they* didn't feel right about it, either.

"Commander?" said Paxton, who had returned to the bridge only a few minutes earlier.

She turned to the comm officer. "Lieutenant?"

"I have a communication for you from Starfleet Command."

Command? "Put it through."

A moment later, the image of an admiral popped up on the viewscreen—a woman with long, gray hair gathered into a ponytail. She looked vaguely familiar to the second officer.

What was her name again? Reagan? Rayburn?

"This is Admiral Rayfield at Starbase Sixty-three," the admiral said, putting an end to the commander's speculation. She looked around the bridge. "Where's Captain Picard?"

"The captain," said Wu, "is on Gnala."

"What's he doing there?"

Wu frowned. She didn't want to make Picard look like the kind of officer who abandoned his ship to take care of personal matters, no matter how well-intentioned.

"He's pursuing a matter of some importance to the Gnalish," she said finally. "First Officer Ben Zoma went with him. I'm Commander Wu. May I be of assistance?"

"I'd rather speak with Captain Picard," the admiral insisted.

The second officer felt her spine stiffen. "Unfortunately," she said truthfully, "any attempt on our part to contact the captain would be seen as a breach of Gnalish custom. And even if we were to ignore that consideration, it might take a while to get hold of him."

Rayfield looked as if she were about to ask for details. After all, Wu's responses to that point had been rather vague. In the end, however, the admiral seemed willing to accept the situation at face value.

"All right," she said. "Commander Wu, you say?"

"That's correct, Admiral."

"An Andorian cargo vessel has relayed us a distress call from the *Belladonna,* a research vessel assigned to the Oneo Madrin system. Familiar with it?"

"I've heard of Oneo Madrin," Wu told Rayfield. "Unfortunately, I've never seen it firsthand."

Rayfield frowned. Obviously, it wasn't the answer she had been hoping for. "It's a binary system with an accretion bridge. You've seen those before, haven't you?"

"I have," the second officer assured her. "Twice, in fact. At Aescalapios and Wells-Parvat."

The admiral seemed to take some comfort in that. "Good. Then you know how tricky they can be."

"You think the *Belladonna* got too close?" Wu asked.

"It's a reasonable assumption in the absence of any real data. The *Belladonna*'s distress call was garbled, to say the least."

As would have been the case if the vessel's comm system had been damaged by unexpected radiation from the accretion bridge. And if her captain had called for help, communications probably wasn't the only system that had been damaged.

But if the *Belladonna*'s shields were functioning, her crew had a fighting chance. They could still be alive—as long as a rescue effort was launched in time.

Apparently, that was where the *Stargazer* came in.

"You're the closest Starfleet ship," said Rayfield. "You know how that works."

"I do," Wu replied.

"Keep me posted," said the admiral. "Rayfield out."

As the admiral's face vanished from the screen and was replaced by their view of Gnala, Wu turned to her helm officer.

"Lieutenant," she said, "take us out of this system."

"Aye," Idun replied.

The commander was under orders not to contact Picard and the away team. The captain had been crystal clear on that point. But with luck, they would be back before Simenon's ritual ordeal was over.

"Navigator," Wu said, "chart a course for the Oneo Madrin system." She watched Simenon's planet slide unceremoniously off the starboard side of the viewscreen. "Best speed."

"Charting," said Gerda, who had begun tapping out commands at her console as soon as she heard the admiral's orders.

Leaning back, the second officer took a deep breath. She would have ample opportunity to get comfortable in the captain's chair. After all, she was going to be seeing a lot of it.

Picard took his right leg, which had been lying across his left one for too long, and planted it on the floor. Then he picked up his left leg and laid it across his right.

Ben Zoma was sitting next to him on a ledge built into the wall. "So," he said, "how do you like your visit to Gnala *so* far?"

The captain frowned. "Just fine, Number One." He indicated the small, high-ceilinged chamber in which they had spent the last two hours. "I was *hoping* I'd be incarcerated in a windowless chamber while this region's Council of Elders—"

"*Assemblage* of Elders," Greyhorse interjected from his seat on the other side of the room.

"While this *Assemblage*," Picard amended, "inflicts who-knows-what-sort of miseries on my chief engineer."

Pug Joseph, who had steadfastly refused to sit since

they were herded here, shook his head. "I still can't believe those monsters in the black pajamas were Gnalish."

"I know what you mean," said Vigo, who sat beside the doctor with his massive arms folded across his chest. "I thought all Gnalish were small of stature like Mr. Simenon."

"You learn something new every day," Joseph remarked.

Suddenly, the door to the chamber creaked open. As the captain watched, he saw Simenon cross the threshold.

Picard sat up. "Where have you been?"

"Are you all right?" Joseph wanted to know.

"Of course I'm all right," the Gnalish told him. "No one's going to injure someone in my position."

Vigo grunted. "What did they tell you?"

Simenon made a sound of disgust. "They didn't tell me *anything*."

Picard looked at him. "Then where have you been all this time?"

The engineer scowled. "I've been meditating. So has the Assemblage—so when we finally discuss your presence here, we can do it rationally and with all of our arguments clear in our heads."

"And when will you make these arguments?" asked Greyhorse.

Simenon jerked his head in the direction of the open doorway. "That, I'm told, would be *now*."

Ulelo was aware of the conversation taking place around him as he sat in the mess hall, but he wasn't paying attention to it. He was too intent on what had taken place in his quarters a few short hours ago.

"Do you believe in Fate?" Emily Bender had asked.

He should have seen it coming, but he hadn't. He had stared at her, barely managing a protest.

"It was *Rayfield,*" said Paxton, Ulelo's superior in the communications section. He placed such an emphasis on the name that it broke in on Ulelo's reverie. "You know, the one with the gray ponytail."

Dubinski, the officer in charge of engineering in Simenon's absence, looked skeptical. "Wait a minute. I thought Takahiro was the one with the gray ponytail."

Paxton shook his head. "Takahiro is the one with the short hair and the mole."

"I thought that was Saturria," remarked Refsland, the *Stargazer*'s senior transporter operator.

"No," said Paxton. "Definitely Takahiro."

Ulelo began to settle back into his thoughts. He could feel Emily Bender's finger pressing gently on his lips. He could hear the huskiness in her voice as she moved closer to him.

"I had a crush on you back at the Academy," she had told him. *"A big crush."*

"So we're headed for Oneo Madrin," said Garner, one of Pug Joseph's senior security officers.

"That's right," said Paxton.

Refsland grunted thoughtfully. "Both those suns are Sol-class, aren't they?"

Paxton nodded appreciatively. "Good memory, Bill. With seventeen planets, none of them habitable."

"Any idea what the distress call is about?" asked Urajel, Dubinski's colleague in engineering.

Paxton shook his head. "None."

"Command must be concerned," said Refsland, "or it wouldn't have asked us to investigate."

"It's a distress call," Urajel told him with a typically

Andorian lack of patience. "Of *course* they're concerned."

"It'll probably turn out to be engine trouble," said Dubinski.

Garner, who had served with Dubinski on another ship before this one, chuckled at the comment. "You *always* think it's engine trouble."

"It's the most common cause of distress calls," Dubinski told her. "You can look it up."

"Never mind all that," said Urajel. She looked around the table. "What are Simenon and the others up to on Gnala?"

Paxton smiled. "That's the billion-credit question, isn't it?"

"It's not a diplomatic problem," Refsland noted. "The captain wouldn't have needed the doctor and Pug and Vigo along for that."

"Then what?" asked Urajel. She turned to Ulelo. "You've been awfully quiet. Care to venture a guess?"

The comm officer shrugged. "I wouldn't know where to begin."

It was at least half a lie.

Ulelo had perused Ben Zoma's correspondence with Tanya Tresh just as he had perused every other correspondence received on the *Stargazer,* so he knew exactly what Simenon was facing on Gnala. He just didn't know what Picard and his officers had planned to do about it.

"I've got a hunch I know what they're up to," said Dubinski. And he went on to describe his theory.

As it turned out, he couldn't have been farther from the truth. But Ulelo didn't say so because it would have meant exposing himself as something other than what he seemed.

The others eventually discarded Dubinski's hunch

and offered a half dozen of their own. But by then, the comm officer wasn't really listening to them anymore.

He had rediscovered the thread of his ruminations. He found himself remembering Emily Bender's kiss, the soft insistence of it. He remembered too the smell of her as she pressed against him.

And he remembered the look on her face when he denied her what she wanted of him. It was a look of pain, of humiliation, of deep and abiding disappointment.

If she had posed a threat to Ulelo before, he had magnified it with the clumsiness of his response. He needed to do something before she placed his mission in jeopardy.

As his colleagues prattled on about Simenon and Gnala, he gradually came up with a plan.

Chapter Eleven

UNTIL HE BEAMED DOWN from the *Stargazer*, Simenon had only heard about his people's ancient Northern Sanctum from his father and his uncles. He himself had never had occasion to set foot in the place.

Now he found himself in the sanctum's Great Hall, an imperious, torturously angular chamber with floors pitted by age and slanted windows ablaze with the glory of the setting sun.

The Assemblage of Elders sat in front of him on a raised stone bench, their High One occupying its center with three of his colleagues on either side. Some Gnalish found it daunting merely to stand in the presence of those august figures, and even more so when they were flanked by their gigantic guards.

But Simenon wasn't here just to stand in their presence. He was here to fight for the future of his family.

Fortunately, he wasn't alone in the effort. His comrades from the *Stargazer* were seated behind him on one of the stone shelves that hugged the perimeter of the chamber. It wasn't as if they could say anything on his behalf, but he was grateful for the moral support.

Not that he would ever have confessed that to them.

There were several others in attendance as well, a few dozen Gnalish with personal stakes in the outcome of the proceedings. The law allowed them to observe and participate as long as the Assemblage had no objection to their doing so.

The High One, who was also the oldest and most loose-skinned of the councillors, got to his feet. Simenon could see the blue mark on the front of his robe.

"The Assemblage has meditated," the High One announced. He eyed Simenon. "I trust you've done the same."

The engineer nodded. "I have."

"You have brought offworlders to engage in the ritual," the High One noted, wasting no time in addressing the matter at hand. "However, the ritual is restricted to Gnalish."

Here goes, thought Simenon. "Normally, that's true. But as I'm sure you know, exceptions have been made in the past."

The councillor frowned, stretching the sac of loose skin under his chin. "Only under the most extenuating circumstances."

"These are extenuating circumstances as well," Simenon said.

The High One's eyes narrowed. "In what way?"

"I have no brothers to take along on my journey. An accident claimed both their lives a few years ago."

The councillor shrugged. "The law states that you may take first cousins in their place."

"I have no first cousins either," said Simenon. "My parents had no siblings who survived to adulthood."

The High One didn't have an answer for that. Sensing that he had gained an advantage, Simenon pressed on.

"As a result," he said, "I have invited the assistance of some of my friends, all of whom are male and roughly my age and should therefore be admissible to the ritual."

Another Gnalish, as tall and heavy and pale of skin as the black-garbed guards, rose from the midst of the onlookers. "I would like to speak," he said in a deep, harsh voice.

The High One nodded. "You have leave."

"I disagree with the one called Simenon. The laws governing the ritual are explicit." His fiery eyes flashed with indignation as he glanced in the engineer's direction. "It's not enough for someone to be the right age and sex. He must also be a blood relative of the individual undertaking the journey."

A second Gnalish got to his feet. He was considerably smaller than either Simenon or his fellow protester, and his skin had a light and dark pattern to it. He too asked to be recognized by the Assemblage and was granted the privilege.

"Kasaelek is right," the diminutive one snapped. "The ritual is intended for Gnalish and their blood kin, not for strangers to our ways—and certainly not for the offspring of other worlds."

Simenon smiled grimly. It was no secret why these two would have a problem with his choice of comrades. In their place, he might have objected with the same vehemence—and maybe even the same arguments.

"My competitors can hardly be considered unbiased judges," he told the Assemblage, his voice ringing passionately throughout the chamber. "It's in their interest to see me undertake the ritual on my own."

"I merely seek justice," countered the giant.

"We must honor our traditions," the light and dark one insisted.

"Of course," said Simenon, his eyes narrowing. "Especially when justice and tradition favor your causes."

His rivals glowered at him. He glowered back, measure for measure.

"The fact remains," Simenon went on, "that it's in the Assemblage's power to grant my request—to give me the help I need to compete on an even footing. Anything less would ensure my defeat."

The High One looked pensive. "What you're suggesting is unprecedented, Simenon. But you're correct in your contention that all competitors should have an equal chance to win."

"High One," the giant spat, "this is—"

The councillor whirled and hissed, imposing silence on the speaker. "You will address us when you're given permission to do so."

The giant inclined his head in contrition. "Of course," he said. "I meant no disrespect."

It was then that someone new entered the chamber through its only door. As Simenon was facing the Assemblage, he couldn't turn to see who it was. It was only after the newcomer had sat down alongside the other Gnalish that the engineer caught a glimpse of him.

And cursed in the privacy of his mind.

"I would like to speak," said the newcomer.

The High One nodded. "You may do so."

Simenon sighed. He hadn't prepared for this possibility, though in retrospect he realized he should have.

"I'm Lennil Ornitharen," the newcomer told the Assemblage. "Phigus Simenon's cousin. Despite his claim to the contrary, he doesn't have to recruit offworlders to help him in the ritual. He has living kin on *this* world. He has *me*."

The councillors muttered beneath their collective breath and exchanged meaningful glances. Only the High One withheld comment until he could present Simenon with the obvious question.

"Is it possible you have a cousin, after all?"

The engineer heaved a sigh. "Ornitharen is my cousin, yes. But he's my *second* cousin. And believe me, I'm grateful for his offer of assistance, which—as you know—extends above and beyond the mandate of our customs and traditions.

"However, I decline to include him in my entourage, which the ritual laws limit to six companions—not as a matter of affection, but as a practical matter. I know from experience that Ornitharen isn't made for physical exertion. He pales in comparison even with other Gnalish of my subspecies, whereas my human and Pandrilite friends are hardy examples of their kind."

He regarded his cousin with an expression of regret. "I don't have the luxury of worrying about his feelings, High One. I've got to think about survival—not only my own, but that of my bloodline."

Ornitharen began to protest the decision, but the High One stopped him. "Simenon is the generational leader of your clan. You lack the standing to argue with him."

If the look on Ornitharen's face was any indication, he wasn't happy about the High One's remark. Nonetheless, he managed to remain silent, bending to his cousin's will.

Apparently satisfied with Ornitharen's response—or rather, his lack of one—the High One told Simenon, "We of the Assemblage must weigh what we have heard here. We will let you know when we've come to a decision in this matter."

The engineer would have preferred an answer then and there—but only if it was the *right* answer. As he had indicated to the Assemblage, the wrong one would ensure his defeat.

"I wait patiently," he told the High One, "trusting in your wisdom." As if he had a choice.

McAteer regarded the Bolian seated on the other side of the black plastic table. Like all Bolians, he had light blue skin and a ridge that ran from the nape of his neck to somewhere under his chin.

His name was Shalay. He was the second officer on the *New Orleans,* a starship that had once been a state-of-the-art prototype and was now far from it.

By human standards, the fellow was quite handsome, quite charming. No doubt, he did well with the ladies. And if the admiral's reports were accurate, Shalay was prepared to make a career move.

"You know," said McAteer, "I've been looking forward to meeting you, Mr. Shalay. I've heard good things about you."

Truthfully, Shalay's file hadn't contained anything spectacular. It wasn't nearly as impressive as Garrett's had been. However, the Bolian had demonstrated a talent for politics that had moved him briskly up the chain of command.

He reminded McAteer of someone: himself.

Shalay nodded, taking the compliment in stride. "It's kind of you to say so, Admiral."

"Kindness has nothing to do with it, Commander. To be blunt, I hate to see an individual with your unlimited potential languishing as second officer on a third-rate ship."

The Bolian smiled—warily, McAteer thought. "That's blunt, all right."

"How do you like serving on the *New Orleans?*"

Shalay shrugged his muscular shoulders. "It's been a valuable experience. I benefited from every minute of it."

He was politic, too. The admiral liked that.

"But you wouldn't be adverse to making a change? Moving to another vessel where there was a greater chance of moving up?"

Shalay's brow puckered. "A *chance* of moving up?"

McAteer smiled. "You were hoping to move right into a first officer's slot. I understand. However, the post I'm thinking of is just as good as a first officer's slot."

"Begging the admiral's pardon," said the Bolian, "I don't see how that could be the case."

McAteer leaned forward and rubbed his hands together. "On the vessel I have in mind, the captain and first officer leave something to be desired. My problem is I'm not present to document their inadequacies. But," he added pointedly, "if I had someone who *was...*"

Shalay seemed to get it. "You want me to transfer to another ship as second officer. Then you want me to supply you with ammunition so you can sink that ship's captain and first officer."

"At which point," the admiral said, "I will see to it that you move up to take their place."

"As first officer? Or as captain?"

McAteer smiled. "Need you ask?"

Shalay's eyes crinkled at the corners. "I've never received an offer like this."

"And you never will again," the admiral told him pointedly. "Not from me, at least."

"So it's take it or leave it."

McAteer nodded. "That's correct."

Shalay pondered the quid pro quo. Finally, he said, "You've got yourself a deal."

The admiral was pleased—he had been right about the Bolian. "I'm glad to hear it," he said.

"Where am I going, anyway?"

McAteer saw no reason to keep it a secret. After all, Shalay had to give his captain the information.

"The name of the ship," he said, "is the *Stargazer.*"

Picard stood outside the door to the Great Hall, in the gargantuan lobby where he and his officers had beamed down, and asked Simenon the question they all had on their minds.

"Do you think the Assemblage has been persuaded?"

His engineer shrugged. "I don't know. They're the Assemblage. They can do anything they like."

His cousin, who bore a striking resemblance to Simenon but was rounder and softer looking, stood by himself in a fluted alcove. It was difficult to tell if he was praying or just thinking.

Greyhorse tilted his head in Ornitharen's direction. "Your chances seemed good until *he* walked in."

Simenon glanced in his cousin's direction. "I can't fault him for what he did. We had the same grandfather. He feels it's his responsibility to help me."

Joseph grunted. "Even if you don't *want* his help?"

The engineer frowned. "Even then."

Picard noticed that Simenon's detractors were standing around as well, each with his own small contingent of supporters. In both cases, those who had spoken in the Great Hall were of the same stature as those who surrounded them.

The captain understood why. But then, once the hearing was over, Simenon had had a chance to enlighten them a bit in that regard.

"Hey," said Joseph, "the door's opening!"

Picard followed his security officer's gesture and saw that the door to the Great Hall—a ponderous wooden affair on ancient metal hinges—was indeed swinging open. Apparently, the Assemblage of Elders had completed its deliberations.

But it hadn't been more than a couple of minutes since the Assemblage had begun them. The captain wondered if that boded well or ill for Simenon's cause.

A hulking bailiff in a black robe emerged from the Great Hall. "You may enter," he told everyone present.

"Let's go," said Ben Zoma, leading the way.

Simenon paused for a moment, seemingly reluctant to go back into the Great Hall. Then he followed Ben Zoma and the rest of their colleagues fell in behind them.

Picard went through the doorway last. But then, he wanted to see the expressions on the faces of Simenon's adversaries. As it turned out, they didn't look any more confident than Simenon did. The captain drew encouragement from that.

The Assemblage of Elders was just where the captain had seen it last, occupying the bench in the center of the room. Simenon walked up to them and stood before them, while Picard and the others again took seats on the stone shelves that protruded from the walls.

It took a moment for everyone to get settled. Then, as before, the High One spoke for the entire Assemblage.

"We have heard the arguments and made our decision," he said, his voice echoing lavishly. "And it is this—that the offworlders will be allowed to participate in the ritual."

The announcement was met with muttered protests

and expressions of disgust from the camps that had spoken against Simenon. The High One didn't respond to them. He simply stood there and waited patiently for them to subside.

"However," he added at last, gazing directly at Simenon, "it will be up to you to keep your companions from violating the ancient laws that govern the ritual—for if they do, rest assured that you will be the one held accountable."

Simenon nodded. "I understand."

The High One regarded him for a little while longer. Then he turned to Picard. "Accommodations will be provided for all participants. However, I cannot guarantee they will be to your liking."

"I'm sure they will be just fine," the captain assured him.

But then, what else could he say? The Gnalish weren't about to build a new wing on their majestic Northern Sanctum expressly for the comfort of meddling offworlders.

"Then," said the High One, "this hearing is over." He took in everyone present at a glance. "As always, the trial begins at first light. May all participants in the ancient ritual face the challenges ahead of them with skill and courage."

There was a chorus of agreement with what was no doubt a traditional blessing. But, clearly, not everyone was happy with the Assemblage's decision. The two who had spoken against Simenon earlier glared at him now with unabashed animosity.

But Ornitharen didn't glare at his cousin. He walked over to him and put his scaly hand on Simenon's shoulder as Picard and the others closed in on them.

"I think you're making a mistake by not including me

among your companions," Ornitharen said. "But I'll still be cheering more loudly than anyone for you to make it to the egg nest first."

Simenon harrumphed—about as close as he ever came to a laugh. "Thanks," he told his cousin. "I'll feel better knowing that."

He sounded sincere, Picard thought. However, it seemed to him that his engineer was simply trying to take the edge off Ornitharen's humiliation. Nothing would truly make Simenon feel better except the knowledge that his ordeal was over....

And that it had ended in victory.

Chapter Twelve

CARTER GREYHORSE FOUND HIMSELF in a dark, drafty place, surrounded by an eerie landscape of blanketed bodies. It took him a moment to get his wits about him—to figure out where he was and what the devil he was doing there.

Finally, he figured it out. Gnala. The Northern Sanctum. He and his colleagues had been given this chamber so they could rest in preparation for Simenon's ritual.

He raised his head and looked out past the last prone body, which was too large to belong to anyone but Vigo. Greyhorse remembered the weapons officer saying he liked to sleep by the exit. Apparently, he had done just that.

But the doctor couldn't make out the outline of the door, which meant one of two things: either it fit its frame too perfectly to let any light in, or it was still the middle of the night. In a place this ancient, the doctor guessed that it was the latter.

He sighed and laid his head back against the wad of clothes he had employed as a pillow. Everyone else appeared to be sleeping soundly, despite the hardness of the surface beneath them. *So why am I awake?* Greyhorse asked himself.

He didn't have to think for very long to come up with the answer. Her name was Gerda.

He had dreamed of her before he woke—dreamed of the two of them, actually. They were embracing in the cloistered confines of a scarlet forest, her face turned up willingly toward his, her blue eyes glittering like sapphires in the moonlight.

Even here, Greyhorse was preoccupied with her, obsessed with her. She invaded his every thought, day and night.

If one of his patients had come to him and described such an obsession, he would have prescribed therapy. It wasn't healthy to dwell on someone so often and so intensely.

He probably needed a psychiatric counselor. Unfortunately, Starfleet crews didn't include such people, and he wasn't going to leave the *Stargazer* to gain access to one of them—because if he did, he would be giving up his only chance to be with Gerda. *A vicious cycle,* he mused, *if ever there was one.*

The doctor propped himself up on an elbow. Whenever he woke in the middle of the night—which was often—he had a difficult time getting back to sleep unless he took a nice, long walk. He had a feeling that this instance would be no exception.

Of course, he reflected, he wouldn't be walking the predictable, temperature-controlled corridors of a starship down here. He would be outside in the open, unfiltered air of Gnala. But then, that might actually make him sleepier.

Besides, his only alternative was to lie there until the others woke up, which might not be for hours, and that was a bleak prospect indeed. Rather than contemplate it, he unrolled his clothes, put them on as quietly as he could, and threaded his way softly past his colleagues until he reached the door.

Fortunately, it didn't creak as he opened it. Feeling a breath of warm, moist air on his face, he knew he had made the right choice. As he stepped out into the darkness, he closed the door behind him.

As luck would have it, the sky was clear and crowded with stars, the air redolent with scents that reminded him of mint and sage and other Earthly spices. A near-full moon frosted the mossy ground underfoot as if eager to guide his steps.

By the light of Gnala's setting sun, the Northern Sanctum had looked like a colossal bloody dagger. By moonlight, it seemed even larger and more ominous. Likewise, the shaggy, wind-driven growth of forest surrounding it, where Greyhorse and the rest of the away team would be toiling after daybreak on Simenon's behalf.

He didn't want to lose his way in the depths of that forest—not after Ben Zoma had briefed him on the perils that awaited the unwary traveler. However, he wasn't ready to go back inside their sleeping chamber yet, so he decided to simply walk a circuit around the sanctum.

As the doctor did this, the architecture of the place revealed itself to him line by craggy line. If the sanctum had seemed intricate and intriguing on the inside, its exterior was even more so.

What's more, it featured a series of little alcoves, each one paved with small, flat stones and separated from the mossy ground by red walls. Greyhorse inspected a couple of the alcoves and found that there was nothing to see in them. By the time he got to the third one, he was ready to assume the same of it.

But he gave it a glance anyway—and discovered that it wasn't quite the same as its predecessors, after all. For one thing, the ground wasn't paved. It was the same mossy stuff that the doctor had been walking on.

For another thing, there was something embedded in it—something oval in outline, its surface rounded like a small hill, and so pale as to appear luminescent in the moonlight. His curiosity aroused, Greyhorse entered the alcove to take a closer look.

And saw that it was a stone.

At first, he thought it had been milled by a machine— that's how smooth and regularly shaped it was. Then he saw the tiny imperfections in its surface. He also noticed a complex network of glyphs that had been incised into it and darkened for greater legibility.

Greyhorse didn't read Gnalish, so he had no idea what sort of wisdom the glyphs were meant to impart. However, he was intrigued by the patterns that seemed to emerge for him.

In fact, the more he looked for them, the more they seemed to reveal themselves to him. And the more they revealed themselves, the more he got the feeling that he had seen them somewhere before.

It can't be, the doctor told himself. *I've never set foot on Gnala before. And I've never seen anything of Simenon's that might have borne these markings.*

But he had seen them *somewhere.* He was certain of it.

Greyhorse had to stare at the stone for some time, kneeling before it and examining it in the moonlight, before he realized why the markings seemed so familiar. They were reminiscent of a genetic data map he had helped to compile back in medical school.

The doctor recalled it as if it were yesterday. He and his classmates had been given tiny batches of cellular material that belonged to an eel-bird, a denizen of the fifth planet in the Regulus system, and were asked to identify each of the creature's genes by its unique sequence of purine and pyrimidine bases.

He had learned more from that simple exercise than almost any other facet of his medical education, perhaps because the professor involved was so passionate about his work. He had promised his students that they would never forget what eel-bird genes looked like—and, in fact, Greyhorse had never forgotten.

He nodded to himself now as he gazed at the markings on the moonlit stone. *Yes,* he told himself, *there is a remarkable similarity to that eel-bird map.*

Was it just a coincidence—or something else? After all, the ritual in which he and his companions were about to take part would determine whose traits would survive in the Gnalish gene pool and whose would be lost to the pool forever.

Could Simenon's ancestors have understood the concept of genetics—and not just at the relatively superficial level of common sense? Could they have had the wherewithal to track the makeup of the species from generation to generation?

The medical officer sat back on his haunches and ran his fingertips over the markings. They were sharp-edged enough to have been carved just the day before. But this was an ancient complex according to

Simenon, one that had been used for thousands of years. More than likely, the stone was as ancient as the rest of it.

And if that were so...

Greyhorse frowned. The Gnalish hadn't climbed the ladder of technological development any more quickly than his forebears on Earth. If anything, Simenon's people had been a little slower. To suggest that they'd enjoyed a grasp of advanced genetics thousands of years ago didn't seem likely.

But then, things weren't always what they seemed. A good scientist had to keep an open mind.

Greyhorse resolved to ask Simenon about the stone in the morning. Maybe he could shed some light on it.

Standing, the doctor stared at it some more, tilting his head so he could appraise it from another angle. Now that he knew where to look for the patterns, they were hard to miss.

Just then, a chill invaded the alcove—a sharp breath of unexpectedly cold air. It reminded Greyhorse that it was time he got back to the sleeping chamber. He would need his strength if he were going to be of any help to his colleagues in the morning.

And he had to be of considerable help to them if he were going to impress Gerda with his accomplishments.

With some reluctance, Greyhorse left the stone behind. Then he made his way back around the perimeter of the sanctum, Gnala's moon diligently lighting his way.

As Errigo Shalay entered his captain's ready room, he saw that she was intent on her monitor.

"Have a seat," said DeMontreville, a stern-looking woman with a square jaw and short, dirty-blond hair.

Shalay sat down opposite his superior and watched her eyes move back and forth in the glare of her screen. *A message from Starfleet,* he thought. *It had to be.*

Finally, DeMontreville grunted, leaned back in her seat, and said, "Damned Romulans."

"Romulans?" the Bolian echoed.

The cold-blooded bastards hadn't been seen in or near the Federation in almost thirty years, ever since they signed the Treaty of Algeron. And as far as Shalay could tell, no one missed them.

DeMontreville nodded. "Every so often, Command receives a report of a Romulan vessel in our space. They all turn out to be false alarms when they're investigated, but we're still apprised of them."

"I see," said Shalay.

His captain regarded him. "So how was your shore leave?"

"Fine," he told her, leaving out the details. After all, his meeting with Admiral McAteer was supposed to be a secret.

DeMontreville looked at him askance. "I know that look, Shalay. You've got something on your mind."

The second officer smiled. "You know me too well." He leaned forward in his chair. "I've heard through the grapevine that there's a position opening for a second officer on the *Stargazer.*"

An expression of disappointment crossed the captain's face. But then, no commanding officer liked to lose a valued officer, and Shalay had done an exemplary job on the *New Orleans.*

"And you'd like to apply for it?" she said.

"I would," he confirmed.

DeMontreville sighed. "I hate to lose you, Commander. But if that's what you want, you've got my permission."

Shalay smiled again. "Thank you, Captain."

"Just remember, there are no guarantees. The *Stargazer*'s a new ship. I'm sure you're not the only one eyeing that post."

"No guarantees," he acknowledged.

What DeMontreville didn't know was that it wouldn't be any contest. The *Stargazer* position was Shalay's, hands down.

Admiral McAteer would make certain of that.

Picard hunkered down next to Greyhorse in the darkness of the sleeping chamber and shook the big man's shoulder. "Doctor?"

Greyhorse looked up at him with eyes so wide they looked almost comical. "Is it time already?"

"It is," the captain confirmed.

The doctor sat up. "All right," he said firmly, as much to himself as to the captain. "I'm awake."

That is a matter of opinion, Picard thought.

Simenon was standing by the door to the chamber already, a scowl on his face, his arms folded impatiently across his chest. Obviously, he was eager to get going, eager to get his ordeal under way.

However, the captain's wrist chronometer told him they had almost three quarters of an hour before the ritual was scheduled to begin. Certainly, that was ample time for a quick bite and some last-minute mental preparation.

Clearly, Simenon could use some calming down. With that in mind, Picard started across the room to join him.

As he passed Ben Zoma and Joseph, he saw that they were just beginning to pull their clothes on. "Let's go, gentlemen," he told them. "We've got work to do."

Ben Zoma grunted good-naturedly. "And here I was thinking we were on shore leave."

"No such luck," the captain told him.

Joseph stretched his arms out and groaned. "I feel like I just went to bed," he complained to no one in particular.

"You *did*," said Ben Zoma. "This time of year, the nights here are only five hours long."

Joseph sighed. "Now you tell me."

As Picard approached his engineer, he could more clearly see the nervousness in Simenon's eyes. It was certainly understandable. If the future of the captain's family were at stake, *he* would have been nervous as well.

The ritual, as Simenon had described it to them the night before, was really a foot race that took place in the wilderness surrounding the Northern Sanctum. Three teams started from the same point but were compelled to negotiate divergent courses.

However, the winners of the race didn't get a trophy, as Picard had done when he came in first in the Academy marathon on Danula II. Instead, they won the right for one of their number to fertilize a cache of two dozen newly hatched eggs, the majority of which would then grow into a clutch of bouncing baby Gnalish.

Earlier in the evolutionary development of Simenon's people, this competition had been a good deal more chaotic. Instead of a few hand-picked teams trying to negotiate a prescribed course in an orderly fashion, it had been a free-for-all, pitting huge packs of instinct-driven Gnalish against each other.

Unfortunately, each pack was more or less decimated in the struggle. Few males emerged from the struggle whole and even fewer reached a ripe old age.

As time went on and civilization took hold on Gnala, the impulse to fertilize was channeled into other pursuits. It became less of a biological imperative and more a matter of personal pride. Finally, a couple of thousand years earlier, the ritual began to resemble its current, considerably less bloody form.

Not that Gnalish didn't get hurt in the course of the ritual; they did. And on occasion, their injuries were fatal. But at least most of them survived to tell the tale.

On the other hand, as Simenon had told them, those who lost the race sometimes didn't wish to survive. That was because each Gnalish male had one chance and one chance only to succeed in the ritual—and the prospect of never seeing one's progeny walk the earth was sometimes too much for them to bear.

So if Simenon seemed grim and fidgety, he had a right to be that way. In a sense, countless generations of his bloodline were depending on him—both those who had come before him and those who might come after. Picard didn't envy him that burden.

And to complicate the matter, Simenon wouldn't be racing against his equals. He would be racing against representatives of Gnala's two other subspecies, the Aklaash and the Fejjimaera.

In this case, they were the Gnalish who had spoken against the engineer in the Great Hall. Kasaelek, the pale-skinned giant at whom the elder had hissed, was a product of the towering subspecies called the Aklaash. The light-and-dark specimen was Banyohla, who represented the small, slender Fejjimaera.

Simenon had outlined the other subspecies' advantages for his colleagues. The captain recalled his engineer's words as if he had spoken them only moments earlier.

"The Aklaash are big and unspeakably strong and they tend to fare well in the ritual, which is why they're easily the most populous subspecies on Gnala."

"I see. And the Fejjimaera?" Picard had asked.

"They're smaller than I am, but a hell of a lot quicker. Also, they have a considerable talent for camouflage."

"And do they fare well in the ritual also?"

"Almost as well as the Aklaash, as a matter of fact. Finally, there's the subspecies to which I belong—the Mazzereht. We perform the worst of all, and by a wide margin."

"I'm sorry to hear that," the captain had said.

Simenon had frowned. *"So am I. But there's no way around it. Strength and speed are big assets in the wild."*

"But if your subspecies has survived at all, Nature must have given it some assets of its own."

"She did," Simenon had told him.

"And what are they?"

"She gave us . . . brains."

Simenon hadn't said it with any real optimism. Clearly, for the purposes of the ritual, he would have preferred that his people possess some more physical attribute.

Nor could Picard blame him.

He regarded Simenon now. The engineer's eyes were hard and alert, the eyes of a being about to meet the challenge of his life. And not just a challenge, but a test of his ability to survive.

The captain and the others could help him here and there. They could lend him support in his struggle. But ultimately, the test was Simenon's to pass or fail.

"Well?" Ben Zoma asked, inadvertently breaking into the captain's reverie. "What are we waiting for?"

The first officer had finished getting dressed and

seemed eager to get going. They all seemed that way—even Dr. Greyhorse, though he still looked a little bleary-eyed.

Picard looked back at Simenon. "Are you ready?" he asked as gently as he could.

The Gnalish scowled at him. "I'd better be, hadn't I?"

Chapter Thirteen

As Picard and the others issued from their sleeping chamber in the thin morning light, a white-robed Elder and two of his Aklaash bodyguards were already waiting for them.

"You will follow me," said the figure in the white robe.

Simenon agreed that he and his comrades would do this. Then they followed their guides into the embrace of the undulating, dawn-speckled forest, leaving the pride and majesty of the Northern Sanctum behind.

Insects chittered at them over the sighing of the wind. There were scraping sounds of tiny creatures making their way from hiding place to hiding place. *The occupants of the lowest rungs on the food chain,* the captain thought, *gathering to witness the trial of the beings on the highest rung.*

Before long, they came to a large clearing ringed by immense crimson trees with mottled bark and broad, spade-shaped leaves. Picard had seen sequoias on the western coast of North America; it seemed to him that these behemoths were bigger.

As the captain and his officers entered the clearing, he saw that they were the last to do so. The other two teams were already standing in closely knit circles, munching on something that smelled vaguely like bananas but sounded a lot crunchier.

Seen in briefer and more informal attire, Kasaelek and his bunch looked even more imposing than they had in the sanctum—more massive and thickly muscled under their scales. The smallest of them was as tall or taller than Vigo, and Vigo was a head taller than Picard. It was difficult for an offworlder like the captain to believe the Aklaash and Simenon belonged to the same species.

The Fejjimaera group was decidedly less impressive-looking, their informal garb revealing small, slender physiques. However, as Ben Zoma had pointed out, it was their speed that had earned them a good track record in the ritual event—and quickness wasn't likely to manifest itself in a display of bulging muscles.

But it wasn't just their body types that distinguished the Aklaash from the Fejjimaera. While Kasaelek and his comrades seemed very much at ease, almost lethargic, Banyohla's team looked fidgety. They kept darting looks at the other two groups and hissing their observations in each other's ears.

Perhaps that was just the way they acted, Picard thought. Or perhaps they were actually worried about the competition the offworlders might offer them.

He chose to believe the latter.

Of course, the Gnalish in the white robes were in evidence here as well. There were three of them in all, including the individual who had led Simenon here—each of them followed closely by a couple of Aklaash in black garb.

According to Simenon, the rest of the Assemblage would be waiting for them at the "finish line." They would sit there patiently, telling stories of their fore-bears and humming ancient melodies, until a victor appeared—the first of the three competitors to reach the nest of unfertilized eggs.

And when he did, they would oversee the fertilization process, as he added his DNA to that of the eggs. Apparently, *that* was one of the Assemblage's duties as well.

Picard was hardly an expert on Gnalish biology, but he could imagine what the fertilization process might be like. It made him cringe a little to think of his engineer performing such an act in full view of both the Assemblage and his colleagues.

But then, he wasn't a Gnalish. No doubt, there were human behaviors that occasionally made Simenon squirm as well.

As Picard thought this, a black-garbed Aklaash came over to the engineers' group and distributed something small and flat to each of its members, with Simenon receiving an extra package of the stuff. When it was the captain's turn, he saw that he had been given a couple of crackers with a strong, bananalike scent to them—the same sort of food the other teams were eating.

"Lovely," said Greyhorse, an expression of displeasure on his face as he inspected the crackers more closely. "What are they?"

"*Layfid,*" Simenon replied, as he tucked the extra package into an interior pocket of his shirt.

"And what's that?" asked Ben Zoma.

"Reconstituted worm waste," said the engineer. He

took a bite of one of his crackers and nodded approvingly. "And nutritious worm waste at that."

Vigo swallowed back his revulsion. "I don't suppose there's an alternative of some kind?"

Joseph grunted. "This from the guy who shoves sturrd down his throat? I'll take worm waste over that stuff any day." And to prove his point, he began munching on one of his crackers.

Picard tried one of his own and found it wasn't nearly as bad as Simenon had made it sound. Besides, they were going to be in the woods for some time, and he would sooner trust a cracker than something he found growing in the wild.

Another black-robed guard came by and gave each of them something else—not food this time, but a tapered wooden club about a meter long and a belted sheath to go with it. The captain turned the club over in his hands.

Then he glanced at Simenon. "This is a *tellek?*"

The engineer nodded. "The only weapon any of us is allowed."

Simenon had described it to Picard and the others the night before. It had sounded formidable. But now that the captain held it in his hands and saw how light it was, he was a good deal less confident about its effectiveness. Nonetheless, he put on the belt and stuck the *tellek* in its sheath, and watched his companions do the same.

For a few minutes, they ate their crackers and watched Gnala's sun come up through the branches of the densely packed forest. Then one of the white-robed ones made his way to the center of the clearing and raised his bony hand.

"Come on," said Simenon.

He led the way to a narrow trail radiating from the clearing—one of three distinct pathways through the woods that began just a few meters apart. Kasaelek approached the trail on their left. Banyohla approached the one on their right.

The Assemblage's representative said something slow and rhythmic, something that seemed to find willing accompaniment in the soft plaint of the morning breeze. Picard's universal translator had a devil of a time making any sense of it.

But then, he didn't have to understand the words. All he had to do was watch for the fall of the elder's hand, because that was the gesture that would signal the start of the race.

The captain glanced at Simenon. He looked like a Markoffian sea lizard, coiled and ready to strike.

As Picard thought this, the elder in the white robe stopped singing. His hand fell like a dying bird. And the captain plunged forward alongside Simenon, for the ritual had begun.

Gerda Asmund was checking her monitors for unexpected obstacles on the course she had plotted when her sister spoke up.

"All right, what is it?" asked Idun, who was sitting beside her at the helm console.

Gerda glanced at her. "What do you mean?"

"Your expression," her sister said knowingly. "You seem concerned about something."

The navigator frowned. Was it that obvious?

"I was wondering how the captain and the others were faring on Gnala," she said. It was the truth, more or less.

"They've been in my thoughts as well." Idun made a sound of disgust, loud enough only for her twin to hear. "They should have taken us with them."

"They couldn't," Gerda reminded her. "The ritual in which they're participating is restricted to males."

Her sister dismissed the idea with a sound of disgust. "If it were a Klingon ritual, there would be no such restriction."

Gerda nodded. "True."

Klingons were more egalitarian than most other species in that regard. When it came to fighting, to killing and being killed, males and females were on the same footing.

"Nonetheless," said Idun, "they will acquit themselves well—I am certain of it. The captain is a brave and clever individual. Likewise, Ben Zoma and Simenon."

"What about the others?" Gerda asked.

Her sister shrugged. "What Joseph lacks in experience he makes up in determination. And Vigo...few humanoids have his strength."

She had failed to mention only one member of the party. What's more, Gerda understood the omission. Despite Greyhorse's size and the handful of lessons she had given him, he wasn't much of a fighter.

Then why had she tutored him in the martial arts? Why had she spent precious hours with him in the gym when she could have been honing her own fighting skills or studying her navigation charts?

Yes, she thought. *That is the question.*

Gerda and Idun had always shared everything with each other. Even their deepest secrets.

When the two of them were taken in by the House of Warrokh, tiny stripling girls in the midst of huge, menacing warriors who roared and snarled at each other for no apparent reason, they had cried themselves to sleep—and shared each other's tears, for they were wrapped in each other's arms.

When they were older and a gang of sneering boys had thought to push "the human girls" around, they had stood back to back and endured their beating together. And in the end, they obtained their revenge together as well, cornering the offenders one by one and returning their injuries measure for measure.

And when their father died defending his family's honor, they had howled together over his ruined body and and shared the joy of knowing he would go to join Kahless in Sto-Vo-Kor.

We have shared everything, Gerda thought. *But I cannot share my feelings in the matter of Carter Greyhorse.*

And what was worse, she couldn't bring herself to say why.

Ulelo stopped when he got to the set of doors he had been looking for and waited for his presence to be announced.

It took longer to get a response than he had expected. But then, having never called on any of his crewmates, his only point of reference was how it felt on the other side of the doors.

Finally, the duranium panels slid aside, giving him a view of an anteroom much like his own. However, this anteroom looked a good deal warmer, decorated as it was with Japanese watercolors and a grouping of Vulcan statuettes.

Emily Bender looked at him. She was standing in front of an unusually shaped teakwood chair, a padd in her hand. "Yes?"

Ulelo recited the words he had rehearsed. "I wanted to apologize for my behavior. I treated you rudely and I'm sorry."

His host regarded him for a moment. "I don't know whether to forgive you or detest you."

"I wouldn't blame you either way," he said.

That seemed to soften her up a bit. "Have a seat," she told him, clearly still a little wary. *Of being hurt again.*

"Thank you," he said.

Emily Bender stepped aside and Ulelo entered her quarters. Once inside, he noticed a number of other personal touches—a geode filled with brilliant violet crystals, a woven wall hanging done in more muted violets, an artifact that might have been a ceramic oil lamp a very long time ago.

And a picture of Emily Bender with two people who seemed to be her parents.

She indicated a Starfleet-issue chair. The communications officer sat. For a heartbeat or two, neither of them spoke, until he realized that she wasn't going to make this easy for him. It was incumbent on him to begin the exchange.

He did so.

"What I said before must have seemed strange to you," Ulelo ventured. "Both in the corridor and in my quarters. After all, you were certain that you knew me, but I wasn't acknowledging that I knew *you.*"

Emily Bender nodded. "It was strange, all right." She was still holding herself back, waiting to hear what he had to say.

"I'm sure everything you told me was true," he continued. "About the Academy, our friends there, how close we were…I don't doubt it for a minute. But what I was saying…that's true too. I honestly don't remember any of it."

She tilted her head to one side as she studied him. "You're saying you have amnesia…?"

Ulelo shrugged. "I was in an accident a little while ago. I lost pieces of my memory. Apparently, my relationships with you and the others you mentioned were some of the pieces I lost."

It was a lie, of course. He hadn't had an accident at all.

So why was he misleading her? Heaven knew it wasn't because he wanted to torment the woman. It would have been a lot easier on him if he could have simply told her the truth.

But that wasn't an option.

"An accident," Emily Bender echoed, making it clear she was skeptical about the information.

He nodded. "I'm not supposed to talk about it." Another lie. He was getting good at telling them. "But it wasn't pleasant," Ulelo added for good measure.

She sighed. "So you really don't remember me?"

"Not at all." That part, at least, was true. "And I don't remember any of the people you mentioned."

Emily Bender seemed to weigh his claims for a while, her eyes searching his. Then she drew a breath and slowly let it out.

"Look," she said, "if you don't remember me, you don't remember me. I guess that's the way it is."

"It's frustrating," Ulelo allowed. "For me more than anyone."

"I'm sure it is. And lonely, I imagine."

"That too." *Painfully so.*

Emily Bender leaned forward in her chair. "So let me get this straight. When you asked me to leave your quarters...you weren't giving me the brush-off after all?"

He started to answer in the affirmative—until he saw where his response might lead her. As before, he acknowledged the fact of her beauty, if only to himself. He tortured himself with the idea that he could bring some joy into his life, just by giving in to a woman who obviously wanted him as much as he wanted her.

A woman who was willing to accept him unconditionally, it seemed. Without reservations. Without *questions*.

Fortunately, Ulelo was still strong. He could still do what his duty—and his sanity—demanded of him.

"I wasn't giving you the brush-off," he conceded. "But please understand...I would feel awkward getting involved with you romantically, given the fact that you know me and I don't—"

Emily Bender held up her hand. "Don't. I can already hear what you're going to say."

Ulelo frowned. "And what's that?"

"That you could use a friend."

He hadn't planned on saying that at all. However, he saw no way to deny it.

She considered him for a moment. Then, looking a little bitter, she shook her head. "If we can't be what I'd like us to be..." Her voice trailed off wistfully.

The comm officer was grateful that the matter had resolved itself without his having to engage in further maneuvers. "I understand," he said softly. Then he added, "I guess I'll be going."

She didn't stop him. In fact, she didn't even turn her head to watch him go.

Picard and his colleagues had been jogging down their ritual trail for less than twenty minutes before Simenon slowed them to a walk.

The captain himself could have continued at a trot for another hour, if necessary. However, it was clear that at least one member of their party could not.

And that member was Greyhorse.

The doctor was breathing heavily even now, still feeling the effects of the quicker pace. But then, he was a big man, not exactly made for long-distance running, and to Picard's knowledge he had never dedicated himself to a fitness regimen.

Of course, Greyhorse had prescribed such regimens for others. Why was it that physicians so seldom practiced what they preached?

Simenon glanced back at the doctor. Then he muttered something beneath his breath.

"What's that?" asked Greyhorse.

Simenon shook his head. "Nothing."

"Don't give me that," Greyhorse said. "You don't mutter at someone that way and then not tell them what you're thinking."

The Gnalish rolled his eyes. "All right. I admit it. I was wishing that you were in better shape."

The doctor frowned. "Really."

"Really. And," Simenon added, "while I was at it, I wished one of the Asmunds could have come in your place."

Picard would have expected Greyhorse to react negatively to such a statement. But if his feelings were hurt, he didn't show it.

Instead, he told Simenon, "Believe me, so do I."

Clearly, the admission caught Simenon by surprise. "You know," he said, "no one told you you had to come."

Greyhorse chuckled derisively. "As usual, my friend, your gratitude knows no bounds."

"Gentlemen," said Picard, "I suggest we table this discussion for the time being. As you may have noticed, the Asmunds are not in evidence here, nor is there any possibility that they will arrive before the start of the ritual."

"And as for the doctor's conditioning," Ben Zoma

chimed in optimistically, "I expect him to catch his second wind any moment now."

Simenon looked at Greyhorse. "Maybe you're right."

"That's the spirit," said Ben Zoma.

"But," Simenon added as he forged ahead, "I doubt it."

Chapter Fourteen

COMMANDER WU HAD HER HELM OFFICER drop the *Stargazer* out of warp near the center of the gargantuan Oneo Madrin system, at a point more or less equidistant from its twin stars.

It was a tricky maneuver, considering the complex balance of planets and gravity wells in the system. However, Idun pulled it off without any apparent difficulty.

"Proceed at half impulse," said the second officer.

"Half impulse," Idun confirmed.

Wu advanced toward the viewscreen, which showed her a substantial section of the slender, golden accretion bridge that linked the system's two young suns. One sun was substantially bigger than the other, which was why it was able to steal a stream of charged particles from its neighbor's photosphere.

Not surprisingly, there was no sign of the *Belladonna*. But then, the research vessel was less than a hundred meters in length. Trying to pick her out visually against the vast backdrop of a binary star system made finding a needle in a haystack seem ridiculously easy by comparison.

Fortunately, the ship's sensors weren't restricted to the visible spectrum. They also included wideband electromagnetic scanners, virtual neutrino spectrometers, and a host of other devices.

It was the nonvisual array that Wu was relying on to pick out the *Belladonna*. She glanced at Gerda, who had primary responsibility for sensor operations.

"Got them?" she asked.

The navigator frowned as she worked at her console. "Not yet," she was forced to report.

Wu was surprised. Turning back to the image on the viewscreen, she wondered what the problem was. The *Belladonna*'s captain had sent out a high-priority distress call. He wouldn't have resorted to that option if his ship had been in any shape to leave Oneo Madrin.

According to that logic, the research ship should still have been here, and Gerda's sensors should have identified it in a matter of moments. But they hadn't done that.

Wu's mind raced, going through the possibilities. None of them was very promising—and the ones that involved hostile intervention were the least promising of all.

She could think of half a dozen species in this part of space that might have been tempted to attack the *Belladonna*—among them the Enniac, the Azhuridai and the Topoli. It was unlikely that any of them would have done so for fear of the repercussions, but one never knew.

Fortunately, there was a way to see if the research vessel might have met with foul play. "Scan for ion trails," she told Gerda.

The navigator looked up at her. "You think they were attacked?"

Wu shrugged. "Let's find out."

It didn't take long. In a matter of seconds, Gerda had called up a graphic identifying ion concentrations in the area.

As it happened, there was only one discernible trail. That pretty much ruled out the possibility of an assault. But the exercise was a valuable one nevertheless, because it showed them the route the *Belladonna* had taken through the system.

And in the process, it gave them a pretty clear picture of where she had gone—a picture that, as it sank in, turned out to be as disheartening as it was unexpected.

Gerda muttered something harsh in the Klingon tongue. Wu didn't speak a word of Klingon, but she had no trouble understanding the gist of the navigator's remark.

"They're in the accretion bridge," Idun said for the benefit of anyone who hadn't figured it out.

Wu nodded. "It seems that way, all right."

She considered the conditions the *Belladonna* would be facing, ticking them off one by one in her mind. *High levels of radiation. Powerful magnetic fields. Near-solar temperatures, mitigated only by the scarcity of material in which thermal energy could be stored.* No one could survive in that environment for long.

"We've got to get her out of there," she said.

Of course, it might already have been too late. If the *Belladonna*'s shields had been compromised even a little...

Nonetheless, they had to try.

The second officer turned to Gerda. "Can you identify them?"

The navigator shook her head. She was rotating sensor modalities, one after the other. "I'm picking up some kind of solid object. But it doesn't look like a ship. At least, not a *whole* one."

Wu bit her lip. Was it possible that the vessel had already blown up? Or been vaporized?

"There's a reason for that," said Kastiigan.

He was standing at the tiny science station aft of the captain's chair, his jowly face caught in the crawl of a moving graphic. Apparently, he had joined his colleagues on the bridge without Wu's noticing it.

"A reason?" she prodded.

"Yes," said the science officer. "According to my readings, only a portion of the *Belladonna* exists within the accretion bridge. The rest...does not."

"You mean she's been ripped apart?" the commander asked, trying to get a handle on the situation.

"No," said Kastiigan. "There's no indication that the *Belladonna* has sustained that sort of damage. Her sensor profile just seems to go so far and no farther."

"Where is she?" Wu demanded. "I want to see her for myself."

"I'll relay the coordinates to Lieutenant Asmund's station," the Kandilkari said obligingly.

A moment later, Wu saw what Kastiigan was talking about. The *Stargazer*'s sensors were picking up a fragment of what might have been a Federation research ship. But it showed no signs of the carbonization or twisted metal that would have resulted from a hull-rending decompression.

It was just as the science officer had said—the *Belladonna* simply wasn't all there.

Wu shook her head. It didn't make sense. She was tempted to say so until she remembered something—that she was the one in charge of the ship at the moment.

She had to keep her head if she expected her subordinates to do so.

"Good work," she told Kastiigan.

"Thank you," he responded.

The second officer stared at Gerda's monitor, coming up with question after question for which she had no ready answers. For instance, how had a piece of the *Belladonna* wound up in the accretion bridge? And what had happened to the rest of the ship?

Then she got something new—an answer for which she had no question. "Commander," said Gerda, "we're detecting life signs."

Wu watched as Gerda magnified the surviving portion of the research ship on her monitor. It was covered with red blips, each of them representing a viable, functioning life-form.

Without question, there were living beings aboard—humanoid, judging from their biochemical makeup. But how could that be? This was only a *section* of the *Belladonna.*

Or was it?

"Commander," said Idun, her voice taut with concern, "we're being drawn in the direction of the accretion bridge."

The second officer eyed the viewscreen and saw a confirmation of what Idun had told her. The accretion bridge was growing larger at a slow but noticeable rate.

Wu didn't get it. Accretion bridges didn't have enough mass to generate gravitic forces. So what in the name of Zefram Cochrane was tugging at them?

As calmly as she could, she made her way to the helm. "Reverse engines," she said. "Full power."

Idun carried out the command. For a tense moment or

two, it wasn't clear whether she would win the battle or not. Then she turned to Wu and reported that the *Stargazer* was moving backward, returning to her original position.

Indeed, the commander could see it on the screen. The accretion bridge was gradually diminishing in size.

"Maintain thrusters," Wu told her, "until we're two thousand kilometers from the accretion bridge."

"Aye, Commander," said the helm officer, and they continued to retreat from the phenomenon.

Wu returned to her seat and regarded the image on the viewscreen. She no longer wondered how the *Belladonna* had wound up in the accretion bridge. Obviously, it had succumbed to the forces the *Stargazer* had just managed to overcome.

But where in blazes were those forces coming from? She couldn't say—just as she couldn't say how all those people had survived on a mere piece of a ship, or how it had become merely a *piece* of a ship in the first place.

Maybe the *Belladonna*'s crew could tell her. "Hail them," the commander told Paxton.

The comm officer did as she asked. But after a moment, he said, "No response."

Obviously, she would have to take another tack.

"Launch a probe into the accretion bridge," Wu commanded, determined to obtain some answers while there was still time to help the living on the *Belladonna*.

Back in his Academy days, Picard had run marathons. What's more, he had fared rather well in them, regardless of whether the course before him was crumbly desert dirt or rocky mountain turf or some smooth artificial surface.

But then, he hadn't run those races on anything even remotely like the stuff he now found underfoot.

"There's a rhythm to it," Simenon told him. "All you've got to do is find it."

Picard frowned and tried to follow his engineer's instructions. However, the springy, reddish-brown moss beneath his feet seemed to want to bounce when he didn't, and vice versa.

"Easy for you to say," he told his engineer.

When they had begun this race, the ground had been pretty much what one found in most forests—an uneven but generally reliable mixture of whatever substances the surrounding trees cared to contribute. But a few minutes ago, that had changed.

"This is most unsettling," Vigo observed. Obviously, he was having trouble making the adjustment, too.

"Get used to it," Simenon told them. "From here on in, the trail will be like this more often than not."

And that wouldn't be a disadvantage to the Aklaash or the Fejjimaera, Picard reflected. But it would be a disadvantage to *them*—a group made up mostly of off-worlders unaccustomed to this kind of terrain—as if they weren't laboring under enough of a disadvantage already.

Suddenly, the trees up ahead seemed to explode into a million fragments and the sky was filled with a flight of green and purple avians. Shading his eyes from the shafts of sunlight that penetrated the forest, the captain saw that the creatures were vaguely reminiscent of a flock of Terran geese.

As they flew, their wings flapping in graceful unison, they shed their plumage over the forest. The green and purple feathers wafted and rolled lazily, glinting with iridescent majesty.

"The colunnu?" Picard asked.

"That's right," Simenon confirmed.

"They're beautiful," Vigo observed, squinting so he could see. "And so fragile-looking."

"Yes," said Ben Zoma. "Hard to believe they would pick us clean if we let our guard down."

Thanks to Simenon, Picard knew exactly what his first officer meant. The colunnu's feathers were extremely poisonous. If any of them were to prick his unprotected skin, they would paralyze him in twenty seconds and shut down his nervous system in another ten.

And the colunnu, who had an uncanny knack for knowing when one of their feathers had claimed a victim, would be on him almost instantly. If Simenon's cautions weren't exaggerations, his bones would be picked clean even before the poison finished its work.

"A gruesome end," said the captain, "to be sure."

That, he mused, was why they were all wearing thick, sturdy boots—to make certain they didn't step on any green and purple feathers and come to regret it.

Suddenly, Joseph stopped in his tracks and looked around. "What's that?" he asked.

Greyhorse stopped, too. "I didn't hear anything," he said.

"Listen," the security officer insisted.

They stopped and listened—all of them, Picard included. That's when he heard it—a barking sound in the distance.

"Simenon?" said Ben Zoma.

"Sanjarra," the Gnalish told them.

"Which ones were those again?" asked the doctor.

Simenon shot him a disparaging look. "Four-legged predators, travel in packs...starting to sound familiar?"

Greyhorse's brow furrowed. "These aren't the ones that can snap our bones with their teeth, are they?"

"In fact," said the engineer, "they are."

"What are the odds they'll pass us by?" asked Vigo.

"Not very good," Simenon told him.

The barking was getting louder. "As I recall," Picard said, "sanjarra hate water."

"That's correct," the Gnalish rasped. "Unfortunately, we're not *near* any water."

"So what do we do?" asked Greyhorse. "Take to the trees?"

Simenon shook his scaly head. "It wouldn't help. Sanjarra are *born* in the trees."

"Then what?" the doctor demanded.

Simenon looked grim. "We get our sticks out and stand our ground—and hope they've eaten recently."

Picard drew his stick from its sheath and watched his officers do the same. Then, without anyone telling them to do so, they put their backs together and formed a knot.

As the beasts got closer, their growling grew louder and more frenzied. They were within a hundred meters now, the captain judged, though the forest still hid them from view.

His heart was pounding and he could feel a trickle of sweat running down the side of his face. Primitive reactions, he noted. But then, this was a primitive confrontation.

Picard would have given much for the reassuring weight of a phaser pistol in his hand. Unfortunately, the nearest directed energy weapon was in orbit high above the planet's surface, securely locked in the *Stargazer*'s armory.

More growling, closer still. Without question, the sanjarra had caught their scent.

"As soon as you see them," said Simenon, "go on the offensive. Keep them off-balance. Once they leap, we're as good as dead."

Another flight of colunnu crossed the sky in close formation. But this time, the captain didn't look up to appreciate them.

He had a more immediate concern.

Chapter Fifteen

Wu FELT AS IF she had been watching the streaming splendor of Oneo Madrin's accretion bridge for hours before the *Stargazer* finally got some telemetry from its class IV probe. In fact, though, it could only have been seven or eight minutes.

"We're receiving," Paxton announced.

"What have we got?" asked the second officer, getting up to join him at his console.

Paxton frowned as he studied his communications monitors. "There's interference from all the radiation, Commander. I'm trying to eliminate it..."

Wu leaned over his shoulder to see how he was doing. Little by little, the comm officer was cleaning up the image on his central monitor. As he did this, Wu could see the outline of a ship emerging.

Or rather, *part* of a ship.

But the part she could make out appeared undamaged, just as their sensors had already indicated. It was as if something had sheared the *Belladonna* in half.

Then Wu saw that there was something else in the accretion bridge—a churning maelstrom of energy that had no business being there, but was dancing around the severed end of the research ship. "What's that?" she asked Paxton.

The comm officer peered at his monitor, its glare casting crimson shadows on his face. "It looks like a graviton storm—though I don't think I've ever seen one of this intensity."

"Is it intense enough to have drawn us toward the accretion bridge?" Wu asked.

"I don't believe so," Kastiigan told her. "Nor do I believe it is intense enough to have trapped the *Belladonna*."

The second officer frowned. *Something* had exerted an attractive force on them. If not the graviton storm, what then?

As if he had read her mind, Kastiigan said, "Graviton storms seldom occur spontaneously. They are usually an incidental effect of some other sort of disturbance."

"So maybe this one is concealing something," Paxton speculated.

"Something that has an attractive force all its own," Wu remarked.

Paxton nodded. "A kind of cosmic sinkhole."

"An interesting thesis," Kastiigan noted. "It would explain why we are only seeing part of the research vessel."

Wu felt a trickle of cold sweat in the small of her back. "You mean because the rest has already been swallowed up by the sinkhole."

Paxton shrugged. "Makes as much sense as anything else."

The second officer studied the telemetry some more.

She had heard of gaps in space–time that pulled matter from her universe into another. They had been documented in the logs of starship captains as far back as the twenty-second century.

"All right," she said at last. "If this is a sinkhole, where does it lead?" She challenged her bridge officers with a look. "What's on the other side?"

"That is difficult to say," Kastiigan responded. "But one thing seems certain, Commander—the *Belladonna* won't have the wherewithal to survive the journey."

Wu didn't like hearing that. However, it was hard to argue the point. The stresses associated with space–time rifts were such that few vessels had a chance of getting through them intact.

She stood up and eyed the viewscreen. "Mr. Paxton," she said, "do you think you can use the probe to punch a comm signal through that mess?"

"I think so," said the communications officer.

"Good," Wu replied. "Try hailing them again."

Paxton's fingers crawled over his controls. Then he sat back and watched his screens for a reply.

"Anything?" she asked.

Paxton shook his head. "I'm afraid not."

Wu frowned. A lack of response could mean one of two things: either their signal still hadn't gotten through to the *Belladonna* or there was no one in a position to answer it.

She hoped it was the former.

"Commander," Kastiigan said abruptly, "we have a problem. The probe is being drawn into the phenomenon as well."

Wu turned to Paxton. "Get it out of there."

The comm officer tried. But after a while, he shook his head. "It's not responding. The pull is too strong."

The second officer considered their options. They

were too far away from the probe to get a tractor beam on it. And if they got much closer, they would be putting the *Stargazer* in jeopardy again.

Had the class IV been a manned probe, Wu would have gone after it without a second thought. But it was just a set of instruments surrounded by a duranium hull. And instruments—no matter how valuable—could be replaced.

"Try a sudden acceleration," Wu suggested.

Paxton looked at her. "You mean slingshot it out the other side of the accretion bridge?"

"If you can."

"It's worth a try," the comm officer said.

His fingers moving with practiced ease, he tapped out the second officer's order on his control panel. Then he implemented it.

On Paxton's monitor, the yellow blip that represented the probe suddenly leaped past the research ship, striving to free itself from the phenomenon's embrace. And for a moment, it appeared to Wu that it might make it.

Then, slowly but certainly, the probe was dragged backward. Paxton gave it all the thrust he could, but it didn't seem to help. Finally, the class IV device vanished from the screen altogether.

Paxton turned to Wu, looking apologetic. "We've lost contact with the probe, Commander."

She sighed. Clearly, she needed more information, and she wasn't going to get it by sending in more unmanned probes.

Wu gazed at the main viewscreen, where all she could see was the accretion bridge. Somewhere inside it, the *Belladonna* was slowly but inexorably slipping into the stormy maw of the phenomenon.

If she were going to do a better job with the research vessel than she had with the probe, she had to do something—and soon. But this wasn't a problem with a simple solution. She couldn't just transport the survivors off the *Belladonna*—not when she couldn't even get a comm signal through.

Turning to the rest of the bridge contingent, Wu said, "I need a plan—and I need it *now*."

The sanjarra were already within twenty meters of Simenon's party when Picard got his first glimpse of the beasts through a gap in the screen of crimson trees.

They looked like sleek, black greyhounds with blood-red tiger stripes and faces like fruit bats. Their eyes were like shiny, black pebbles and their mouths were full of long, curved teeth. A strange combination to be sure, but hardly the strangest the captain had seen in the course of hundreds of planetary surveys.

It was difficult to tell precisely how many there were, but Picard reckoned that there might be a dozen. As they got closer, their growls deepened and they bared their fangs.

The sanjarra looked completely undaunted by the fact that they had never seen the likes of the offworlders before. But then, the captain supposed, meat was meat.

As they emerged from cover, they got lower to the ground and their muscles seemed to bunch. Picard was reminded of Simenon's instructions: *"As soon as you see them, go on the offensive. Keep them off-balance. Once they leap, we're as good as dead."*

Taking the Gnalish's advice to heart, the captain lunged as if he were on a fencing strip and swung his *tellek* at the nearest bat-face. Its plans interrupted, the beast gave a deep-throated snarl and jumped back out of harm's way.

Picard's companions lashed out as well, with much

the same results. The sanjarra looked angry, discomfited by the turn of events. But then, they were predators. They weren't accustomed to defending themselves from their prey.

Again, the captain leaped forward and took a swing at the nearest of the bat-faces. And again, it withdrew with a dangerous-sounding rumbling deep in its throat.

Ben Zoma narrowly swung and missed another one. "When do we get to the part where they run away?" he asked.

Picard had been wondering the same thing. "Why do I get the feeling we're just making them madder?"

"Keep at it," Simenon told them, "and they'll get the idea." Taking his own advice, he drove back one of the beasts with a vicious two-handed attack. Then he added, "Eventually."

Suddenly, someone cried out and fell in a heap. Glancing to his left, the captain saw that it was Greyhorse who had gone down, his leg caught in a thick, leafy vine.

Nor was Picard the only one who had noticed. A couple of sanjarra appeared to have taken note of the doctor's fall as well. Their tiny eyes glittered with a fierce, undeniable hunger.

As the captain looked on, the beasts coiled to spring. *Not good,* he thought. *Not good at all.* Once they pounced on Greyhorse, he was as good as dead.

Someone would have to stop them before they could spring. Determined that he would be the one to do that, Picard started to move in the doctor's direction.

But Joseph beat him to the punch. Leaping forward and swinging his *tellek* in big, savage arcs, the security officer made the beasts think twice about claiming their prey.

Then help came in the form of Simenon and Ben

Zoma. Overmatched now, the sanjarra who had been eyeing Greyhorse grudgingly gave ground. But at the same time, it gave some of the other beasts an opening.

And when Picard and Vigo went after *those* bat-faces, it created an opportunity for the sanjarra to attack from still another quarter. It was as if the bat-faced predators were a deadly flood and Picard's people were trying to maintain a leaky seawall in which they could only plug one hole at a time.

"Watch out!" someone cried, his voice thick with urgency.

"Behind you!" shouted someone else.

They whirled, swung their *telleks,* whirled again to face a new threat. None of them ever quite managed to hit anything, but neither did they let the sanjarra gain the advantage.

Picard blinked away sweat that had fallen into his eyes and tried desperately to hold up his end of the bargain. They all did—Greyhorse too, now that he was on his feet again.

Finally, after what seemed like a very long time, the beasts' frustration seemed to overcome their hunger. They didn't growl any less loudly or viciously when they were beaten back, but they also weren't as quick to come forward again.

Then the breakthrough came. One of the bat-faces, perhaps the largest of them, appeared to lose interest in his prey. He turned around and began to pad away through the forest, not even bothering to give Simenon's party a second look.

A moment later, a second beast admitted defeat as well. And as if by tacit agreement, the rest of the sanjarra followed suit.

In a matter of moments, they were gone. It was only

then that Picard realized how much his arms hurt. Taking a deep breath, he looked around at his comrades. They were breathing hard but no one seemed to have sustained any damage.

Not even Greyhorse.

"Everyone all right?" Ben Zoma asked.

His question was met with tired murmurs of assent.

Vigo slipped his *tellek* back into its sheath. "Well," he said, grpping Joseph's shoulder, "that could have turned out worse."

Joseph nodded. *"Much* worse."

Ben Zoma swiped perspiration from his brow with the back of his hand. "I'd call it a good omen."

Simenon cast a skeptical look at him. "That is," he amended, "if you believe in such things."

"Come on," the first officer told him. "Even you have to admit we did well just now."

Simenon's nostrils flared stubbornly. "All right," he said at last. "I'll admit it."

Then he started off down the path again.

As he fell in behind the engineer, Picard smiled through his weariness. If even Simenon could show a hint of optimism, their venture might turn out well after all.

Chapter Sixteen

"WELL?" SAID WU, scanning the faces of her bridge officers.

She could feel the hum of the *Stargazer*'s engines through the deck plates, hear the control consoles' unrelenting chorus of beeps and chirps. Normally, she tuned those things out the way any veteran officer would, but they seemed all too obtrusive now in the silence that followed her challenge.

"Who's got a way to get those people off the *Belladonna?*" she asked, her voice echoing throughout the bridge.

No one spoke for a moment. Then Paxton broke the ice.

"We could try using a tractor beam. But that would require us to get a lot closer to the accretion bridge."

"And we can't do that," said Idun, "because the pull would drag *us* into the phenomenon as well."

Kastiigan nodded at his science console. "True."

"We can't transport them off," Gerda thought out loud. "Not when we can't get a reliable lock on them."

"And," Kastiigan added, "the radiation and the magnetic fields in the accretion bridge would wreak havoc with a confinement beam."

"So the transporter isn't an option," Wu concluded. "What *is?*"

Silence ruled the bridge again. Wu found herself missing the captain, Ben Zoma, Simenon, and Vigo. Had they been aboard, there would no doubt have been a few more suggestions in the air.

Paris, who was manning the weapons station in Vigo's absence, hadn't spoken to that point. But now he said, "We've established that we can't use our tractor beam to pull the *Belladonna* out. But why couldn't we use it to send in an unmanned shuttle?"

Wu looked at him. "You mean as a rescue vehicle?"

The ensign nodded. "If we can get it to the *Belladonna,* they can offload their people one group at a time."

The second officer considered the notion. It was interesting, all right. She turned to Lt. Dubinski, Simenon's stand-in at the engineering console. "What do you think?"

The engineer took a moment to run some calculations. When he looked up, it wasn't with a great deal of optimism. And when he spoke, it was with even less.

"Even if a tractor beam could be effective in an accretion bridge environment, we'd have to stretch it pretty thin to keep the *Stargazer* out of trouble. It wouldn't be able to handle the mass of a shuttle *pod,* much less a full-fledged passenger craft." Dubinski glanced at Paris. "Good try."

But the ensign didn't seem especially gratified by the compliment. His expression said he wouldn't be content until he had come up with something better.

Wu looked around the bridge. "Anyone else?"

No one seemed to have an idea—not even Paris, for all his obvious determination. Under different circumstances, that might not have bothered the second officer so much.

But under *these* circumstances, with a ship full of lives hanging in the balance, it bothered her a lot.

Picard sat down heavily and rested his back against the rough bark of a tree trunk.

"I just need a minute," Greyhorse gasped, collapsing against another tree on the opposite side of the path.

Of course, this was the fourth time the doctor had said that since the beginning of the race a few hours earlier. Though no one had complained out loud, it was growing difficult to ignore the fact that he was slowing their team down.

To Simenon's credit, he was managing to withhold comment on Greyhorse like everyone else. He just stood there a little farther up the trail, glancing occasionally at the paths of their adversaries to either side of them and frowning.

"Thanks a lot," Greyhorse rasped in the Gnalish's direction.

Simenon turned. "For what? I haven't said a word."

"You don't have to," the big man told him. "The way you're standing there is comment enough."

The engineer's ruby eyes narrowed. "What would you have me do? There's nothing more important to a Gnalish than winning this race. *Nothing*. And we're sitting here wasting time when we could be looking after the future of my clan."

"No one's trying harder than I am," Greyhorse wheezed.

"I didn't say you weren't *trying*," Simenon shot back. "All I'm saying is that—"

He stopped in midsentence as something dark darted

across the path and leaped into his backpack. Muttering a curse, the Gnalish reached for the pack, but he was too late.

Whatever it was had emerged with Simenon's package of extra crackers and was dragging it off into the forest.

"Stop it!" the Gnalish cried.

Picard, who was closest to it, managed to head the thing off. It was then that he got his first good look at it.

The creature was small and slender with black, matted fur, a long reddish tail, and tiny paws. Picard would have sworn it was a Terran rat if not for the high, bony ridge in the center of its skull.

It stopped and looked at him for a second with its black, oval eyes, as if it were wondering what kind of smooth-skinned monstrosity had wandered into its forest. Then, with blinding speed, the creature whirled and darted back toward the path, still dragging Simenon's cracker package along with it.

By then, the others had come after it as well. But when the thing scampered back into their midst, it made them spin and dance with the awkward determination of Tellarites at a Regency ball.

"It's behind you!"

"Over there!"

"No," said Picard, pointing to the thing as it scurried past him, "over *there!*"

Every time the creature made a move to elude them, someone blocked its escape route. And after a while, their efforts began to take a toll on the rodent. It moved less quickly and unpredictably, became easier to track with one's eyes.

It still could have slipped into the brush and eluded its pursuers if it had relinquished its hold on their food supply. But having come this far, the creature seemed reluctant to part with its prize.

Finally, Picard and his officers surrounded it, blocking its escape at every turn. At that point, it was just a matter of retrieving the package of crackers.

"Stay where you are," the Gnalish snapped. "I'll get it." And he moved in to recover what was his.

"Feel free," said Ben Zoma.

"It's all yours," Joseph told him.

Hunkering down low, Simenon eyed the rodent. Then he advanced on it with a hunter's purposefulness. "I'll teach you to steal my food," he said softly.

"You can teach him to steal mine, too," Greyhorse remarked dryly.

The rodent didn't move a muscle. It just sat there on its hind legs, its furry, ridged head tilted to one side, watching the engineer as if mesmerized by him.

"That's right," Simenon hissed approvingly. "Just stay there *one* moment longer, you filthy duwiijuc—"

Suddenly, he darted forward and grabbed for the creature. But as he did so, the rodent darted forward, too—right between the Gnalish's legs. And before Simenon could do anything about it, the thing had grabbed hold of his tail.

A cry of rage and indignation boiling up from his throat, the engineer switched his appendage back and forth in an attempt to dislodge his tormentor. But it didn't work. The rodent hung on as if its life depended on it—and maybe it did.

Cursing like a drunken Klingon, Simenon bent over and tried to reach for it through his legs. But that didn't work very well either. The rodent managed to remain just out of reach.

By then, everyone was laughing so hard it hurt. They

couldn't help themselves. The only exceptions were Greyhorse, who *never* laughed, and of course Simenon himself.

Finally, Picard couldn't stand it any longer. "Stay in one spot," he told his engineer, "and I'll get it off."

"Easy for you to say!" Simenon hissed. "You haven't got a duwiijuc eating you inch by inch!"

Nonetheless, he managed to remain still until the captain could grab the rodent by its furry torso. Trying not to get bitten himself, Picard pulled the creature off Simenon's appendage. Then he flung it into the crimson brush.

As soon as Simenon was free of the thing, he brought his tail up and inspected it. "The damned thing drew blood!" he groaned.

"Stay where you are!" mimicked Ben Zoma, "I'll get it!" And with that, he incited another wave of laughter.

"Thank you," said the engineer, stoically watching his superior guffaw at his expense. "Thank you very much. I'll remember your compassion next time *you're* injured."

"Oh, don't be such a baby," Greyhorse told him. He grabbed hold of Simenon's tail and took a look at it. "It barely broke the epidermis. I'll bandage it and you'll be fine."

By then, the laughter had begun to die down. Joseph and Ben Zoma had to wipe tears from their eyes as they made an uphill attempt to recover their sobriety.

The security officer took in a deep breath. "Now that," he said, "was worth the price of admission."

"*Twice* the price," Greyhorse decided as he delved into his pack for a plastiskin bandage and a dressing.

"Don't let anyone ever tell you you're not a good host," Ben Zoma chipped in.

Simenon scowled. "I'm glad I had the opportunity to provide you with some entertainment."

The doctor managed to keep his expression deadpan as he approached his colleague with the bandage he had found. "So am I. Now stand still. I can't treat a moving tail."

And they started laughing all over again.

Wu leaned back in Captain Picard's chair in the captain's ready room and pondered what she had learned from Lt. Kastiigan.

The *Belladonna*'s descent into the sinkhole was slower than she would have guessed. Assuming the research vessel's shields continued to hold up, it probably had a few hours before it was lost forever.

That was good news. It gave her some breathing room, some time to come up with an option she and her officers hadn't considered yet. *If there is one,* she found herself adding.

There is, she insisted. There had to be.

But there were only so many methods of getting a crew off an endangered ship. She ran down the list again in her mind, hoping to somehow find something she had missed.

One way was to beam them off. However, she and her bridge officers had already ruled out that possibility because of the conditions that prevailed inside the accretion bridge.

The other method was to put them in a shuttlecraft. But that was an impossibility as well because a shuttle couldn't escape the pull of the sinkhole.

Wu leaned back in her chair and closed her eyes. She had always found it easier to think with her eyes closed, even as a little girl back at the Aramis III agricultural colony. Her younger sister, Victoria, had made fun of her for that all the time. Then Victoria saw some of the things her sister was accomplishing in school and she secretly began to close her eyes as well.

Wu sighed. Her accomplishments in school had meant a lot to her—much more than they might have to other children her age. They had paved the way for her to realize her dream of joining Starfleet, of ascending the chain of command—of reaching a moment like this one, when people depended on her for their survival.

I can't let those scientists down, she told herself stubbornly. *I've got to get them out of there. Any other outcome is unacceptable.*

Of course, there *was* a third way; there had been one all along. If the *Belladonna* could generate enough thrust, and the *Stargazer* brought her tractors to bear at the right moment, they might be able to wrench the research ship free of the sinkhole.

But that required a willing partner in the *Belladonna*, not to mention a considerable contribution from her impulse drive. And so far, they had been unable to obtain a response to their hails, much less any evidence that the *Belladonna*'s engines were still in working order.

Wu frowned to herself. If not for those two small problems, the plan couldn't miss.

If only Ensign Paris's idea had proven workable. They would already have sent out a shuttlecraft on a tractor beam, offering the crew of the *Belladonna* a lifeline. The survivors might have been boarding it at that very moment.

But Dubinski's calculations had thrown a wrench into the ensign's plan. Too much mass on the end of the beam. Too much radiation, too many uncertainties presented by those magnetic fields.

Even a pod would have been too much, the engineer

said. But then, even the smallest one weighed nearly a metric ton. And there wasn't anything lighter than a pod....

Or was there?

Wu's eyes snapped open.

Could they send in a probe with instructions for the scientists? Maybe one they had stripped of its instruments and propulsion capabilities, to reduce the mass their tractor beam had to handle?

For a moment, it sounded as if it might work. Then the commander thought about it some more and her heart sank. Sure, they could send in a probe. But what would it do when it got there? How would it gain access to the interior of the *Belladonna?*

Probes couldn't open hatches. Probes couldn't canvass the research ship for survivors among the crew regardless of where they might have decided to gather.

Only a rescue team could do that. And no rescue team Wu had ever heard of could survive in a radiation-shot environment full of fierce, bone-crushing graviton waves.

All of a sudden, it came to her that she was wrong about that. Dead wrong. There *was* such a rescue team. And it was waiting for her in blissful ignorance on a lower deck of the *Stargazer.*

Chapter Seventeen

PICARD WAS JOGGING side by side with Simenon, the rest of their party a bit behind them, when he remarked that the trees ahead of them seemed to be thinning.

"You're right," the Gnalish observed.

It wasn't until a few minutes later that Picard saw the reason for it. That was when he found himself standing at the brink of a narrow but remarkably deep crevasse that appeared to cut the wild tangle of forestland in half.

Fortunately, there was a way at hand for the group to make their way across the half-dozen meters of treeless space. But it wasn't one that inspired a great deal of confidence.

"A bridge," said Greyhorse, a lock of his dark hair lifting in the swirling winds that held sway here.

"If one can call it that," Ben Zoma added.

To Picard, it looked more like a quartet of thick, scarlet ropes, two above and two below, with the latter supporting a series of short, wooden planks and the former serving as crude handrails. There were also a few short lines that connected the upper ropes with the lower ones.

"Looks old," said Vigo.

"And rickety," Joseph added.

"It was built some time ago," Simenon confirmed.

"Decades?" Greyhorse asked.

"Centuries," the Gnalish told them.

Picard looked at him, an expression of surprise on his face. "And it's still standing?"

"It was built to last," Simenon explained. "Also, it's maintained on a regular basis."

"What's *regular?*" Joseph asked.

"Every few weeks," the engineer replied.

"So it should be safe," the captain concluded, though he didn't sound as sure of himself as he might have intended.

"*Should* be," Simenon agreed.

"You think it can hold me?" Vigo asked.

"If it can hold an Aklaash," the Gnalish reasoned, "I would think it can hold a Pandrilite."

Joseph looked at him. "How do you know it can hold an Aklaash? I thought this route was just for Mazzereht."

"*This* time it's for Mazzereht," Simenon told him. "Last time, it might have been for a party of Aklaash, or Fejjimaera. The routes are doled out at random."

"Hey!" said Joseph. He was standing on the brink of the ravine and pointing to something far to their right. "There's another bridge down that way. Maybe it's sturdier than this one."

"It's not," the engineer assured him. "And even if it were, we couldn't use it."

"Why not?" asked Greyhorse.

"Because," said Simenon, "that's the one the Fejjimaera are going to use. We've all got to cross the ravine somewhere. The Fejjimaera are going to cross it down *there*."

Ben Zoma grunted. "So we're stuck with *this* bridge."

"In a manner of speaking," said the Gnalish, "yes."

As he said that, the wind whistled a little more insistently and the bridge swayed drunkenly under its influence. Seeing it, they all fell silent—Simenon included.

"Listen," said Picard, breaking the spell, "it's not as if we have a lot of choice in the matter."

Greyhorse shaded his eyes as he examined the bridge from one end to the other. "So it would seem."

The captain took his companions in at a glance. "So what are we waiting for?"

There were murmurs of agreement. However, no one seemed very eager to try the span.

"I'll go first," Simenon volunteered.

He didn't get any arguments from the others.

Jiterica was sitting at her workstation in the science section, dutifully inspecting yet another set of sensor readings, when she heard someone call her name.

Turning, she saw that it was Commander Wu. The second officer was crossing the science section, headed her way.

"Commander?" Jiterica said in response.

Wu looked serious. "I need your help with the research vessel," she told the Nizhrak.

Her curiosity piqued, Jiterica swiveled to face her superior. "I will assist you in any way I can."

Wu held a hand up. "Don't say that until you've heard me out. What I have in mind will involve considerable personal risk. If you decline, I'll understand."

"I would like to help," Jiterica maintained.

Wu nodded. "I was hoping you would say that."

"What do you need me to do?" the ensign asked.

The commander didn't tell her right away. Instead, she described Ensign Paris's idea. Its flaw, apparently, was that a shuttle would have too much mass to be manipulated by a tractor beam under the conditions that existed in the accretion bridge.

"But not a single crewman," Wu continued pointedly. "That would be a different story entirely."

Jiterica looked at her. "A single crewman," she repeated thoughtfully. The conclusion was an obvious one. "You mean *me.*"

Wu nodded. "That's right."

"Because I'm accustomed to the conditions in a gas giant."

"Exactly. Radiation and magnetic fields aren't a problem for you and neither is high gravity, and your mass is no greater than that of the average human being."

Jiterica took a moment to consider the idea. The more she thought about it, the more sense it made—except for one fairly significant problem.

"Given the inefficiencies of projecting a tractor beam into the accretion bridge, the ship will have to come rather close to it. Won't she run the risk of being drawn inside?"

"She would," Wu agreed, "if she had to come that close. But what if she simply maintained a tractor lifeline to a shuttle...and it was the shuttle that sent in the crewman on a beam of its own?"

"Two tractor beams," Jiterica said. "One from the ship and one from the shuttle. An interesting approach."

"I'm glad you think so," Wu told her. "Of course, the beam would only get you so far. You would still have to find a hatch and gain access to the *Belladonna.*"

It seemed to Jiterica that she was capable of doing that. Then something occurred to her. "Commander... unless I'm mistaken, our shuttlecraft aren't equipped with tractor assemblies."

"Normally," said Wu, "that's true. But we're going to take one of ours and make it an exception."

The ensign nodded. "I see." She had just one other question. "Who will pilot the shuttle?"

Wu told her who she had in mind.

Simenon wasn't nearly as matter-of-fact about crossing the crevasse as he had made himself out to be.

Like most Mazzereht, he was discomfited by heights. It was one of the reasons his subspecies didn't succeed in the ritual more often.

On the other hand, what was the point of mentioning such a shortcoming? He had to cross the chasm. They all did. It was just a matter of looking straight ahead and doing it.

All right, Simenon told himself, *you can do this.*

Clenching his jaw, he grasped the rope rail on the right side and took a step onto the bridge. Then another. And another.

As it turned out, the span wasn't half as wobbly as it looked. It wasn't as easy as walking down a corridor on the *Stargazer*—after all, corridors didn't bounce as one negotiated them—but neither did it require a particularly sophisticated sense of balance.

After Simenon had advanced a couple of meters, he was inspired to turn around and look back at his comrades. "Coming?" he asked them.

Joseph frowned and ever so carefully followed the engineer onto the bridge. It didn't appear to take him long to discover what Simenon had discovered—that the crossing simply wasn't as prodigious a feat as it had appeared.

"This isn't bad at all," the security officer observed.

"All the same," Picard said, "let's not all pile on at once. We'll go no more than two at a time."

"You're the captain," Simenon told him.

Or rather, that was what he meant to say. Before he could quite get the words out, he felt the bridge give way.

It all happened so fast, the Gnalish barely knew what he was doing. But somehow, he managed to snatch one of the ropes that attached the span's rail to its floor and hang on for dear life.

For a heartbeat, he couldn't tell if only one end of the bridge had given way or both. Then he realized that it was only one—the one on the far side—and he was swinging back in the direction of the cliff he had left behind.

That was the good news. The bad came when Simenon crashed into the sheer rock surface with bone-crushing force, squeezing the air out of his lungs and awakening a terrible, sharp pain in his side.

Blackness threatened to overwhelm him. It seeped in from the edges of his vision, offering him the warm, welcome balm of oblivion.

But the Gnalish fought it off, pulling in air as hard as he could. His throat burned with the effort—burned horribly as if it were on fire. But he didn't let that stop him. He kept gasping, kept sucking down what little his tortured windpipe would accommodate.

And somehow, he held onto the twisted remains of the bridge. The taste of blood filled his mouth and his ribs throbbed as if someone were taking a hammer to them, but he didn't allow himself to fall to the bottom of the chasm.

"Simenon!" someone cried. "Pug! Are you all right?"

"Yes," said the security officer, who was dangling just above Simenon. "I'm fine."

The engineer couldn't answer. He was too busy trying to fill his lungs with air.

"Simenon!" someone called again.

"Here," he croaked.

"He's below me," Joseph shouted over the wind. "Just a couple of meters."

"Can you reach him?" someone asked. This time, Simenon recognized the voice as the captain's.

The wind keened through the valley as Joseph made his assessment. "I think so," he said.

"I'll go down, too," someone added. *Vigo,* thought Simenon.

"No," the captain told him. "You're too heavy."

"Me, then," suggested Ben Zoma.

A pause. "All right," said Picard. "But first, we'll secure this end of the bridge as best we can."

While they did that, Simenon caught his breath. But the easier it came, the harder his side began to throb. And his right arm—the one that had borne the burden of his weight to that point—was beginning to ache with the effort.

"Take your time," he rasped with false bravado.

Wu regarded Paris across the captain's ready room. The ensign looked surprised by the assignment she had just given him—more so than she might have expected.

"Me, Commander?" he replied after a moment.

"Why not?" said Wu. "You may be young, Mr. Paris, but it's clear to me that you're the best pilot we have—with the exception of Lieutenant Asmund, of course. And we need her to pilot the ship, which won't be any mean feat."

"I suppose not," Paris responded.

Wu briefed the ensign on the particulars of the mission—how far he would have to go and what he would have to look out for, that sort of thing. By the time she finished, he seemed to have gotten past his surprise and was again exuding the confidence that had distinguished him from other young men of Wu's acquaintance.

It was a good thing, she reflected. She would need Paris at his best if they were going to pull this off.

"Then go get ready," the second officer told him. "Mr. Chiang tells me he'll have that shuttle ready in the next twenty minutes."

The ensign lifted his chin. "Acknowledged."

Then he turned and made his way out of the room. As the doors hissed closed behind him, Wu nodded to herself. If anyone could do this, it would be Cole Paris.

Simenon winced as Greyhorse used his fingers to probe the Gnalish's tortured flank. "Careful," Simenon groaned.

"I'm *being* careful," the doctor told him.

"Well?" asked Picard, who was standing over them, a couple of meters back from the crevasse and the dangling bridge.

Greyhorse rolled back onto his haunches and made a face. "You're lucky," he told Simenon. "I don't think those ribs are broken, after all. And your arm's in remarkably good shape considering it could have been torn out of its socket."

Somehow, Simenon didn't feel that fortunate.

After all, his hope of progeny had just been crushed. Unless he could get across the chasm, one of the other teams would claim the eggs waiting for them at the finish line. And without a bridge, the odds of their making it across seemed slim indeed.

Not that it was impossible. The chasm was only six or

170

seven meters from one side to the other. An Aklaash might have had the size and the power to leap across it.

But not a Gnalish of Simenon's stature—especially one who had injured himself the way the engineer had. For someone like that, leaping the gap simply wasn't an option.

"We still need to get across," Ben Zoma said.

"Someone's going to have to jump it," Joseph added.

There was silence for a moment. Then someone said, "I think I can make it."

The Gnalish looked around, eager to see who had spoken. So did everyone else in his party—with one exception.

That of the captain.

Chapter Eighteen

"You?" Simenon said.

He had already blurted it out before he realized how derogatory it sounded. But he hadn't intended to disparage the captain. It was just that he hadn't thought of Picard as the most likely candidate to negotiate the chasm.

Vigo, perhaps, with his Aklaash-like strides and his muscular physique. But not a normal-size human with a normal-size human's strength and speed.

"I mean," the engineer added quickly, "are you certain you want to risk it?"

The captain still looked as if his ego had been bruised. "Though you may not be aware of it, Mr. Simenon, I've always been a rather decent track-and-field man. With a little luck, I'll be able to make the jump. Then, if someone can toss me the loose end of the bridge, I can make it fast again on the other side."

Simenon frowned. He had seen Picard engage Captain Ruhalter in some sort of swordplay, even work out a bit on the pommel horse in the ship's gymnasium—and he had certainly seemed proficient in those activities. But he had never seen the man perform a long jump.

And as much as he wanted to win the race, he didn't want to do it at the cost of his captain's life.

"I can't ask you to do that for me," he told Picard.

The captain's eyes crinkled at the corners, as if he had managed to find some humor in their predicament. "I'm not doing it for you," he said evenly. "I'm doing it for generations of brilliant but irascible Gnalish to come."

Simenon looked to his other colleagues. No one was objecting to Picard's proposal—not even Ben Zoma, who was supposed to protect his commanding officer at all times. In fact, the man was smiling as if in appreciation of the captain's quip.

But Simenon didn't find it funny. He didn't find it funny in the least. It was *his* fault they were down here, *his* fault that they were placing life and limb in jeopardy. If Picard came up short in his jump and hurt himself— or worse, *killed* himself—that would be the Gnalish's fault, too.

"Sir," he said, meaning to talk the captain out of it. "If anything happened to you, I'd—"

"It won't," Picard told him unequivocally. He glanced at the chasm, then nodded. "I'll make it."

"But, sir—"

"Belay that," the captain said. His eyes narrowed as he regarded Simenon. "That's an order, Lieutenant."

The engineer scowled. It didn't seem he was being given much of a say in the matter.

"All right," he said, yielding to his superior. "But for the gods' sake, be careful."

"I will be as careful as the situation permits," the captain promised him. Then he turned to the crevasse again and focused his attention on the task ahead of him.

First, he approached the chasm and inspected the turf at its edge. It appeared to be as spongy as the rest of the forest floor, hardly optimum for takeoff. Nor would the spongy surface on the other side lend itself to an easy landing.

Simenon was glad that Picard was taking the time to prepare for his effort. It gave the Gnalish some confidence that his captain might actually survive it.

Next, Picard turned his back on the chasm and walked back into the depths of the forest, brushing aside the odd branch as he retraced the steps their team had taken to get here. By Simenon's reckoning, the man was nearly thirty meters from the group before a tree trunk that had fallen across the trail prevented him from going any farther.

Turning around, the captain regarded the chasm again. He took a breath and let it out slowly. Then he said, "Would someone be so kind as to get those branches out of my way?"

Even with his side aching and his right arm all but useless, Simenon was able to pull a branch back and hold it there. Each of his comrades did the same thing, clearing all obstructions from Picard's path.

Simenon saw the captain's brow furrow. He half-expected Picard to finally yield to reason and admit that the feat was too much for him.

But as he was thinking this, he saw Picard lower his head and launch himself forward. Arms pumping, legs churning, he pelted past the Gnalish a good deal faster than Simenon would have ever predicted, the heels of his heavy-duty boots tearing up the spongy ground and throwing up bits of it in his wake.

The captain gained speed all the way to the near edge

of the chasm, then sprang suddenly into the air. For a moment, he rose like a big, dark bird, arms and legs cycling ferociously. Then, as his momentum died, he began to lose altitude.

"Come *on*," Simenon heard someone say.

Come on, he echoed silently.

For one heart-stopping fraction of a second, the engineer was sure that Picard would fall short of the other side. Then the captain tucked his legs beneath him and threw his arms forward, giving himself the added impetus that he needed.

Simenon cheered inwardly when he saw Picard's heels hit the ground just past the sheer drop of the ravine. The captain had surprised him. He had *done* it.

But as Simenon watched, horrified, it became clear to him that there was something wrong. The captain was still in jeopardy after all.

He seemed to be struggling to keep his weight forward on the spongy, uncertain turf. And little by little, he was losing the battle. Before the Gnalish's disbelieving eyes, Picard staggered back just half a step—but half a step was all it took to send him sliding toward the depths of the crevasse.

"No!" Simenon cried out.

And somehow, as if in response to his anguished cry, the captain stopped falling.

Apparently, he had latched onto something before he could be swallowed by the abyss. As pieces of turf and debris spiraled down into the crevasse and were lost to sight, the Gnalish saw that it was a protruding root that had saved Picard's life.

"Hang on!" Ben Zoma shouted. "I'll be right there!" And he darted back into the depths of the forest to get the same kind of running jump the captain had gotten.

"No, you won't!" Picard bellowed back at his first officer. Then, still dangling from the errant root, he added in a voice full of forced calm, "Stay where you are, Number One. I can do this on my own."

Ben Zoma didn't look happy about it, but he returned to the brink of the crevasse. Then he stood there with Simenon and the others, watching as the captain swung a leg over the edge of the cliff and—finding a dependable handhold hidden under the lip of turf—laboriously wrestled himself to safety.

For several seconds, Picard lay on his back on the spongy ground, breathing deep draughts of air. It occurred to Simenon that he might have injured himself in his climb.

Just what we need, the Gnalish told himself.

"Are you all right, Captain?" Greyhorse called, obviously thinking the same thing.

"I'm...fine," Picard called back, gasping between words. "Couldn't...be better."

Slowly, he rolled over onto his belly, pushed himself up, and got to his feet. Then he pointed to the loose end of the bridge, which lay in a pile on Simenon's side of the chasm.

"Toss it over," Picard said.

Vigo, the strongest of them, was the one who tossed it. Even so, it took him three tries to reach the captain.

Picard secured the end of the bridge temporarily with a few of the heaviest rocks around. Then he found a big, dead tree trunk in the brush and rolled it on for good measure.

Unfortunately, what was left was no longer something one could walk all the way across. The line of the handrails converged with the bridge's floor by the time they reached the captain's side of the ravine, making it necessary for Simenon and the others to crawl across.

But at least there was something to crawl on. If not for the captain, there wouldn't even have been that.

As before, Simenon figured he would be first to use the bridge. After all, he was the reason they were all out here. But before he could take a step onto the wooden planks, Ben Zoma stopped him.

"Let *me*," he said.

The engineer's first impulse was to protest. But when he thought about it, he had to admit that it made sense. If the bridge failed them again, Ben Zoma could save himself. It would be a lot more difficult for a Gnalish with bruised ribs and strained muscles in his arm.

Simenon held his breath as the first officer made his way across the span. But it actually swayed less than when it was whole, and Ben Zoma passed the halfway point without anything catastrophic happening. A couple of moments later, he reached out for Picard's hand and joined the captain on the other side.

"Vigo's next," Picard said.

Again, a rational approach. The weapons officer was heavier than any of them, though Greyhorse ran a close second. If the bridge could hold Vigo's weight, it could hold anyone's.

Picard's construction methods passed that test, too. As Vigo completed the crossing, the captain nodded approvingly. "Now the rest of you. One at a time, of course."

Simenon wouldn't have had it any other way. He went next, using his tail to support and steady himself in place of his right arm. Then came Joseph and a shaky-looking Greyhorse.

Once the doctor was across, Simenon was ready to

get going again. But Joseph knelt by the end of the bridge and lingered there.

"What is it?" Picard asked him.

The security officer held up the end of one of the ropes where it stuck out from beneath a rock. "Take a look at this, sir."

The captain came over to inspect the rope-end more closely. So did Simenon, his curiosity aroused.

"It's not frayed," Joseph pointed out to them. "It's been *cut.*"

Simenon could see that the man was right in his assessment. The end of the rope had been neatly sliced.

Greyhorse frowned. "It looks like someone didn't want us crossing this bridge."

"Or winning the race," Vigo added.

Picard turned to Simenon, his expression a stern one. "Who do you think it might have been?"

The Gnalish was at a loss. "I have no idea. "Kasaelek's party, Banyohla's...who knows?"

"These might tell us something," said Joseph.

He had hunkered down next to a patch of dried mud— a *rare* patch, given the ubiquitousness of the spongy ground cover on which they had made most of their trek.

"What are they?" asked Vigo.

The group gathered around the security officer now. "Footprints," he said. He looked up at Simenon. "And they're recent, by the look of them."

Simenon moved to the spot and placed his foot beside one of the prints. Then he shook his head. "Unfortunately," he told Ben Zoma, "these are my size. They must have been left by the Mazzereht party that came through here last cycle." A cycle was about the length of a Terran week.

"And a party of Mazzereht wouldn't have sabotaged

the bridge," Greyhorse noted. He glanced at the engineer. "Would they?"

"Of course not," Simenon said. He stared at the prints for a moment longer, then turned to the bridge and considered that as well. It had to be one of his competitors.

But which one?

"It's a mystery," Ben Zoma said.

Simenon nodded. "A mystery indeed."

He turned to the trail ahead. It led through another dense expanse of crimson forest. And unless his competitors' bridges had been sabotaged as well, they had obtained a healthy lead on him.

"Come on," he said, fighting off his weariness and the ache in his side. "We're losing time."

Wu was about to contact Lt. Chiang and see how things were proceeding down in the shuttlebay when the door chime sounded.

"Come in," she said.

The doors slid aside, revealing Lt. Kastiigan. "I beg your pardon," he said, "but if I could have just a moment?"

Wu shrugged. "Of course."

Kastiigan threw out his chest. "I volunteer to accompany Ensign Paris and Ensign Jiterica on the shuttlecraft."

The offer seemed a little out of place to the second officer. However, she understood the impulse that had spurred it—or thought she did.

"I'm impressed by your scientific curiosity," she told Kastiigan. "But rest assured, the shuttle's sensors will record all we need to know about the phenomenon."

"It's not scientific curiosity that propels me," the Kandilkari explained. "It's a desire to serve my commanding officer, no matter how perilous that service may be."

Wu wondered if she were missing something. "Beyond making scientific observations, what kind of service did you have in mind?"

Kastiigan shrugged. "Nothing specific. But if you should think of some way I can be of assistance on the shuttle, I hope you'll not hesitate to order me aboard."

"Why would I hesitate?" the second officer asked, positive now that she was missing something.

"It has been my experience," Kastiigan said, "that my commanding officers have placed an undue emphasis on my survival. I am only a single cog in a very large and sophisticated machine."

Wu could hardly argue with the metaphor. However, she didn't see what it had to do with the rescue mission.

"I promise I won't place an undue emphasis on your survival," she told the Kandilkari. "However, considering I can't think of any reason to send you on that shuttle..."

"I'll stay here," he concluded correctly, though he looked rather grim about it. "I understand."

"Good," said Wu, though she wasn't sure *she* understood.

"Thank you for your time," Kastiigan told her.

"No problem," she said.

And with that, the science officer departed.

Wu expelled a breath. Kastiigan was proving to be a most interesting fellow. She resolved to learn more about him—and she decided it might as well be now, since the only alternative was to sit and wait for Chiang to complete his work.

She had begun calling up Kastiigan's personnel file when the door chime sounded again. *What now?* she wondered. Was Kastiigan going to *insist* that she place him on the shuttle?

"Come in," Wu said.

As it turned out, it wasn't the science officer seeking another audience. It was Ensign Paris. And he looked troubled somehow, distracted—a stark contrast to the confident young man the second officer had seen a few minutes earlier.

"May I speak with you?" the ensign asked.

Wu nodded. "Of course. Have a seat."

Paris sat down in the chair opposite hers and looked at his hands for a moment. Then he met her gaze.

"It's hard to know where to begin," he told her.

The commander knew they didn't have much time— or rather, the people on the *Belladonna* didn't. But she resisted the impulse to rush the ensign, sensing that whatever was bothering him had to come out at its own pace.

"Begin anywhere," she said.

Chapter Nineteen

WU WATCHED THE MUSCLES WORK in Paris's temples.

"Back at the Academy..." he said, "my very first semester, I had a class in Particle Physics. One day, our professor decided to spring a surprise test on us. I had barely read the first question on my monitor when my hands began to shake.

"They didn't just tremble a little, Commander. They *shook,* as if I had some terrible neurological disorder." The ensign winced as if in pain. "I was horrified."

Wu had never experienced anything like what Paris was describing. However, she had no trouble imagining how uncomfortable it would have made him feel.

"I tried to hide my hands from the other cadets," Paris continued, "in the hope that no one would see. And to my relief, no one did. But I needed my fingers to tap out answers on my keyboard, so I couldn't keep them hidden forever."

He swallowed. "Taking that test was the worst kind of torture. But I got through it somehow, shakes and all. And I earned a passing grade, while half the other first-year students flunked."

"So you came through," Wu observed.

"Yes," said Paris, "but that's not the point. It was just an exam, and not even a particularly important one. It wasn't as if my whole career was hanging in the balance."

"In other words," the commander translated, "you shouldn't have reacted that way."

"That's right," he said. "And if I were someone else, maybe I wouldn't have. But as I've been reminded all my life, I'm not just anybody." The muscles worked in the ensign's jaw. "I'm a *Paris.*"

Wu was beginning to understand the problem.

"In the years that followed," he went on, "the same problem surfaced over and over again. Most of the time I was fine, as calm and controlled as anybody. But when I was under pressure, when I felt there was a chance I might fail, my hands shook and my stomach clenched and I had to struggle to conceal it."

The ensign paused, his nostrils flaring with emotion. He seemed to be staring not *at* Wu but through her.

"But I *always* found a way to hide it," he said softly, "because I was a *Paris.* Because I had a standard to live up to. Because I had inherited a reputation for courage and dedication and grace under fire."

"Ensign," said Wu, seeing how much it hurt him to talk about it, "you don't have to—"

But Paris was like a dam that had finally burst. Obviously, he felt the need to get this out in the open. And if that's what he needed, she was willing to listen.

"First," he told her, smiling bitterly, "there was my grandfather, Daniel Paris. You may have heard of him at the Academy. He distinguished himself on the *Potemkin* and the *Excalibur* before he came back to Earth, where he was asked to assist Admiral Kirk during the admiral's stint as head of Starfleet operations."

In fact, Wu *had* heard of Daniel Paris—even *before* she had read the ensign's personnel file.

"Then," said Paris, "my grandfather became an admiral himself. His plaque at Starfleet Headquarters says he earned a reputation for wisdom and courage unmatched by any of his peers."

Wu had never seen it. But then, there were lots of plaques at headquarters, lots of officers who had been honored.

"Next came my father, Iron Mike Paris. He was decorated no less than seven times as second officer and then executive officer of the *Agamemnon*." The ensign's voice dropped. "Unfortunately, his career was cut short when his ship was obliterated by the Romulans in what's become known as the Tomed Incident."

The run-in with the Romulans that precipitated fifty years of Romulan isolationism. Wu knew it as well as anyone.

"I never knew my father," Paris told her. "I was just an infant when he died. All I had were holograms and my mother's stories, all of which made him seem bigger than life."

"I'm sorry," said Wu.

The ensign acknowledged her sympathy with a nod. But there was more, apparently.

"Then there's my Aunt Patricia, who's five years younger than my father. She was on the *Maryland* at the Battle of Ankaata, where she lost an arm saving two of her fellow officers. She retired about the time I entered the Academy."

hadn't always relied on his head. More often than not, he had relied on his heart.

And not just *his* heart, but the hearts of others.

With that in mind, Wu looked across the table at Cole Paris. Clearly, the young man was scared stiff of bringing disgrace to his family's name, and even more scared of being responsible for Jiterica. He didn't want to let anyone down.

But Wu had seen him working at the *Stargazer*'s helm console. He wasn't just good. He was a rare talent, a prodigy. At his best, Paris was still the number one choice for what she had in mind. In her heart, the commander was sure of it.

She just had to make sure she could get his best out of him.

"I've sat here and listened patiently to what you had to say," Wu told the ensign. "Now you listen to me. Your grandfather, your father, your aunt...you may see them as superhuman figures, as gods. But they were people like you and me. And people get scared. I've never met anyone who *didn't*, myself included.

"Ever been in combat?" she asked him.

Paris shook his head. "No."

"You can't imagine how you'll ever get through it. Your knees tremble and your belly clenches like a fist and your heart pounds so hard you think it's going to shatter against your ribs. And it's even worse when other people's lives depend on what you do and say. Then you feel their weight on you, a mountain of it, and you hate to make a move because you're sure it'll be the wrong one.

"But you make it, Ensign. Somehow you make it and you get through to the other side."

Paris looked at her. "But—"

"Your hands shake?" she said, refusing to let him finish, refusing to let him slide back into his morass of self-doubt. "Maybe mine are shaking right now. Maybe I'm wondering if there's a better way to save those scientists—or a way that doesn't involve putting my own people's lives at risk.

"Maybe I'll be wrong. Maybe I'll disgrace myself and my family and have all those deaths on my head, and be haunted by my choice for the rest of my life. But that's the chance I've got to take."

Wu leaned forward in her chair. "I picked you for this job because I thought you were the best, Ensign. I still think it—and not because you're a Paris. Frankly, that couldn't matter less to me. The reason I think you're the best is because you *are*—and I'd be a whopping great fool to send anyone else out on such an important mission."

Paris didn't seem inclined to protest what she was saying any longer. He just sat there, his mouth hanging open.

"Any questions?" the commander asked him.

The ensign didn't say anything. He just shook his head from side to side.

"Then report to the shuttlebay."

Paris nodded, looking as if he had just been slapped across the face. Then he got up and made his way out of the captain's ready room. As the doors opened, he looked back at her for a moment.

"I'll try not to let you down," he said.

And with that, he went through the open doorway.

Wu slumped back in the captain's chair. Apparently, her words had had the desired effect. Paris would do what she had asked of him.

She could only hope it would be enough.

It was late in the day when Simenon and his companions came to the obstacle he had been dreading the

Chapter Twenty

Wu ARRIVED IN THE SHUTTLEBAY just as Jiterica was entering the specially rigged shuttle. Paris, it seemed, was already inside the craft. The commander turned to Chiang.

"Everything checks out," he said before she could ask.

She nodded. "Good."

Then she approached the shuttle and watched Jiterica take her place inside it. Ironically, the Nizhrak seemed to have less trouble negotiating the cramped quarters of the auxiliary craft than she'd had taking a seat in the mess hall.

Paris was running a last-minute instrument diagnostic. When he noticed Wu standing at the hatch, he acknowledged her with a nod.

"Commander," he said.

He seemed to have regained his confidence. The second officer certainly hoped that that was the case. There was a lot riding on Paris and his abilities.

"Ensign," she said by way of a reply. Then, after she was certain that Jiterica had taken notice of her as well, she said, "Do either of you have any questions?"

Neither of them seemed to have any. But then, their assignment was a simple one in concept. It was only in its execution that complications seemed likely to set in.

"Then good luck to you," said Wu.

"Thank you, Commander," Paris replied.

"Thank you," Jiterica echoed in her tinny, unnatural-sounding helmet-audio voice.

Then the hatch closed and Wu stood back from the shuttlecraft. She watched as it lifted off the deck and headed for the permeable force field that separated the bay from the airless void.

The shuttle seemed to hesitate for a fraction of a second as it neared the force field. Then it sailed through it with a gentle flash, wheeled to starboard, and was lost to sight.

And Wu, who wished she could have accompanied the ensigns in their shuttlecraft, instead returned to the bridge to direct the rescue effort from the captain's chair.

Ben Zoma considered the triangular cave mouth in front of him, which was little more than a meter high but as many as three meters wide. It was dark inside the opening, but not too dark to catch a glimpse of the water through which they would all soon be swimming.

Joseph turned to Simenon. "How far did you say it would be?"

The Gnalish shrugged. "Not that far. Thirty meters or so. But there's no light and it's not quite a straight path. That's why you've got to hug one of the walls as you go forward."

Ben Zoma filed the information away for when his

turn came. But that wouldn't be for a while. Vigo would be the first one in the water, followed by Simenon.

Vigo smiled at the Gnalish, no doubt hoping to inspire confidence in his abilities. "I'm ready to try it if you are," he said.

Simenon frowned as he studied the cave mouth. "All right," he said after a moment. "But now that I think about it, I want someone to tie the end of the vine around my waist. That way I don't have to worry about losing my grip."

"But," Greyhorse protested, "if you get stuck, you won't be able to free yourself. You'll be lost down there."

Simenon looked grim as he glanced at the doctor. "That's a chance I'll have to take."

No one else argued with him. It was, after all, his life at stake. He had a right to do what he thought best.

"Here goes," said Vigo.

He checked the vine wrapped around his middle and pulled the knot that held it a little tighter. Then he hunkered down, made his way into the cave, and took a series of deep breaths. After the last and deepest, he submerged himself and was gone.

The water gurgled and churned as the length of vine broke the surface in the Pandrilite's wake. Like the others, Ben Zoma watched it disappear, meter by meter.

As long as it kept moving it signified that Vigo was moving as well. The last thing any of them wanted to see was slack in the line. And they didn't see anything of the sort—not until half of the last vine had been claimed by the passageway.

Then the safety line stopped flowing into the water. Ben Zoma glanced at his friend Picard. If they were lucky, Vigo had reached the other side. If not...

Suddenly, they heard a shout—a booming cry that

could only have come from the powerful throat of a Pandrilite, audible despite the soaring wall of rock that stood between them. The first officer breathed a sigh of relief.

Vigo had made it. It was time for step two.

In recognition of the fact, Simenon came forward and wrapped the end of the vine around his waist. Then Picard and Joseph tied a knot in it and pronounced it secure.

The prearranged signal of the Gnalish's readiness was a series of three tugs on the end of the vine. Ben Zoma did the honors. A moment later, he saw the line rise off the ground and go taut.

And a moment after that, it tugged Simenon in the direction of the cave mouth. The engineer looked at each of them in turn, his expression uncomfortably like that of a man condemned to death.

"My turn," he said grimly.

Then, pulled by Vigo, he vanished into the water and left a swirl of current in his wake.

"Leave it to Simenon to get a free ride," said Ben Zoma, hoping to break the tension.

But no one laughed. They would only do that, he suspected, after they knew their colleague had reached the other side.

They waited for a few seconds, then a few more. If all went well, it wouldn't be long before they heard from Vigo.

But after what seemed like enough time, the signal still hadn't come. Ben Zoma and the others looked at each other.

"He's been down there too long," said Greyhorse.

The doctor was right. "Someone's got to go after him," the first officer said.

And without another thought, he scrambled through the cave mouth and hit the water.

It was cold, shockingly so. But then, its source was probably some mountain lake only half-redeemed from the grasp of winter. Ignoring the temperature, Ben Zoma propelled himself through the gloom with his legs, using his hands to feel his way along the wall beside him.

He couldn't see Simenon, but he could hear some kind of bubbling up ahead. It got louder and more insistent as he swam forward, telling Ben Zoma that he wasn't too late.

Simenon was alive. At least, for the moment.

But something had stopped him from getting through the cave chain. And in the now-perfect darkness that surrounded him, Ben Zoma couldn't tell what it was.

There was only one thing he could do—get hold of Simenon and feel around until he found the problem.

With that in mind, he scissored forward until his hand brushed against one of the Gnalish's frantically churning legs. Grasping it, he felt the kicking stop—a sign that his comrade was either acknowledging his presence or had run out of air.

Hoping it was the former, Ben Zoma used Simenon like a ladder and pulled himself up to what he imagined was the Gnalish's face. Then he found Simenon's shoulder and upper arm and felt for the tautness that would suggest his friend's hand was stuck.

As it turned out, it wasn't. In fact, it seized the first officer's wrist and directed it to where Ben Zoma had come from—toward Simenon's feet.

By then, the human was starting to feel light-headed. The impulse to breathe, to replenish the supply of oxygen in his lungs, was becoming almost impossible for him to deny. But he put it aside somehow and focused on the task at hand.

Working his way down Simenon's body again, Ben Zoma felt one leg moving. But not the other one. *Finally,* he thought.

A moment later, he found the problem. Simenon's foot was wedged in a crevice. But as long as the vine rope was pulling on him, he wouldn't be able to get free.

Darting upward, Ben Zoma found the vine and swung his feet in the direction of the cave wall. When they met something solid, he planted his heels there and hauled for all he was worth.

Just as he had hoped, the vine rope relaxed—probably because he had pulled it right out of Vigo's unsuspecting hands. Freed of its pull, Simenon would be able to back his foot out of the crevice.

But just in case, Ben Zoma felt his way down the wall of rock and tried to lend a hand. He arrived just in time to realize that the Gnalish wasn't stuck anymore.

In fact, as the first officer groped for his comrade, he realized that Simenon was gone.

Then he put together what must have happened. Vigo had regained his grip on the rope vine and pulled the Gnalish through.

At least, that's what Ben Zoma hoped. With his lungs screaming for air, he launched himself forward alongside the wall, intent now on only one thing—saving *himself.*

For a single, terrifying heartbeat, it seemed to him that he had waited too long and would drown in the darkness. Then he saw a hint of light up ahead and arrowed through the water with the desperation of a man who knew his life depended on it.

Kick, he thought, a different kind of darkness closing around him. *Kick, dammit!*

He kicked—and broke the surface just in time.

As Ben Zoma dragged in draught after draught of warm, welcome air, he noticed Vigo a couple of meters away on a shelf of flat, dark rock. He was hovering over Simenon, who was gasping even harder than the first officer was, his ruby eyes looking as if they were about to pop out of his head.

"Are you all right, sir?" the Pandrilite asked Ben Zoma.

But the human couldn't speak yet. All he could do was pull in one shuddering breath after another as he joined his companions at the water's edge.

Paris brought his shuttle to a stop as close to the unholy glow of the accretion bridge as he dared, then immediately redirected all available power to his forward thrusters.

As he had anticipated, they held the shuttle in equilibrium. However, it was a rather uneasy equilibrium.

The pull exerted by the sinkhole was so powerful here that he could feel it in his bones. Without some timely assistance, the shuttle would either have to abandon its position or be sucked inside the accretion bridge.

Fortunately, that assistance was just a comm message away. Touching the communications pad on his control console, he said, "Paris to Wu. I've reached the coordinates we talked about."

The return signal was a sloppy one as a result of all the graviton activity, but the ensign was still able to make out the second officer's words. "...establishing tractor lock...stand by."

"Acknowledged," said Paris.

He glanced at Jiterica, who was sitting quietly in her seat, staring at the accretion bridge through the shuttle's forward observation port. He wondered what she was thinking about.

Him, perhaps? How he and his tractor beam would soon be all that stood between her and the sinkhole?

"Tractor lock...established..." Wu told him over the comm link.

Paris could see it reflected in his readouts. "Confirmed."

Of course, at the distance the *Stargazer* was compelled to maintain, the beam couldn't do much. But if it cut the stress on the shuttle's thrusters by twenty percent and lent them a little stability, it would be all the help they needed.

Providing I do my job, Paris added silently.

Frowning, he put the thought out of his mind. It wasn't productive for him to try to anticipate how he would perform. He would simply do his best.

Paris turned to Jiterica. "Ready?"

She turned to look at him, the golden glare of the accretion bridge reflected in the face mask of her helmet. He could barely see the spectral features that lurked beneath it.

"Yes, Mr. Paris," the Nizhrak said calmly, almost mechanically. "I am ready."

She got up from her seat and moved aft through the shuttle. With the press of a pad set into the bulkhead, she activated a selectively permeable force field like the one in the *Stargazer*'s shuttlebay—another of the improvements Lt. Chiang had been forced to engineer into the craft on short notice.

Then she opened the hatch.

Thanks to the force field, the atmosphere in the shuttle remained inside instead of rushing to join the vacuum of space. Still, it was disconcerting for Paris to look past Jiterica and see the gleam of naked stars.

Without a second look, the Nizhrak took hold of the hatch frame and swung out into space. The field sizzled around her for a moment, as if nettled at her interrupting its integrity. Then it was intact again—and Jiterica was floating outside the shuttlecraft, her momentum carrying her slowly toward the accretion bridge.

"Ensign Jiterica has exited the shuttle," Paris reported.

"Keep us...posted...," Wu instructed him.

"Will do," he said.

Then Paris activated the tractor beam device that Lt. Chiang had installed minutes earlier, trained its shimmering shaft on Jiterica, and established a lock. The procedure went every bit as smoothly as he had hoped.

But the hard part was still ahead.

Keeping an eye on his helm instruments, the ensign ever so carefully used the tractor beam to propel his colleague forward. Unaware that there was any reason not to trust Paris's abilities, Jiterica wafted in the direction of the accretion bridge until Paris had to squint to see her through the viewport.

A little farther, he told himself. Farther still.

And then she was gone from sight, immersed in the furious stream of plasma moving from Alpha Oneo Madrin to Beta Oneo Madrin—her life and those of the *Belladonna*'s surviving scientists dependent on how Paris handled himself.

He told himself that he wouldn't let them down, and he meant it. It's just that he wasn't prepared for what happened next.

Chapter Twenty-one

PARIS CLENCHED HIS JAW as he struggled to reestablish control of the shuttle's tractor beam, which had suddenly begun whipping about as if it had a mind of its own.

With all the graviton flux in the accretion bridge, Commander Wu had anticipated that it would likely affect tractor integrity. She had warned Paris that it might be difficult to keep Jiterica on target.

But she hadn't told the ensign to expect anything like *this*. It was like trying to thread a needle with a strand of overcooked spaghetti.

Frantically, he consulted his monitors. The graviton emitter seemed to be functioning within expected parameters. The same with the subspace field amplifiers.

So it wasn't a malfunction. The graviton storm was just a lot more turbulent than it had a right to be. No doubt, with some careful analysis, Kastiigan and his people would figure out the reason for it after Paris got back.

But that wasn't any help to him right now. And it wasn't any help to Jiterica, either. She was at the mercy of a bizarre and chaotic environment, a small and very fragile leaf in a violent, howling windstorm.

If the graviton flux jerked her around like this much longer, Paris would lose his tractor lock on her. And if he did, he didn't think he could catch hold of her again.

Chilled by the prospect of watching Jiterica spiral off into the sinkhole, the ensign expelled a breath. *You can do this,* he told himself, working his controls. *You're a good helm jockey, as good as any man or woman in the fleet.*

But try as he might, he couldn't steady the tractor beam. The forces acting on it were just too fierce, too unpredictable. Every time Paris tried to compensate, he found himself taking the beam the wrong way.

Come on, he told himself, a bead of sweat making its way down his face. *Do it. Do it* now.

But his controls felt funny—as if they were shivering in his hands. Paris looked down and saw that it wasn't the controls shivering. It was *him.* His hands were trembling just as they always did when he found himself under pressure.

He could feel the weight of his family descending on him, crushing him, making it impossible for him to function. "No," he groaned out loud. "Now *now.*"

He was a Paris. It was his destiny to succeed. But he wasn't *going* to succeed. He was going to fail—not just himself and his family, but all those people on the trapped research ship.

And he was going to fail Jiterica, too. That felt worse to him than all the rest of it.

No, the ensign heard a voice tell him, a voice that rose from the depths of his psyche. *You're not going to fail. You're going to straighten out this beam and complete your mission.*

It took him a moment, but he figured out whose voice it was. It belonged to the woman who had refused to accept his fear and uncertainty, who had bared her own doubts to free him of his.

You make it, she had said. *Somehow you make it and you get through to the other side.*

The ensign could see Commander Wu staring at him across the captain's desk, demonstrating a faith that had taken him by surprise. *Not because you're a Paris. Frankly, that couldn't matter less to me. The reason I think you're the best is because you are.*

Paris's teeth ground together. If Wu believed in him, who was he to give up on himself? If he failed in this mission, it sure as hell wouldn't be for lack of trying.

Shakes or no shakes, he wrestled with the shuttle's tractor controls, doing his best to keep Jiterica on something remotely resembling her intended course.

Picard was the last member of Simenon's party to crawl out of the cave on the far side of the rock wall. As he did so, he saw his comrades shading their eyes and looking back.

"What is it?" the captain asked, using his fingers to comb back an unruly lock of hair plastered to his forehead.

Vigo pointed to the immense, dark gray barrier, first to a spot far on their left and then to another on their right. "We've taken the lead," he said.

As Picard followed his weapons officer's gestures, he saw that Vigo was right. Both of Simenon's rivals and their teams were visible from here, and neither had benefited from the decision to go over the wall instead of under it.

The Aklaash were little more than halfway down, slowly and laboriously using a series of vines to lower each member of their party from ledge to narrow ledge. And the Fejjimaera group hadn't even come that far. They were still in the vicinity of the summit, descending by use of hand- and footholds alone.

The captain nodded his approval. It was the first glimmer of hope they had gotten since the beginning of the contest. And it couldn't have come at a better time.

After all, their underwater ordeal had been a grueling one. They were cold, their legs were rubbery, and their energy was at a decidedly low ebb. But the sight of the other teams' positions was a tonic.

"Let's go," said Simenon, always the driving force behind their efforts. Still breathing heavily, he dragged his battered body away from the cavern mouth. "We've still got seven or eight kilometers to go."

Ben Zoma looked as if he would have liked to rest for a moment. Like the engineer, he hadn't quite caught his breath yet. Nonetheless, he followed Simenon without complaint into the towering woods on the other side of the wall.

Picard could do no less. "Come on," he said to the others. "This lead will evaporate all too quickly if we don't get a move on."

Nor was he offering that simply as a spur. They might be ahead now, but the other teams could do a lot of catching up over the course of seven or eight kilometers.

And no doubt, they *would*.

* * *

Ensign Jiterica had a problem.

could see the unconsumed portion of the *Belladonna* through the visual-analog apparatus built into her containment suit. It wasn't far away, either—less than a kilometer, perhaps, its gray hull only partially obscured by drifts of fiery golden plasma. But the way she was whipping about on the end of the shuttle's tractor beam made her wonder if she would ever reach the beleaguered vessel, much less get inside it.

The Nizhrak wanted to rescue the research scientists as much as anyone. To accomplish that goal, she would suffer any hardship, assume any risk. However, she couldn't get herself across the space separating her from the *Belladonna*. That was the job of her colleague, Ensign Paris.

Commander Wu had said that Paris was a good pilot. She had told Jiterica that she would be in good hands. But clearly, the rescue effort wasn't going as the commander had hoped.

And the Nizhrak had no illusions about the deadly seriousness of her predicament. If the tractor beam lost its grip on her, if she tore loose from her tether, it wouldn't matter that she could survive the radiation and magnetic forces that seemed to permeate this environment, or that the ebb and flow of the graviton storm couldn't pulp her the way it would pulp a being of greater density.

All that would matter was that she possessed mass, however widely distributed, and that she would be inexorably drawn into the sinkhole like the *Stargazer*'s probe and the *Belladonna* before her. And if the research ship wasn't likely to remain intact through such a passage, there was even less of a chance that she would do so.

Jiterica didn't want to die. But more than that, she didn't want to die for *nothing*.

204

She had barely completed the thought when she noticed something—that the intensity with which she was being cast about was diminishing. The tractor beam seemed steadier, more resistant to the graviton eddies that assaulted her. A brief respite, she wondered, or the first sign of an actual improvement in her situation?

In the seconds that followed, the beam seemed to assert itself even more. And though the ensign's progress in the direction of the *Belladonna* was a little slower than before, a little more deliberate, it was also markedly less erratic.

Once again, she had reason for hope.

Simenon was losing his battle.

Despite the terrible urgency that coiled in his belly, despite the dark, looming knowledge of what would happen if he failed, he was slowing down kilometer by kilometer. He couldn't help it. His strides were getting shorter, his legs heavier, his bruised ribs more excrutiatingly painful with each ragged, throat-searing inhalation.

Nor was the Gnalish the only one nearing the limits of his endurance. Greyhorse, who hadn't kept up right from the beginning, had managed to slow down even more. And for that matter, so had Ben Zoma, Vigo, and Joseph.

Of them all, only Picard seemed to have the stamina to maintain their original, ground-eating pace. But it wouldn't do Simenon any good if the captain reached the end ahead of everyone else. After all, it wasn't really a question of who got to the clearing first.

It was a question of who got there last—because none of the teams would be considered to have finished until its last member arrived at the cache of unfertilized eggs.

So if Picard got there in record time and Greyhorse

reached the end behind the last Aklaash or Fejjimaera, Simenon would lose. That was why he had gotten so irritated with the doctor in the beginning—because no matter what any of the others did, it was Greyhorse who would most likely determine their fate.

And that of Simenon's bloodline.

As the Gnalish considered that, he stumbled on an exposed root. *Damn,* he thought, sure that he would go sprawling on his face. But almost instantly, a hand reached out and righted him. Glancing at its owner, Simenon saw that it was Picard.

The Gnalish cursed himself out loud and roused a flock of colunnu in the process. *Keep your mind on what you're doing,* he thought. *Concentrate on that or nothing else will matter.*

Suddenly, Joseph cried out, "I see a star!"

Simenon cast a glance back over his shoulder at the security chief. What in blazes was the man babbling about?

He was still trying to figure it out when Ben Zoma called out a moment later, "I see it as well!"

It was then that the engineer realized what they were up to—a song sung by cadets back at Starfleet Academy, usually accompanied by copious quantities of alcoholic beverages until it became slurred entirely beyond recognition.

"To reach that star!" Vigo trumpeted.

"I'll go through hell!" Picard barked between breaths.

The second verse was considerably less tasteful than the first, but Simenon's comrades didn't let that stop them. They made the forest ring with that one as well. And then the third verse, which was even bawdier than the second.

Before the Gnalish knew it, he was singing as breathlessly as the rest of them. It wasn't like him to sing at all, much less in front of anyone else, but he was singing nonetheless. And as he sang, his spirits seemed to lift.

His legs seemed to churn more easily and his pain seemed to fade into the background.

He looked at Joseph, who saw him looking and winked. Simenon frowned at him. *Singing in the midst of the ritual,* he thought disdainfully. Then he sang some more.

Jiterica knew exactly when she would come in contact with the *Belladonna*'s weakening deflector shields.

After all, her suit's sensor pack had warned her about it soon after she entered the accretion bridge. But she hadn't worried about the research ship's defenses because Commander Wu had conceived a way for her to bypass them.

As Jiterica understood it, ships' deflectors—like other force fields, including the one inside her own containment suit—were emitted at certain frequencies. They were designed to fend off solid objects as well as directed-energy barrages, but not other fields generated at the same frequency.

So if the ensign extended her personal force field outside of her suit, and set it for the frequency most commonly used by Federation vessels, she would be able to penetrate the *Belladonna*'s protective barrier. At least, in theory.

Of course, Commander Wu might have guessed wrong about the frequency of the research ship's shields, in which case the challenge facing Jiterica would suddenly become a good deal more complicated. However, she had decided to—as humans seemed fond of saying—cross that bridge when she came to it.

With the outer surface of the *Belladonna*'s deflector wall getting close enough to reach out and touch with the fingers of her gauntlet, that bridge was now at hand.

As Wu had instructed her, the ensign extended her force field beyond the skin of her suit, instantly placing a much greater burden on herself to maintain an unnaturally dense form. If she had to do this on her own all the time, it wouldn't be possible for her to remain on a ship like the *Stargazer*. But for a short span of time, she could handle the considerable strain of self-containment.

Next, Jiterica matched her field's frequency to the deflector's—or rather, what she expected the deflector's to be. At that point, there was only one thing left for her to do.

She let the shuttle's tractor beam carry her forward.

The ensign's sensors ticked off the distance between her and the *Belladonna*. Twenty-five centimeters. Twenty. Fifteen. Ten. None.

She braced herself for an impact—because if the deflector remained impervious to her, she would bounce off it like any other solid object. But she didn't bounce.

She went right through it.

Wu's theory had proven out. Jiterica had pierced the *Belladonna*'s defenses. And the tractor beam was still carrying her forward.

Once she was certain she was past the deflector barrier, the ensign withdrew her force field into the fabric of her suit again. Then she relaxed, allowing it to reassume the burden of containment.

Better, Jiterica thought with a sense of relief. *Much better.*

The still-visible portion of the research ship was looming in front of her, looking strangely truncated. Also a little curved, an effect of the churning gravitor activity in the area.

As luck would have it, one of the vessel's exterior hatches was almost directly ahead. The ensign could make her way toward it as soon as the tractor beam released her—which it would do in a matter of seconds, judging by the rate at which she was approaching the *Belladonna*'s hull.

Again, she braced herself—not for contact with a deflector shield, but with the duranium surface used by the Federation in the construction of spacegoing vessels. But the impact, however gentle, never came. And somehow, though it seemed the research ship was mere centimeters away, Jiterica was still moving forward—propelled dutifully by the shuttle's tractor beam.

At first, she didn't understand. Then she checked her sensors and realized what was happening.

The *Belladonna* wasn't nearly as close as it looked. But then, her suit's visual-analog device was designed to respond to light in the manner of flesh-and-blood optical organs, and lightwaves would be distorted in the presence of all those gravitons. Fortunately for the ensign, her suit's sensor suite responded to other sorts of stimuli, which were more dependable gauges of distance under the circumstances.

Intent on her sensors this time, she tracked her progress toward the research ship's hull. Thirty meters. Twenty. Ten. And then, as if it had been there all the time and had only now decided to take on substance, the hull pressed back against the palms of her gauntlets.

Jiterica had arrived at her destination.

What's more, Ensign Paris must have known it, because she didn't feel any more pressure from the tractor beam. It had carried her as far as it could. She was on her own now.

Activating the magnetic anchors built into her suit, Jiterica latched onto the duranium surface—first with her right palm and then her left, followed by her right foot and finally her left one. Each time she made contact, she felt a reassuring *clunk*.

When she was done, she found herself in a shallow crouch, all four limbs of her suit adhering to the hull. Had she been a human, she would have taken the opportunity to smile. Despite everything, she had reached the *Belladonna*.

Chapter Twenty-two

JITERICA TURNED THE HELMET of her containment suit as she hung onto the *Belladonna*'s outer skin.

The hatch that she had seen was above her and to her left, almost hidden by the curve of the ship. It appeared to be no more than ten meters away, but she had learned better than to trust her visual-analog faculty in this place. Consulting her other sensors, she saw that the actual distance was more like twenty meters.

Detaching her right palm-magnet, the ensign brought it alongside her left and reattached it to the *Belladonna*'s hull. Then she did the same with her right foot. Once her right-side appendages were in place, she detached those on her left, extended them as far as she could in the direction of her goal, and resecured them. And in this manner, she made her way toward the hatch.

She was more than halfway there when she detached her right palm again and realized that something was amiss. Looking down, she saw the feet of her suit drifting away from the hull.

Commander Wu had warned her about this phenomenon as well. The magnetic eddies that existed in the accretion bridge were wreaking havoc with her anchors. If Jiterica wasn't careful, she might go drifting off—and if she did that, it was unlikely that Ensign Paris would be able to reassert his tractor lock on her.

First, she reattached her sole anchors to the hull. Then she moved more slowly and cautiously than before, making sure not to detach any of the magnets until she was certain that the others were secure.

It took a while, but the ensign at last reached the hatch. It was locked, of course—no surprise there. But she had a remedy for that. Removing a hyperspanner from its sheath along the leg of her suit, she went to work on the hatch.

As it turned out, the mechanism was in perfect working order. With the proper tool in hand, it was the work of a minute to swing the hatch door open. Resecuring the hyperspanner, Jiterica maneuvered herself about until she could lower herself into the aperture.

Unfortunately, she still hadn't gotten any better at moving in tight places. However, the hatch was made to accommodate the bulk of a containment suit, so she was able to thrust herself down through the opening without too much trouble. At the last moment she felt one of her hand anchors slip off the hull, the victim of a competing magnetic wave, but by then she was mostly inside the hatch.

Deactivating her magnets, Jiterica pulled the hatch closed. She found herself in a small compartment—an airlock, not unlike those that existed on the *Stargazer.*

It took a moment for air to shoot in and a few more to fill the lock. Though oxygen was of no use to the Nizhrak except as an occasional source of nutrition, she was compelled to wait for the process to run its course. When the readout on the bulkhead indicated that an atmosphere had been established, Jiterica pressed the pad that would give her access to the interior of the ship.

A pair of doors parted, revealing a corridor. Moving out into it, the ensign scanned its length in either direction. There was no evidence of any living humanoids.

But the *Stargazer*'s scan had indicated a number of survivors. Since Jiterica's personal sensors didn't have the range to locate them, she picked a direction at random and set out in search of the *Belladonna*'s crew.

Not much longer now, Simenon thought as he pelted over the dark, spongy ground, barely able to feel his legs.

A couple of kilometers at most, he promised himself. *Just a couple of kilometers. Then the ritual would all be over, one way or the other.*

His friends were all around him, ahead and behind, coping with varying degrees of exhaustion. Their breath rasped in their throats and they grunted every so often, evidence of how hard they were struggling not to let him down.

Simenon hadn't seen any sign of the Aklaash or the Fejjimaera since he left them on the stone wall, but he had a feeling they weren't far behind. If he stopped and listened, he would probably hear them thrashing through the woods on an unseen trail, desperate to close the distance between Simenon's party and their own.

All the more reason to keep going, he told himself. To fend off any thoughts of slowing down for a moment, no matter how tempting they might be. To ignore the savage throbbing in his banged-up ribs and the ache in his damaged arm.

Funny, Simenon thought. In the end, his intellectual

superiority over his competitors hadn't made the slightest bit of difference. The only smart thing he had done was refrain from arguing too much when he found Picard and the others standing on that transporter pad. If not for them, he would have lost this race a long time ago.

Suddenly, he felt something sticky on his face. He brushed it aside with his good hand. Then he felt it again. And again.

Sedgmaya, Simenon realized with disgust. Ugly little creatures not much bigger than one of his fingers. They stretched their secretions from tree to tree to catch insects, in the manner of Terran spiders.

Actually, he was lucky. Fully spun sedgmaya webs would have been a lot heavier—heavy enough to wrap themselves around him and slow his progress along the trail. Obviously, it had rained in the last few days, forcing the slimy little beasts to begin spinning new webs.

No, Simenon thought, even in the midst of his exertions. *That can't be right.* If it had rained, he wouldn't have seen those footprints back at the bridge.

Or maybe it *had* rained, he allowed, and the footprints weren't as old as he thought—not even as old as the last ritual. If that were so, someone other than a ritual runner had left them there—having snuck into the forest without anyone noticing and sabotaged the bridge.

But who? Other than one of Simenon's rivals, who would have had something to gain if he fell into the chasm? Who would have benefited if he had died or couldn't finish the race?

And then it came to him, like a bolt of lightning in a vast summer sky.

Anger rose into his throat and threatened to choke him. *No,* he insisted. *I can't afford to think about this now. I need to concentrate on reaching the clearing.*

"Damn!" said Ben Zoma, who was running just ahead of Simenon.

"What is it?" the Gnalish demanded.

The first officer jerked a thumb over his shoulder. "It's the Aklaash," he said with uncharacteristic solemnity. "They're making a race out of it."

Simenon didn't want to look at them. He knew it would only slow him down. But he looked anyway—and his heart sank.

He could see the Aklaash moving through the scarlet trees, showing not the least sign of fatigue, their long strides devouring the ground in gulps. Slowly but surely, they were catching up. And Simenon's party still had at least a kilometer to go before it reached the finish line.

The Gnalish darted a glance back over his shoulder at Greyhorse. As usual, the doctor was bringing up the rear. Simenon swore beneath his breath. What had ever possessed him to let the doctor take part in the ritual?

An inexcusable ignorance of his physical conditioning, the Gnalish thought. A complete and utter failure to question whether Greyhorse would be an asset or a liability.

He knew the answer to that question now, though, didn't he? Unfortunately, it was a bit too late for him to do anything about it.

Just then, Simenon saw Vigo move to the side of the trail and fall behind. *What now?* he thought. Had the weapons officer chosen that moment to pull up lame?

Then he realized that Vigo wasn't hurt, after all. He had just dropped back to join the doctor. Pulling Greyhorse's arm over his right shoulder, the Pandrilite threw his own arm around the doctor's middle and started forward with him.

What's more, Greyhorse didn't utter a protest. He had run out of steam and he knew it. With Vigo helping to support him, the two oversize beings lumbered toward the clearing.

And they still had a lead on the Aklaash. As long as they maintained that, they couldn't lose.

The muscles in Simenon's legs burned like fire. His throat hurt so much he couldn't swallow. But he was close to the end, just a few minutes away from it. He could endure anything—any pain, any suffering.

Especially if it meant avoiding a lifetime of regret.

Then he saw it—the clearing. *The eggs,* he thought, his primal instincts coming to the fore. He could feel them somehow, a presence that drew him on unerringly.

But the Aklaash must have sensed the egg cache, too, because they began to close the gap more quickly. Simenon could hear them cursing each other, taunting each other, inciting their comrades to demand more and more of themselves.

The engineer's heart pounded in his chest, spurred by anxiety as much as by the nearness of the eggs. He would never have believed he could run so far or so fast, especially after the beating he had taken in the crevasse. But he was doing it. He was dredging up every last bit of strength as he closed in on the clearing.

The trail rose, dipped, and rose again. Simenon could hear the Aklaash, their voices cracking like whips. He didn't have to look back again to know that they were gaining ground, driving toward the finish line with all the power they could muster.

But Vigo was a powerhouse, too. And he was using his strength to propel Greyhorse along faster than the doctor could ever have managed on his own.

Come on, Simenon thought. *Come on...*

The clearing was right in front of them now. He could see the white robes of the Elders, waiting to proclaim a victor. He could see the black robes of their bodyguards, there to make sure that all transpired in accordance with the law.

The Aklaash started cheering as if they had already won. But Simenon resisted the temptation to cast another glance in their direction. He would see them soon enough.

The trees parted before him and the path widened, giving him a better view of those who awaited him. His breath was coming in sobs now, in strangled groans, his lungs incapable of taking in enough air to meet the demands of his straining body.

A little farther, Simenon told himself, his mouth dry as dust, his eyes starting to lose their focus. *For your brothers. For all those who came before...*

And with that thought burning in his brain, the Gnalish burst into the sacred clearing.

He wasn't alone, either. There were bodies plunging past him on either side. Human bodies. Three of them.

Falling to his knees, Simenon turned and looked for his last two comrades. They were close, closer than he had thought they would be, Greyhorse's arm still slung across Vigo's massive shoulders as they lumbered forward.

But the Aklaash were close, too. They raged toward the clearing down their separate trail, a juggernaut of muscle and bone, the evolutionary apogee of Gnalish strength and endurance.

Run! Simenon thought, urging his comrades on. *For love of the gods, run!*

Wheezing and gasping every bit as badly as Greyhorse, Vigo all but carried the doctor into the clearing. At the last moment, the two of them stumbled and fell in a tangle of long, powerful limbs.

But it didn't matter anymore. They had made it.

Unfortunately, so had the Aklaash. With Kasaelek in the lead, they came pounding into the clearing at what appeared to be the exact same moment as Vigo and Greyhorse.

At least, that was how it appeared to Simenon. But then, his opinion didn't matter. All that mattered was how it looked to the Elders standing in front of the egg cache.

If they thought the engineer's group had come in first, Simenon would be awarded the right to fertilize the eggs. But if they thought Kasaelek's group had beaten them...

Simenon didn't even want to think about that.

His comrades gathered around him, their faces flushed and their breath coming fast. "Don't worry," Ben Zoma told him. "We took them, no question about it."

"I think so, too," said Joseph.

But Picard wasn't venturing an opinion. Like his engineer, he seemed to think it was too close to call.

Simenon studied the Elders, waiting for their decision. As wisdom dictated, they turned and consulted with each other. Then, with both parties hanging on their words, one of them stepped forward and rendered their verdict.

"The race has ended in a draw," he said.

"A draw?" Ben Zoma muttered in disgust.

Picard turned to Simenon. "What does that mean?"

The Gnalish sighed. "It means the winner will have to be chosen another way."

The captain's brow creased. "*What* way?"

Simenon regarded Kasaelek, who was grinning and clenching his fists at the news. The engineer wished he felt like grinning, too.

"In single combat," he said softly.

Commander Wu stared at the blazing section of the accretion bridge on her forward viewscreen as if she could see into it and follow Jiterica's progress.

But of course, she couldn't. All she could see was the tiny speck that represented Ensign Paris's shuttle, its position supported by a tractor beam emanating from the *Stargazer.*

Her officers, on the other hand, could keep track of Jiterica's movements via ship's sensors. And as time went on, they periodically brought the second officer up to speed. But they couldn't say the words she was waiting to hear, the words that would enable her to breathe easily again.

Finally, she heard from the one who *could* say those words. "Paris here," came the transmission from the shuttle.

Wu leaned forward in her seat. "Go ahead."

"She's in," the ensign said.

The commander nodded. "That's good news," she told Paris.

But she knew the Nizhrak's trial wasn't over yet. There was still the small matter of what she had to accomplish on the *Belladonna.*

"Come on home," she instructed the ensign. After all, his shuttle could only get in the way now.

"Aye," Paris said—and cut the comm link.

On the viewscreen, the shuttlecraft could be seen wheeling about, its portion of the mission accomplished. Obviously, Wu had been right to place her faith in Ensign Paris.

"Commander?" said Kastiigan, interrupting Wu's thoughts.

She turned to him. "Lieutenant?"

The science officer didn't look happy. "There's something here I think you should see."

Wu got up and made her way to his side. "What is it?"

Kastiigan pointed a long, wrinkled finger at his central monitor. "I don't know why, but the *Belladonna*'s rate of descent into the sinkhole seems to have accelerated."

"Accelerated...?" Wu echoed, a chill climbing her spine.

She took a look at the Kandilkari's monitor, hoping he had jumped to the wrong conclusion. However, the data bore him out. The scientists' vessel was slipping into the sinkhole faster than before.

Much faster.

No, thought Wu. *She can't do this to us.* She forced herself to ask Kastiigan the obvious question: "How long before she reaches the point of no return?"

The science officer frowned. "It's difficult to say, Commander. But if she continues at this pace, I would say the *Belladonna* has no more than thirty minutes left."

Thirty minutes, Wu thought. *And Jiterica had gone in thinking she would have a couple of hours.*

If there were a way to contact the ensign and warn her, the commander would have done it in a heartbeat. But had it been possible to communicate with the research vessel, Jiterica wouldn't have had to make the trip in the first place.

Wu would just have to hope that Jiterica noticed the change in the *Belladonna*'s situation and acted accordingly. Otherwise, the ensign and everyone else on that ship were doomed.

Chapter Twenty-three

JITERICA WAS PREPARED to spend whatever time it took to find the crew of the *Belladonna*.

However, she believed she would accomplish her objective more quickly if she headed for a place where survivors were likely to congregate. One such place, she decided, was the bridge.

Following the corridor, she stopped at the first turbolift she came to and summoned a compartment using the pad set into the bulkhead. But she didn't have to take it to the bridge to make contact with the crew of the *Belladonna*. One of them was in the lift when the doors opened, ready to emerge into the hallway.

"Damn!" the scientist cried and took an involuntary step back, obviously surprised to see her there. He was a tall man with deepset eyes and a receding line of dark hair. Recovering, he said, "You're the one who opened the hatch, aren't you?"

"I am," Jiterica confirmed.

He looked at her through the faceplate of her containment suit and his eyes narrowed. Her insubstantial-looking visage must have appeared strange to him. But then, it appeared strange to the ensign as well; she had only created it to make her colleagues feel more comfortable in her presence.

"What—?" the human began. Then he stopped himself. "No. Never mind that. Just tell me…are you here to help us? That's what everyone seems to think, and I sure as hell hope they're right."

"I am indeed here to help you," she told him. "My name is Jiterica. I hold the rank of ensign on the Federation starship *Stargazer*."

The man nodded. "I guess that explains the Starfleet insignia on your containment suit."

"How many of you are there?" Jiterica asked.

"Twenty-three," the human told her.

She made a mental note of it. "Casualties?"

"A few injuries, but no deaths," he said. Then he added, "So far."

So far, so good, Jiterica thought, quoting an expression she had heard on the ship.

"My commanding officer has come up with a plan to get you out of here," she said. "However, it will require your cooperation."

Just then, someone rounded a bend in the corridor. It was an Andorian, a female. As she approached Jiterica, her brow creased and her antennae bent all the way forward.

"I guess you got here before I did," the Andorian remarked.

"She's with Starfleet," the human explained before his colleague could ask. "They've come to help us escape this thing." He turned back to the ensign. "What do you need us to do?"

"To begin with," said Jiterica, "I need you to take me to your captain."

Simenon steeled himself for yet another ordeal—one for which he was poorly equipped, to say the least.

"You're sure we can't help?" Joseph asked.

"Surely the Elders can see you're in no shape for this," Vigo pointed out.

Simenon shook his head. "Single combat, to take place immediately after the race. That's the ancient law."

Picard frowned. "Your arm—"

"Has felt better," the engineer agreed. "But I'm going to try not to let Kasaelek know that."

Not that it was likely to matter. In the few times his subspecies had been involved in such combats, they hadn't even come close to winning. And as the captain had noted, Simenon wasn't operating at full strength.

But there was no alternative. He had to face Kasaelek or concede the contest—and the prize.

The Elder who had announced the decision looked to Simenon. "Are you ready, ritual runner?"

"I am," the engineer told him. As if to underline the fact, he moved into the center of the clearing.

The Elder looked to Kasaelek. "And you?"

The Aklaash moved into the center of the clearing as well. "Ready," he said, obviously eager to get the combat over with.

The Elder regarded them. "Let it begin."

Jiterica looked at the captain of the *Belladonna*, a thickset man with close-cropped hair and a full, blond beard, across the confines of his ready room. "That is," she said, finishing her outline of Commander Wu's plan, "if you still *have* impulse power."

"Oh," said the captain, "we've still got it, all right. We just don't know how *much*. After all, we gunned the engines pretty hard trying to get out of this mess on our own."

"I will need to speak to your engineer," the ensign told him.

The captain sighed. "Unfortunately, he was injured early on. His assistant is running things." He leaned forward. "And between you, me, and the bulkhead, he's not the brightest star in the firmament."

The captain of the *Belladonna* was an unusual man, Jiterica observed. Despite the dire nature of his circumstances, he seemed to take it all in stride.

"If you like," the ensign said, "I can offer him assistance. I was trained in engine operations at the Academy."

The captain nodded. "Sounds like a plan. Let's go."

But when the ready room doors opened for them, a human youngling was revealed standing outside them. His mouth fell open as he caught sight of Jiterica.

"My son," the captain explained, throwing his arm around the young man. "Little shy, but he's a whip. Curious about everything. Mind if he tags along?"

The ensign said she didn't mind at all.

Simenon had expected Kasaelek to try a preemptive strike at the outset of their winner-take-all combat. As it turned out, he was right.

The Aklaash had barely gotten leave to begin before he launched a meaty fist at his opponent. It was only because Simenon was expecting it that he was able to duck and shuffle past the attack.

But Kasaelek wasn't done yet. Not nearly. Unlike the

engineer, he seemed to have plenty of energy left in him even after his catch-up sprint through the woods.

As the Aklaash wheeled and came at him again, Simenon had a moment to appreciate how mismatched they were. Kasaelek was proportioned just like him from his scaly head to the tip of his tail, but he towered over the engineer the way an adult might tower over his offspring. And the Aklaash wasn't hurt. It was only a matter of time before he used his superior reach to land a blow from which Simenon couldn't recover.

Unless, of course, Simenon used his vaunted Mazzereht intelligence to even up the contest somehow.

Easier said than done, he told himself, as he ventured to duck Kasaelek's second rush. This time, however, he couldn't avoid it entirely. The Aklaash landed a glancing blow to his right shoulder—the one above his injured ribs.

The resulting wave of pain made Simenon lightheaded, but he managed to scurry away. *Damn,* he thought, unable to keep from wincing. He couldn't keep this up much longer. He had to *do* something.

Think, Phigus. Use that nimble brain the gods gave you. If you can fix a warp drive, you can beat a big, dumb Aklaash.

And then it came to him.

Truthfully, he hadn't come up with the idea on his own. *But if you're going to borrow,* he thought, *borrow something you know has worked.*

He waited until Kasaelek came about for another go at him. Then he braced himself, legs apart for balance, knowing he might not get a second chance at this.

The Aklaash bared his teeth and charged—but this time, he wasn't trying to bludgeon Simenon senseless with a single blow. He was coming on with his muscular arms spread wide, hoping to wrap them around his adversary and *then* batter him senseless.

It's now or never, Simenon told himself.

Marshaling what little energy he had left, he scooted between Kasaelek's legs and grabbed his adversary's tail—just as the duwiijuc had done to *him* earlier in the day.

No doubt, it was the last thing Kasaelek had expected of him. With a cry of rage, he whirled about in the clearing, dragging Simenon with him. The engineer felt as if his arm muscles were shredding, as if his ribs on that side were going to crack in half. But he didn't let go of Kasaelek's tail. In fact, he hung on that much harder.

Kasaelek tried to reach behind him, to peel Simenon off. But he couldn't. Even *his* mighty arms didn't reach that far. And the more he tried, the more the effort took its toll on him.

"Coward!" he rasped. "Pile of dung!"

Simenon didn't let the taunts get to him. If anything, they gave him the courage to keep going, to endure the agony in his side—because if Kasaelek was resorting to curses, he had to be faltering.

"I'll rip you apart!" the Aklaash railed at him. "I'll tear out your entrails and feed them to the sanjarra!"

The engineer barely heard what he was saying. He was too busy biting back his pain. But he wouldn't let go.

And Kasaelek, who hadn't shown any signs of fatigue when the combat started, began to show them with increasing rapidity. His breath came harder and harder. He staggered and flailed with arms that looked as if they had weights attached to them. And his fiery insults turned into a long, formless snarl of anger and frustration.

Finally, he couldn't take it anymore. His gigantic

frame began to sag. And wracked by exhaustion, he crashed to his knees.

It was exactly the opening Simenon had been waiting for. Thrusting aside his own red storm of pain, he scrambled for a rock at the edge of the clearing.

It wasn't more than a couple of meters away, but it might as well have been a light-year. If the engineer didn't grab it and put it to good use before Kasaelek got to his feet, all the torment he had endured would go for nothing.

As the Aklaash drew in a deep, shuddering breath, Simenon's fingers closed on the rock. Then he changed direction and launched himself at his bigger, stronger adversary.

By then, Kasaelek had planted his right foot on the ground and was preparing to get up. But he hadn't cast a glance in Simenon's direction. At least, not yet.

Calling on his ancestors for strength, the engineer lifted the rock and cracked Kasaelek over the head with it. The Aklaash slumped and grabbed the ground, but didn't fall. Simenon smashed him in the skull a second time, forcing the knee Kasaelek had raised to crumble, but the giant was still fending off unconsciousness.

One last time, Simenon thought.

Clinging to that promise, he raised the rock as high as he could and brought it down on the Aklaash's cranium. And to his relief, it knocked Kasaelek flat, stripping the Aklaash of what little sense still rattled about in his head.

I've won, the engineer told himself.

But it didn't sink in until he looked around and saw his comrades cheering for him at the top of their lungs. Even the captain, who usually kept his emotions to himself. Even *Greyhorse,* for the gods' sake. They were shaking their fists and roaring with triumph as if it were they who had toppled Kasaelek.

I've won, Simenon repeated.

And he had—not only for himself but for his father and his brothers, who would have been celebrating his victory now if they had lived long enough to join him in the ritual.

Someone put a hand on Simenon's shoulder. Looking up, he saw that it was the Elder who had called for the combat.

"Rise," he said.

Simenon heaved the rock away, shuddering at the pain it cost him. Then, ever so slowly and carefully, he stood.

He noticed that the Fejjimaera had entered the clearing. They were standing at its edges, looking downcast at their defeat. Especially Banyohla, who seemed to be injured and was leaning on one of his comrades for support.

Simenon almost felt sorry for Banyohla. *Almost.*

"You have won the running of the ritual as prescribed by law," the Elder told him. "You have triumphed over your rivals."

The engineer liked the sound of that.

"All you need do now," said the Elder, "is produce the insadja'tu and complete the ceremony. Then the nest is yours."

The insadja'tu, Simenon thought, his mind numb and distant in the aftermath of his struggle. It was the stone his father had made for him when he was young, an exact replica of the one the Elder Simenon had carried in his own ritual victory.

The engineer knew what he had to do. He had to present the insadja'tu to the Elder and finish what he had started. With that in mind, he fished in the interior pocket of his garment—a deep, narrow slot into which he had inserted the stone before he left the *Stargazer.*

How proud his father would have been of him, he reflected. How jubilant to see his bloodline go on uninterrupted.

It was then that Simenon's fingers reached the bottom of his pocket—and felt nothing. *Nothing at all.*

"Is something wrong?" the Elder asked.

The engineer felt dizzy all of a sudden. Dizzy and weak in the knees. *It can't be,* he thought wildly.

"Is something wrong?" the Elder asked a little more insistently.

Simenon swallowed and probed his pocket again. It had to be in there somewhere. *Where else could it be?* he asked himself, knowing full well that it could have been *anywhere.*

In the underground waterway. In the crevasse. In the place where they fought off the sanjarra.

Anywhere.

Chapter Twenty-four

JITERICA STUDIED THE MONITOR on the engineering console as she ran yet another diagnostic on the impulse drive. There was still a problem with the driver coil assembly, apparently.

She believed she knew how to fix it. It would take some time, of course, but there was no shortage of that. According to the chronometer in her suit, she still had more than an hour and forty minutes to get the engines ready.

"Ensign Jiterica?" said the captain's son, who had been standing alongside her since she came down to engineering, watching her every move.

"Yes?" Jiterica responded, though her attention remained fixed on the console.

"What kind of being are you?" the human asked.

"I'm a Nizhrak—a low-density being from a gas giant. You've probably never seen one of my people before."

"You're right," he said. "I haven't." A pause. "I hope you don't think I'm being rude but...I'm kind of curious about your suit."

"Curious?" Jiterica echoed.

"About what it does for you."

"I see," she said.

She went on to describe how the suit helped her to contain her mass, how it made it possible for her to ambulate throughout a starship, and how it facilitated periodic nourishment. When she was finished, she turned to face him.

"Is that what you wish to know?"

The captain's son nodded, his brow pinched as he absorbed the information. "That's exactly what I wished... I mean *wanted* to know."

Assured that she had satisfied his curiosity, Jiterica returned to her work. But a moment later, she heard the human speak up again.

"May I ask you another question?"

She gave him permission to do so.

"How does it feel," he asked, "to be a biological being that has to interface with a mechanical device?"

The ensign considered the question. "To me," she admitted, "it feels awkward. How does it feel to you?"

The captain's son looked confused. "What do you mean?"

"You interface with this ship, do you not?"

"Well," he said, smiling a little, "sure. But not in the same way."

It seemed to Jiterica that he was about to ask her another question about her interaction with the suit—something along more technological lines, perhaps. But before he could do that, she heard his father's voice over the ship's intercom.

"Ensign Jiterica?" the captain said.

"I am here," she responded.

"We've got a problem—or should I say a bigger problem. My sensor officer tells me we're slipping into the sinkhole faster than before. I hope you're almost done down there."

"How much time do we have?" the ensign asked. She didn't think she would like the answer.

"Twenty minutes," the captain told her. "Tops."

Her prediction had been accurate. She didn't like the answer at all.

Picard didn't understand.

What in blazes was an insadja'tu? And why did it have such significance to the elder?

He saw Simenon turn to the Gnalish in the white robe. "I can't find it," the engineer said, his voice uncharacteristically subdued and full of disappointment. "I must have dropped it somewhere along the way."

The elder's brow furrowed above his scaly snout. "Without the insadja'tu, there can be no consummation." He turned to Kasaelak, who was holding his head as he began to regain consciousness. "If the Aklaash has retained his insadja'tu, he may be declared the victor."

Picard frowned. That hardly seemed like an equitable conclusion.

"Kasaelek," said one of his comrades. The Aklaash knelt beside him. "Show the elder your insadja'tu."

Kasaelek was still dazed, but not to the point where he couldn't understand his comrade's instructions. Delving into a pocket of his own, he felt around for a moment. Then he drew his hand out and showed the elders a white stone with black etchings.

The insadja'tu, Picard thought. Little more than a pebble. And this would decide the outcome of the ritual?

They had come so far, gotten through so much. They

had won by every reasonable standard. It wasn't fair for Simenon's bloodline to be ended forever on a mere technicality. At least it seemed that way to his Terran mode of thinking.

But that weren't on Earth, the captain had to remind himself. They were on Gnala, and what seemed like a mere technicality to him here may have made perfect sense to Simenon's people.

"I have no choice," the elder said, "but to award Kasaelak the victory. That is, if he can transcribe the glyphs that appear on his insadja'tu without error."

Kasaelak laughed despite the bludegeoning he had endured. Clearly, he didn't believe he would have any trouble doing what the elder had suggested—not when he had his little white stone for reference.

Simenon's head drooped and he looked away. It didn't seem he could bear to watch.

Nonetheless, the Aklaash moved into the center of the clearing, where he found a patch of soft, dark ground unconcealed by the spongy stuff. Then he pulled out his tellek and used it to make a line.

"Wait a minute," said Greyhorse, who was standing next to the crestfallen Simenon. "That's what the insadja'tu is for? So you can draw glyphs in the ground?"

"That's what it's for," the engineer confirmed.

"What if you could draw the glyphs *without* the stone?" asked the medical officer.

"What if I could *fly?*" Simenon rasped bitterly. "Without the stone, I can't do a thing."

For the first time, Picard saw Greyhorse become angry. "Answer me, damn you," said the doctor.

Surprised, the engineer looked up at him. "The law of ritual calls for a drawing. That's it. But—"

Greyhorse didn't let him finish. Limping out into the

center of the clearing, he stopped in front of where Kasaelak was kneeling.

"Get out of my way," the Aklaash growled, an unmistakable promise of violence in his voice.

But the chief medical officer didn't answer him. He spoke to the elders instead. "I stand for Simenon," he said.

The foremost elder regarded him. "In what capacity?"

"In *this* capacity," Greyhorse told him.

With difficulty, he lowered himself to his knees alongside another open patch of ground. Then, looking as humble and miserable as Picard had ever seen him, the doctor took out his own tellek and began to draw. And as the captain watched—as they all watched—Greyhorse began to produce a set of glyph-like lines.

Simenon's eyes narrowed as he looked on. "They're the ones on my insadja'tu," he muttered. He turned to Picard. "But how does he—?"

The captain shook his head. "I don't know."

Clearly, however, Greyhorse knew what he was doing. Though he worked intently and exercised great care, he didn't stop even once. He inscribed glyph after intricate glyph as if he had known them from the moment of his birth.

Ben Zoma chuckled. "Amazing."

"It is indeed," Picard agreed.

"This is an outrage!" Kasaelak growled, his ruby eyes full of fury. He got up and charged the elders, stopping just in time to keep from bowling them over. "You gave *me* the victory!"

"We gave you the opportunity to inscribe the glyphs," said one of the elders, unruffled by the Aklaash's display. "But only because Simenon could not. Now, it seems, he *can.*"

"But that's not Simenon!" Kasaelak snarled, pointing

a thick, long-nailed finger at Greyhorse. "That's an off-worlder! Bad enough he was allowed to accompany the Mazzereht on his journey. But to let him inscribe glyphs in our sacred ground...that is beyond reason!"

The elder shook his head from side to side. "We have already determined that the offworlder may stand for Simenon—not just in one aspect of the ritual, but in all of them."

Kasaelak sputtered with anger, but he had to see that he wasn't going to make any headway with the elders. Which was, no doubt, why he whirled and faced Greyhorse instead.

Too late, Picard saw the Aklaash lower his head and go after the doctor. All he could do was cry out a warning. But Joseph wasn't too late. He bolted for Greyhorse as well, embarking on an intercept course with the powerful Kasaelak.

For a moment, Picard wasn't sure which of them would reach the doctor first. Then, with a desperate burst of speed that surprised the captain, the security officer interposed himself between Greyhorse and Kasaelek and took the brunt of the attack.

Aklaash and human rolled across the clearing in a tangle of arms and legs. Predictably, the larger and stronger Kasaelek got to his feet first, intent on doing further damage to Joseph.

But someone intervened. Not Vigo, who was best equipped to have done so. Not Picard or Ben Zoma or Simenon or any of the black-robed Aklaash who stood at the edges of the clearing.

Someone else got to Kasaelek first, tackling him at the knees and toppling him, and then leaping on top of him to deliver a crude but enthusiastic right to the Gnal-ish's jaw.

It was Greyhorse.

Before Kasaelek could shrug off the blow, the Aklaash guards surrounded him and pulled him to his feet. And Greyhorse backed off, holding his right hand with his left.

"Are you all right?" Picard asked as he joined him there.

The doctor frowned as he inspected his hand. "As if tracing those glyphs wasn't *already* difficult. Now I'll be doing it one-handed."

The captain glanced at the elders, who didn't look very happy with Kasaelek's behavior. "I think you'll be granted a certain amount of leeway," he said.

It turned out that Picard was right. Greyhorse was given all the time he needed to complete the glyphs on Simenon's insadja'tu—time enough to describe where he had seen them before and how they came to be planted so firmly in his mind.

For all the captain knew, they might all have been perfectly accurate. Or then again, they might not have been. All that was important was that the elders accepted them.

Maybe by then, they had recognized that Simenon had earned his posterity many times over.

Finally, the engineer was officially declared the victor. But he didn't celebrate. More than anything, he looked relieved.

"As my teammates," he told Picard and the others, "you can stay and watch me inseminate the eggs." But his tone and his expression indicated that he would rather they didn't.

"I don't think so," the captain said.

Ben Zoma smiled. "Maybe some other time."

So Picard and his officers left the clearing, walked back into the scarlet woods and waited. And when Simenon came to get them a short time later, it was after he had done his part—injuries and all—to add to the longevity of his bloodline.

Wu couldn't wait any longer.

According to Kastiigan's sensors, the *Belladonna* had slipped into the sinkhole almost to the point where it would be futile to try to drag her out again. If they were going to try to stage a rescue, they would have to do it *now*.

But the *Stargazer* couldn't do it alone. As long as the scientists on the research ship had recognized the urgency of their situation and gotten their engines ready, they had a chance. If they had failed in that regard, perhaps because the impulse drive was just unsalvageable at this point, the *Belladonna* and all hands would be lost.

It was that simple.

Wu turned to Idun. "Helm, take us within a hundred kilometers of the accretion bridge."

The helm officer did as she was told, her fingers moving nimbly over her controls. Almost instantly, the plasma stream began to loom larger on the forward viewer. After a while, all Wu could see from one side of the screen to the other was brilliant, red-gold turbulence.

Paris had returned from the brink of that chaos with his shuttle safe and sound. But Jiterica was still trapped inside the accretion bridge along with the people she had tried to save. Wu prayed that the ensign's efforts there had paid off.

Finally, Idun turned to her. "One hundred kilometers," she reported, though from the look in her eyes she would have liked to dare more.

Wu glanced at Gerda. "Give me a tractor lock."

The navigator carried out the order. "Got it," she said a few moments later.

The second officer frowned. This was it. If Jiterica

had succeeded, they would know it soon enough. "Reverse engines and proceed at one-quarter-impulse. Let's get them out of there."

"Reversing engines," Idun told her.

"Come on," Wu breathed, staring at the screen as if that could make a difference. "Give us a hand."

"I'm reading engine activity in the *Belladonna*," Kastiigan announced from his science station. He looked up. "They appear to be operating at rated power."

Wu nodded. Jiterica had done it. She had gotten the impulse drive ready in time. But would it be enough?

She felt a shudder in the deckplates. The *Stargazer* was straining to carry out her part of the bargain. But if the research ship was emerging from her trap, Wu couldn't tell from the image on the viewscreen.

Needing to see what was going on, she got up and joined Kastiigan. "Progress?" she asked hopefully.

"None to speak of," he said, intent on his monitors.

Wu bit her lip. The longer this went on, straining both their engines and the *Belladonna*'s, the less likely they were to pull the research ship out of there.

"All available power to the engines!" she snapped. "Shields, life support...everything but the tractor feed!"

The lights dimmed on the bridge and she felt another tremor run through the deck. Then she turned to Kastiigan's monitors, which seemed brighter in the relative darkness, defying them to tell her that her order hadn't helped.

In fact, it *had*. More of the research ship had crept out of the sinkhole. But she still wasn't free. Wu needed to do more for her.

"We need more power," she said out loud.

But there *wasn't* any more power. They had already tapped all their vessel's resources. Or had they?

They were still pumping incredible amounts of energy into their tractor beam—enough to maintain its integrity in this titanic tug-of-war across a hundred kilometers of graviton-riddled space.

They didn't dare compromise the strength of the beam. But if they cut down its length, even by thirty kilometers, and shuttled that suddenly-available power to the engines...

"Take us in closer," Wu told her helm officer. "Within seventy kilometers of the accretion bridge."

Idun looked at her. "Aye, Commander."

And she brought them in closer.

Of course, there was a problem with Wu's idea—a flaw of which she was well aware. At some point, the sinkhole would begin to exert a pull on the *Stargazer* again as well. Then they would be trying to drag two ships at the same time—the scientists' and their own.

Wu could only hope that flaw wouldn't become a fatal one.

"Seventy kilometers," Idun told her. She studied her instruments and frowned. "We're being drawn in."

Wu's heart sank. "What about the *Belladonna?*" she asked Kastiigan, too discouraged to look for herself.

A pause. "She's moving," the science officer replied, a note of surprise in his voice. "Yes...she is definitely moving."

But so was Wu's ship—and in the wrong direction. If she allowed that go on much longer, the *Belladonna* wouldn't be the only victim of the rift. The *Stargazer* would be sucked in along with her.

The only prudent course of action was to deactivate the tractor beam and retreat while they still could. After all, Wu had the lives of her crew to consider. But she couldn't do it. Not with all those scientists depending on them, clinging to the slender thread of hope only Wu and her officers could offer them.

And it wasn't just the *Belladonna*'s crew she was thinking about. Jiterica had trusted her, risked her life at Wu's request.

How could Wu fail to return the favor?

Pull, she urged the *Stargazer,* intent on the yellow blip that represented the research ship on Kastiigan's monitor. *Pull with everything you've got.*

And as if her invocation had given the *Belladonna* the courage she needed, the vessel surged free of her prison, a flying thing too long denied flight.

Gerda turned to Wu, her eyes alight with triumph. "She's escaped the sinkhole!"

"So she has!" the commander returned.

But it wasn't over yet. The *Belladonna* still had to escape the sinkhole's *pull.*

"Her impulse drive is giving out," Kastiigan said, putting a damper on his colleagues' enthusiasm. He pointed to the monitor that showed him the other ship's energy levels. "Another few seconds and she will be without propulsion."

But in the meantime, she was getting closer to the *Stargazer.* And the closer she got, the less energy it took to maintain the tractor beam that held her in tow.

Wu felt a muscle in her jaw begin to spasm. *Wait,* she told herself. *Just a little longer...*

To their credit, none of her bridge officers questioned her judgement. Paxton, Dubinski, Kastiigan...they remained silent and uncomplaining, watching along with Wu as the *Belladonna* slowly climbed out of the swirling plasma of the accretion bridge.

And just as the commander had hoped, the *Stargazer* began to win *her* battle as well. Even without any help from the research vessel's impulse drive, the starship pulled away from the sinkhole—further and further, giving her crew more reason for optimism with each passing moment.

Then something strange happened, something Wu had never experienced in all the time she had spent on the *Crazy Horse*. Someone on the bridge began to *cheer.* And someone else joined him. And before the second officer knew it, everyone around her was cheering or applauding or grinning at her with unmitigated pride.

Part of her noted that it was very much against regulations to cheer on the bridge of a starship. But it was a very small part. The rest of her enjoyed every second of it.

Chapter Twenty-five

JITERICA FELT A WAVE of relief as she studied the readout on her console in the *Belladonna*'s small but efficient engineering facility.

Despite her best efforts, the ship's impulse drive had failed. But it had held out long enough to do what was required of it.

The *Belladonna* was out of danger, the sinkhole falling farther and farther behind her with each passing moment. Her crew was safe. The ensign took pride in that outcome.

Abruptly, she realized that there was a hand on the shoulder of her containment suit. Turning her helmet, she saw that the appendage belonged to the *Belladonna*'s captain. He and his son had come down to engineering without her realizing it.

The captain smiled in the depths of his beard. "Thank you," he said, "from the bottom of my old, black heart." Then he held out his hand.

Jiterica knew what she had to do with it. After all, she had seen humans do it often enough on the ship. Exerting the requisite control over her containment suit, she placed her gauntlet in the man's hand.

His smile widened as he clasped it. "Ever have a yen to visit the colony on New Stockholm, Ensign?"

"No," Jiterica had to confess. She didn't even know what system New Stockholm was in.

"Well," the captain said, "you should. It's a beautiful place. If you ever feel like seeing it, look me up. I'll be happy to show you around." As he looked around the engineering facility, his face finally showed the stress he had been under. "I think after this, I'll be content to stay at home for a while."

It occurred to Jiterica that she *couldn't* "look him up." She lacked an important piece of information.

"What is your name?" she asked.

The captain's eyes opened wide as he realized his omission. "Hansen," he said. "Erik Hansen." He put his arm around his son's shoulder. "And this is Magnus. I'm sure he'll be happy to show you around as well. But you'd better visit soon, or he'll be off on a voyage of his own."

Magnus rolled his eyes. "I'm only thirteen, Dad."

"In years," said his father, who was obviously proud of him. "But you've already got more smarts than most grown men."

The boy looked at Jiterica and shrugged. *Parents*, he seemed to say. *They'll embarrass you every chance they get.*

The ensign knew the feeling. Hers were the same way.

Simenon stopped pacing the small meeting room when he heard its only door open.

"Phigus?" said his cousin Ornitharen as he poked his scaly head in.

"Yes," Simenon said, "I'm in here." He gestured for Ornitharen to come in and join him.

Ornitharen took a deep breath. "I wasn't sure which room it was. Those Aklaash in the black suits don't give very good directions. If I hadn't been here in the Northern Sanctum just the other day, I never would have found you."

"I'm glad you did," said Simenon.

His cousin frowned at him as if realizing something for the first time. "You look terrible, Phigus."

The engineer grunted. "I *feel* terrible."

Ornitharen looked sympathetic. "You lost the race, didn't you?"

Simenon shook his head. "Actually, I won."

"You *won?*" his cousin echoed wonderingly.

"Yes. Fertilized the eggs and everything. Our bloodline will go on at least another generation."

Ornitharen grinned. "That's...that's incredible. I'm so happy for you. For us, I mean."

"I knew you would be."

His cousin looked at him askance. "Something's wrong."

"What makes you say that?" Simenon asked.

"You should be happier about this. What's going on?"

Simenon frowned. "Someone sabotaged the vine bridge at the crevasse."

Ornitharen gazed at him wide-eyed. "Are you sure?"

"Quite sure."

"But who—" Ornitharen thought about it for a moment. "You mean Banyohla? Or Kasaelek?"

"Neither of them."

"Then who, Phigus?"

Simenon looked at him. *"You,* Ornitharen."

His cousin looked hurt. "You must be insane. What would make you say such a spiteful thing?"

The engineer's frown deepened. "There's no longer any point in feigning innocence, Ornitharen. I found Mazzereht-sized footprints near the bridge and had them compared with yours on a hunch. They turned out to be a match."

"Then the records people made a mistake," Ornitharen insisted.

Simenon shook his head. "There's no mistake. It was you who was trying to kill me. And the more I think about it, the more I believe you had a hand in my brothers' deaths as well."

"But why would I do that?" asked his cousin.

"That's what I asked myself," said Simenon. "Why would Ornitharen try to kill me? What could he gain by spilling my blood? And then I came up with the answer."

Ornitharen remained silent.

"I was the progenitor," the engineer told him, "the one whose seed would carry on our line. But you didn't like that situation, did you? You wanted it to be *your* seed. And if I were dead, it would be *you* running in the ritual instead."

Again, his cousin failed to respond to the accusation.

"You can save us all some trouble," said Simenon, "and admit what you've done. You're going to be found guilty in any case."

Ornitharen glowered at him for a moment. Then he made his reply, his voice dripping with resentment.

"Do you have any idea what it's like to be second-best, Cousin—to know you'll *always* be second-best? Do you know what it's like to have to kowtow to a *sedgmaya* who doesn't give a *columnu* feather about your family's affairs?"

Simenon shook his head. "If you weren't happy with me, you should have brought it up a long time ago. We might have been able to work something out. As it is..." He shrugged. "It's a bit too late for that."

Ornitharen spat at his feet. "Had I been born a week earlier, it would have been *me* racing Kasaelek and Banyohla."

"I might have been content with that," said Simenon, "if it meant my brothers would still be alive."

His cousin didn't say anything more. He just glared at the engineer one last time and left the room for the corridor outside, where the black-garbed Aklaash were waiting to take him into custody.

For a little while, Simenon remained alone, contemplating the lengths to which people will go when they're thwarted in their ambitions. Then there was a knock at the still-open door.

"Come in," he said.

Picard led Simenon's other colleagues into the room. All five of them.

"You and your cousin appear to have completed your business," the captain observed.

"They're taking him away?" Simenon asked.

"Yes," Picard confirmed.

The Gnalish heaved a sigh. "Families can be a great responsibility."

Picard nodded sympathetically. "They can indeed."

Simenon looked around at his comrades, who—until his progeny hatched—were the only *real* family he had. "And once in a while," he found himself adding in a wildly uncharacteristic display of generosity, "something of a comfort."

Ben Zoma looked at him as if he had grown another

head. "I must be dreaming. Was that an expression of *gratitude* I heard? From our chief engineer?"

"I believe it was," said Greyhorse, joining in.

The Gnalish made a sound of dismissal. "Don't get too accustomed to it, either of you. You're not likely to hear it again."

"Now that," said Ben Zoma, feigning relief, "is the Phigus Simenon we've come to know and love. For a minute there, I thought you'd been exchanged for your evil twin."

That drew a few chuckles from the others.

Enough banter, Simenon thought. And enough time spent risking his skin in primitive forests. He longed for the civilized simplicity of his life back on the Stargazer.

Not that he would give his colleagues the additional satisfaction of hearing him say that. He was grateful, yes—but he had already expressed his gratitude far too extravagantly.

Assuming his trademark scowl, he said, "Shouldn't someone be contacting the ship for a transport about now? Or would you like to run that course again just for the hell of it?"

As no one seemed eager to do so, Picard agreed to make the call.

Commander Wu arrived in the transporter room just in time to see Ensign Jiterica materialize on the hexagonal platform.

She turned to the operator on duty, and said, "Good work, Mr. Refsland."

He wiped a bead of sweat from his brow. "Thank you, Commander."

Wu knew it wasn't easy to transport a Nizhrak—particularly one in a force field-reinforced Starfleet containment suit. However, Refsland and the other transporter operators would have to get used to it.

Jiterica had proved for the second time in as many months how valuable she was to this ship and crew. Captain Picard would be a fool to let her get away, even if he had to build a special chair for her so she could join her fellow crewmen in the mess hall.

"Commander," said the ensign as she stepped down from the platform. The visage behind her faceplate looked surprised.

Wu smiled at her. "I wanted to congratulate you as soon as I could. What you did out there was..." She couldn't find the words. "You should be proud of yourself, Ensign. I know I am."

Something amazing happened then. Jiterica *smiled*.

"Thank you," she said in her tinny, mechanical voice. "I am pleased to hear you say that."

Wu was about to tell her that she hoped to say it a lot. Then she remembered that that wouldn't be the case—not with her rejoining Captain Rudolfini on the *Crazy Horse*.

Just then, the doors to the transporter room opened again and someone else came in. Glancing over her shoulder, the commander saw that it was Ensign Paris.

He was grinning like a hyena, looking nothing like the doubt-ravaged young man who had poured his heart out to Wu in Picard's ready room. It was only after he saw the second officer standing there that he assumed a more professional demeanor.

"Commander Wu," he said. "I hope you don't mind my coming here. I just wanted to make sure Ensign Jiterica got back all right."

Wu understood. She would have given into the same impulse if she had just risked her life with someone.

"Actually," she said, "I'm glad you're here, Ensign."

Paris became concerned. "You are?"

"Yes. I was just telling Ensign Jiterica what a wonderful job she did—and the same goes for you."

He seemed to take the praise in stride. "I appreciate that, Commander. But…" He shrugged. "I would never have had the chance if someone hadn't had more confidence in me than I had in myself."

Wu felt a lump grow in her throat. She shook her head until it went away. "Don't flatter me, Mr. Paris. Any commanding officer worth her salt would have had confidence in you." She turned to Jiterica and added, "In both of you."

It was a pity that she was leaving, the commander reflected. It would have been fun to watch these ensigns grow—both as people and as professionals.

"See you on the bridge," she told them, and left them to each other's company.

Chapter Twenty-six

PICARD EMERGED from the turbolift and took in his bridge at a glance. The Asmunds were at their usual posts. Paxton was at communications. And Dubinski appeared to be instructing Ensign Nikolas in the proper use of an engineering console.

It was good to be home, the captain thought.

Nikolas was the first to glance his way. "Captain on the bridge," he announced dutifully.

Picard saw everyone present come to attention, the ensign included. "As you were," he told them.

As his officers resumed their duties, he turned to Kastiigan, who was working at the science console. "Do you know where I can find Commander Wu?"

The Kandilkari jerked his head in the direction of the captain's ready room. "I believe she's in *there,* sir."

"I see," said Picard. "Thank you, Mr. Kastiigan."

"I'm glad to be of service, sir," the science officer told him, and returned to his work.

Crossing the bridge, the captain waited outside his ready room doors for a moment—as a courtesy to Wu. When they slid aside, he walked in and saw his second officer standing behind his desk.

"Welcome back," she said.

He smiled. "It's good to *be* back. I understand you had a little excitement in my absence."

"A little," Wu told him. "But nothing we couldn't handle, thanks to the crew. And in particular, thanks to Ensigns Jiterica and Paris."

The captain was pleased to hear it.

"They demonstrated valor and resourcefulness," his second officer continued. "I couldn't have been prouder of them."

It was high praise. "I look forward," he said, "to reading about it your report."

"Which will be available for your inspection first thing in the morning," she assured him.

If Picard had been the second officer, he would taken the opportunity to leave the room at that juncture. However, Wu didn't show any intention of leaving.

He was about to ask why when she said, "I have a request, sir."

He shrugged. "What is it, Commander?"

Wu hesitated. "If it's all right with you, I would like to rescind my request for a transfer to the *Crazy Horse*."

At first, the captain thought he had heard incorrectly. "You want to *stay?*" he asked, just to make sure.

"That's correct, sir."

Without question, he was pleased with the decision. But he had to admit to a certain curiosity. "If you don't mind my asking," he said, "what made you change your mind?"

Wu smiled. "I've given it some thought—and I've concluded that I can do more good *here* than on the *Crazy Horse*. With certain crewmen in particular, you understand."

Picard looked at her. Given the way she had talked about Paris and Jiterica, he had a feeling he knew who those crewmen might be. But he was a bit puzzled.

Do more *good?*

The Nizhrak had been disoriented and isolated from the rest of the crew from the moment she had come aboard. It was clear that she had needed a helping hand from someone. But Paris didn't seem to have needed any such help. He had appeared comfortable on the *Stargazer* from the beginning.

No doubt, Picard would gain a better understanding of the situation once he read his second officer's report. "Have you apprised Captain Rudolfini of your desire to stay with us?"

"Not yet," said his second officer. "I'd like to do that now, if it's all right with you."

"It is," Picard told her.

After Wu left his ready room, he sat down in his chair and leaned back contentedly. Not only did he get to keep a good officer, he wouldn't have to pore through personnel files searching for her replacement.

It was shaping up to be a very pleasant homecoming. Very pleasant indeed.

Ulelo was sitting in the mess hall, eating by himself because he couldn't see any opportunities for intelligence-gathering among the junior-grade crewmen seated around him, when a tray full of food landed next to his own.

He looked up and saw that the tray belonged to Emily Bender. "Fancy meeting you here," she said.

The comm officer didn't know what to make of her joining him. Stalling for time to think, he glanced at her plate. "What's that?"

Emily Bender smiled accusingly. "Chicken and rice. I'm sure you've seen it before."

He had, in fact. "It just looked different," he explained—rather lamely, he thought.

She didn't respond to his excuse. Instead, she dug her fork into her chicken and rice and said, "When we spoke in my quarters, I turned down your offer of friendship. But I've had some time to think about it."

Ulelo didn't know what to say. The best he could do was "Oh?"

"And I think I'd like to be your friend after all."

"My...friend."

"Yes." She looked up at him. "If that's what you want, of course."

Ulelo frowned. He didn't know the answer to that question.

It was critical that he put his mission above all else—and without question, a friend could complicate that mission. That was why he had been careful to keep all his acquaintances on the ship at arm's length.

But mere acquaintances left his need for companionship unfulfilled—and mission or no mission, a man still craved companionship. Emily Bender would fill that need if he let her—if he could cope with the idea of her getting closer to him but not *too* close.

"Yes," Ulelo found himself saying. "It's what I want."

He only hoped he wouldn't come to regret it.

Vigo found Kastiigan in the science section, where he was running a diagnostic on a sensor bank.

"Ah," said the Kandilkari, favoring him with a glance. "I see you're back from your away mission. I heard it went well—though regrettably, no one got the opportunity to perish for his comrades."

"Er...that's right," Vigo agreed. But he hadn't come here to speak of his adventures on Gnala or how close they had come to perishing. "I was hoping we could talk for a moment."

"Of course," said Kastiigan. He gave the weapons officer his full attention. "What about?"

"It's...about your talk of dying." Vigo searched for some diplomatic way to make his point, but finally had to settle for the direct approach. "I find it disturbing."

Kastiigan looked surprised. "Disturbing...?"

Vigo nodded. "You have to understand...we Pandrilites never speak of such things."

The Kandilkari's brow furrowed. Clearly, he was making an attempt to understand his colleague's feelings in the matter. Finally, his purple eyes brightened.

"I see what you mean," he said.

Vigo smiled. "You do?"

"Of course. Talk is of no value. All that matters is what one does—and to this point, I have not been aggressive enough in my struggle to perish for the good of my comrades."

The Pandrilite shook his head, horrified. "That's not—"

"No," said Kastiigan, holding up a hand for silence, "there's no need to elaborate. You have made your point most eloquently. When I perish, it will be with your friendship and kindness foremost in my mind."

"You don't understand," Vigo started to tell him.

But before he could get all the words out, he was interrupted by the captain's voice coming over the intercom system. "Picard to Lieutenant Kastiigan."

The science officer looked up. "Aye, sir?"

"These readings you took of the sinkhole are quite remarkable. I'd like to discuss them with you in my ready room."

"Of course, sir. Kastiigan out."

"Listen," said Vigo, still intent on clearing up the Kandilkari's misapprehension, "I didn't—"

"Sorry," Kastiigan told him, "duty calls."

And before the weapons officer knew it, his colleague was on his way out of the science section. It occurred to Vigo that he could go with him, explain the matter en route.

But by the time he decided to do that, it was too late. Kastiigan was out the door, down the corridor and out of sight, headed for the nearest turbolift.

Vigo frowned. Perhaps he would get through to the science officer another time. But somehow, he had his doubts.

Carter Greyhorse was lying in bed, trying to endure the assorted aches and pains he had accumulated on Gnala without the benefit of medication, when his door chimed.

He swore beneath his breath. Swinging his legs over the side of the bed, he sat up and steeled himself. Then he got up, defying cramps in his quadriceps, his calves, and his lower back.

"Be right there," the doctor muttered, and began making his way from bedroom to the anteroom that stood outside it.

The door chimed again.

"For the love of heaven," he sighed, "what is so urgent? I *said* I'd be right there."

The door had chimed a third time before Greyhorse made it to the center of the anteroom. Taking a deep breath, he gritted his teeth and stood up straight.

Then he said, "Come in."

That's when the doors parted and revealed the last person Greyhorse had expected to see there.

"I heard about your adventure on Gnala," Gerda said. She walked in and the doors hissed closed behind her. "It appears you acquitted yourself rather well."

Greyhorse had a feeling the navigator had only heard part of the story. Quite clearly, his comrades hadn't told her how he held the team back by lagging behind.

"I made a contribution or two," he allowed modestly.

Gerda didn't respond. She just stood there, eyeing him with an intensity he had never seen in her before.

"So...you've come to congratulate me?" he asked, feeling increasingly uncomfortable with the way she was looking at him.

The navigator's lip curled. "More than that, Carter Greyhorse. Judging by what you accomplished on Simenon's behalf, I believe you're ready to attempt a new level of confrontation."

Greyhorse swallowed back his nervousness and looked at her askance. "I beg your pardon?"

Gerda came closer. And as she did so, she raised her hands in a kave'ragh posture, elbows up and knuckles extended, her right hand coiled and poised to strike.

"A warrior does not beg," she told him, her voice suddenly seething with emotion. "A warrior *takes*."

"This is going to be good," said Nikolas as he made his way to the ship's gym.

"Are you certain that you wish to go ahead with this?" asked Obal, who was doing his best to keep up with the human's longer strides.

Nikolas grinned incredulously at his friend. "Am I certain? Do Vulcans have pointed ears?"

The Binderian made a face as he bounded along. "It is

only that I am concerned about the possibility of injuries."

The ensign waved away the idea. "I'll take it easy on her, I promise. Believe me, the last thing I want to do is *hurt* her."

Then they had arrived at the gym. Nikolas pressed the pad set into the bulkhead and watched the doors slide apart in front of him, revealing a single figure waiting for him in the gym.

A single, very *lovely* figure.

"Ensign Nikolas," said Idun, by way of acknowledgement. She glanced at his companion. "Lieutenant Obal."

"Lieutenant Asmund," the Binderian said, though it sounded to Nikolas more like a sigh.

Nikolas's original date with the curvaceous helm officer had been postponed because of the *Belladonna* crisis, which had required her continual presence on the bridge. But Idun hadn't been the least bit reluctant to reschedule.

"Thanks for walking me over," the ensign told his friend, keeping his gaze locked on his sparring partner. "I can take it from here."

"You're absolutely sure?" Obal asked.

Nikolas nodded. "Never been more sure in my life."

"All right," the Binderian told him. "I will see you..." He hesitated for a moment. "Later."

"Later," the ensign agreed.

He waited until Obal had departed and the doors to the gym had slid together again. Then he rubbed his hands together in friendly anticipation and approached his partner.

"Have you had a chance to warm up?" Nikolas asked.

"I have," Idun acknowledged. "You?"

"It'll take just a moment," he said.

Usually, the ensign warmed up slowly, not wanting to

invite injury. But this time, he rushed it a bit. After all, he didn't want Idun to change her mind.

"All right," he said. "Ready."

Idun nodded. "Good."

She began to circle him, her hands curled like claws. She held her left hand forward and the right back near her chin.

"Interesting stance," Nikolas observed.

"It's Klingon," she told him.

He smiled. "Really."

"Really," said Idun.

Then she came at him, shooting her right hand at his face. Nikolas moved his head to one side and avoided the blow without any trouble. Then he returned it with one of his own.

It wasn't anything like his best shot, of course. He had meant it when he told Obal that he didn't want anyone getting hurt.

As it turned out, the ensign's attack missed by more than he expected. Idun was fast. Almost as fast as he was, it seemed.

Abruptly, she changed her stance. Turning her palms inward, she held her hands in front of her chest.

"Don't tell me that's Klingon too," he said.

"As a matter of fact," she returned, "it is."

Idun came at him again, but this time she didn't use her hands. Her body rolled gracefully and her right foot lashed out, her heel headed for his mouth.

As before, Nikolas avoided the maneuver without too much trouble. And this time, he put a little more mustard on his counterpunch.

His opponent handled it flawlessly, showing him that her earlier move was no fluke. She really *was* fast.

"Nicely done," he said.

Idun didn't answer him. Instead, she changed her stance again, reverting to the one with the clawlike fists. And she continued to circle him, her eyes as hard and blue as sapphires.

"You know," Nikolas said, "I have a confession to make."

"What's that?" she asked.

He smiled. "I only staged this match because I wanted us to become better acquainted."

"Really," she responded.

"That's right," he confirmed.

"I assume," said the helm officer, "that you want to become acquainted with *all* of me."

Nikolas felt himself blush. He had hoped this little "date" of theirs might eventually lead to something amorous, but he hadn't expected Idun to be so blunt about it.

"Well, yes," he replied. "Yes, I do."

"With every facet of me?" she asked.

Nikolas couldn't believe it. "Every facet," he assured her. "Every last bit of you."

"Thank you. I wanted to make certain," Idun told him. Then she came at him in a blur of motion.

Admiral McAteer looked out his office window at the San Francisco Bay and the island of Alcatraz that sat in the center of it, and decided that it was officially a beautiful day.

Not that he cared all that much about the view. It only mattered to him as a symbol of how far he had come and how much he had achieved to get there.

What made the day so beautiful was the prospect of having Lt. Shalay on the *Stargazer*.

Picard might very well recognize the Bolian for what

he was—McAteer's spy. But even if he did, he couldn't keep Shalay from observing what went on there. And with a 28-year-old in charge of the ship, a *lot* had to be going on. The admiral was confident of that.

Once he got his hands on the right information, Picard would be cannon fodder. Likewise, his first officer. And next to fall would be the esteemed Admiral Mehdi, who had made the rash decision to promote those two in the first place.

As McAteer was thinking that, his intercom came alive with the voice of his assistant. "Admiral?"

"Yes, Mr. Merriweather?"

"Sir, I have a communication from Captain Picard on the *Stargazer.* I believe it's a response to the orders you sent."

McAteer smiled to himself. He had looked forward to seeing Picard's face when he learned that yet *another* second officer was being foisted on him. Now was his chance.

"Thank you," he told Merriweather.

Then he tapped out a command on his keyboard, brought up a list of messages that had been sent to him, and noted the one that was labeled "Picard." With a deep feeling of satisfaction, he opened the message and saw the captain's face appear on the monitor screen.

McAteer leaned back in his chair. *I've got you now,* he thought.

Picard looked nettled, even a little annoyed. However, the admiral didn't sympathize in the least. There was no room for 28-year-old captains in Starfleet, nor was there room for men like Mehdi who tried to put them there. If Picard thought he was discomfited now, he would absolutely *hate* what was in store for him.

"I must say, sir," the captain of the *Stargazer* began,

"I'm at a bit of a loss. You seem to think Commander Wu is inclined to transfer off this vessel. In fact, nothing could be further from the truth. Wu tells me she has every intention of staying right here."

McAteer felt his face go hot. "What?" he said out loud.

"It's true," said Picard, "that she spoke with Captain Rudolfini and discussed the openings that have occurred on the *Crazy Horse.* But she wanted me to emphasize that she is not going to fill *either* of those openings." He smiled. "I repeat, Admiral, so there will be no further confusion—Commander Wu isn't going *anywhere.*"

McAteer cursed long and volubly. Either his source on the *Crazy Horse* had been lying to him—which he sincerely doubted—or Picard had somehow gotten Wu to change her mind.

But why would in heaven's name she do that? Wu prided herself on her efficiency, sometimes to a fault. What could possibly keep her shackled to a captain several years her junior, a man as raw as one of the oysters the admiral had eaten at lunch?

And what was he going to tell Shalay? That Wu had decided to stay on the *Stargazer* after all? That he had resigned his position on the *New Orleans* for nothing?

Maybe, the admiral told himself, he could come up with a reason to relieve Wu of her duties on Picard's ship. Then he could insert Shalay as he had planned.

No, he argued inwardly. *You can't.*

It was *his* order that had placed Wu on the *Stargazer* in the first place. If he got rid of her now, it would look like he had made a bad choice, and he hadn't gotten to be an admiral in Starfleet by making himself look bad.

McAteer pounded his fist on his wooden desk, shivering everything on it. Damn Picard, he thought. Damn

Wu. And damn Mehdi for putting him in this position in the first place.

But the war wasn't over. Eventually, Picard would make a mistake. And when he did, McAteer would be there to capitalize on it.

Nikolas opened his eyes and found himself in sickbay. "What am I—?"

"Doing here?" Greyhorse said, finishing the question for him. The doctor was standing to one side of the ensign's biobed, checking its readouts. "You had a little accident."

"Accident...?" Nikolas muttered.

"That's correct. In the ship's gymnasium."

It started to come back to him. He was sparring with Idun. She had asked some pretty startling questions. And then...

"She hit me," the ensign realized.

"Several times in succession," said Greyhorse, "if the bruises you sustained were any indication."

Nikolas shook his head. "Amazing."

"I agree," said the doctor.

He wasn't speaking to the ensign when he said it. He was gazing in another direction, as if lost in thought.

"Doctor Greyhorse?" said Nikolas.

Greyhorse turned to him, his eyes still a little out of focus. "Sorry. I was just thinking of...another patient."

He didn't mention who it might be. But then, Nikolas didn't really care. He had other fish to fry.

Swinging his legs aside, he sat up and said, "I think I'm okay now. Mind if I go?"

Greyhorse gave him a disparaging look. "What sort of physician would I be if I released someone who had just been worked over by one of the Asmund sisters?"

The ensign frowned. "Just how long do you think it'll be before I can get out of here?"

The doctor shrugged. "That's hard to say. Mr. Nikolas. In the meantime, just out of curiosity...what did Lieutenant Asmund do to catch you at such a disadvantage?"

Nikolas described the maneuver to Greyhorse—at least, to the extent that he could remember it. Then, a little curious himself, he said, "Why do you ask?"

To the ensign's surprise, Greyhorse went red in the face. "I'm your doctor," he said, a note of annoyance in his voice. "If I'm to treat you, I need to know how you were injured."

It made sense, Nikolas thought. But for just a moment there...

No, he told himself. Not again. He had gotten into enough trouble lately by misinterpeting what someone was thinking.

From now on, the ensign resolved, he would stay out of people's heads—especially when they fought like a Klingon.

263

Look for STAR TREK fiction from Pocket Books

Star Trek®

Star Trek: The Next Generation®

Star Trek: Deep Space Nine®

Star Trek: Voyager®

Enterprise™

Star Trek®: New Frontier

Star Trek®: Stargazer

The Valiant • Michael Jan Friedman
Double Helix #6: The First Virtue • Michael Jan Friedman and Christie Golden
The Gauntlet • Michael Jan Friedman
Progenitor • Michael Jan Friedman

Star Trek®: Starfleet Corps of Engineers (eBooks)

Have Tech, Will Travel (paperback)• various
    #1 • *The Belly of the Beast* • Dean Wesley Smith
    #2 • *Fatal Error* • Keith R.A. DeCandido
    #3 • *Hard Crash* • Christie Golden
    #4 • *Interphase, Book One* • Dayton Ward & Kevin Dilmore
Miracle Workers (paperback) • various
    #5 • *Interphase, Book Two* • Dayton Ward & Kevin Dilmore
    #6 • *Cold Fusion* • Keith R.A. DeCandido
    #7 • *Invincible, Book One* • Keith R.A. DeCandido & David Mack
    #8 • *Invincible, Book Two* • Keith R.A. DeCandido & David Mack
    #9 • *The Riddled Post* • Aaron Rosenberg
#10 • *Gateways Epilogue: Here There Be Monsters* • Keith R.A. DeCandido
#11 • *Ambush* • Dave Galanter & Greg Brodeur
#12 • *Some Assembly Required* • Scott Ciencin & Dan Jolley
#13 • *No Surrender* • Jeff Mariotte
#14 • *Caveat Emptor* • Ian Edginton
#15 • *Past Life* • Robert Greenberger

Star Trek®: Invasion!

#1 • *First Strike* • Diane Carey
#2 • *The Soldiers of Fear* • Dean Wesley Smith & Kristine Kathryn Rusch
#3 • *Time's Enemy* • L.A. Graf
#4 • *The Final Fury* • Dafydd ab Hugh
Invasion! Omnibus • various

Star Trek®: Day of Honor

#1 • *Ancient Blood* • Diane Carey
#2 • *Armageddon Sky* • L.A. Graf
#3 • *Her Klingon Soul* • Michael Jan Friedman
#4 • *Treaty's Law* • Dean Wesley Smith & Kristine Kathryn Rusch
The Television Episode • Michael Jan Friedman
Day of Honor Omnibus • various

STAR TREK
SECTION 31

BASHIR
Never heard of it.

SLOAN
We keep a low profile....
We search out and identify
potential dangers to the
Federation.

BASHIR
And Starfleet sanctions
what you're doing?

SLOAN
We're an autonomous
department.

BASHIR
Authorized by whom?

SLOAN
Section Thirty-One was
part of the original
Starfleet Charter.

BASHIR
That was two hundred years
ago. Are you telling me
you've been on your own
ever since? Without specific
orders? Accountable to
nobody but yourselves?

SLOAN
You make it sound so
ominous.

BASHIR
Isn't it?

No law. No conscience. No stopping them.
A four book, all <u>Star Trek</u> series beginning in June.

Excerpt adapted from *Star Trek:Deep Space Nine*®
"Inquisition" written by Bradley Thompson & David Weddle.